TRAITOR'S MANDATE

KELLY ST. CLARE

TRAITOR'S MANDATE

To the incredible friends in my life.

ABOUT THE AUTHOR

When Kelly is not reading or writing, she is lost in her latest reverie.

Books have always been magical and mysterious to her. One day she decided to unravel this mystery and began writing. Her works include *The Tainted Accords, Last Battle for Earth, Pirates of Felicity, Supernatural Battle, and The Darkest Drae.*

Kelly resides in New Zealand with her ginger-haired husband, a great group of friends, and whatever animals she can add to her horde.

Join her newsletter tribe for sneak peeks, release news, and disjointed musings at kellystclare.com/free-gifts/

"There's two of one number and three of another." Elara stared at her cards, a small wrinkle between her brown brows.

Phobos cocked his head for a second, saying, "A full house? I think that's a good hand."

Romy held back a smile, glancing at her row of cards. She had that thing where all of the hearts cards were in a row, including the king, queen, and what she assumed was a prince. Romy knew it was good.

Really, really good.

Peeking up, she saw Phobos and Elara watching her with narrowed eyes. Without a word, they tossed their cards down on the concrete floor of Atlas's room.

"I'm folding," Phobos said, green eyes bright.

Elara nodded. "Yep."

"Why?" Romy asked.

The couple snorted at the same time, and Phobos replied, "You have no poker face, Ro. You were literally grinning at your cards like they were chocolate cake." His eyes fell to her hands. "And you're currently showing us all your cards, proving we were right to fold. Royal flush, huh?"

Crap. Romy tilted the cards back, but after a beat, she gave up and threw them down. "You guys cheated. You're not supposed to look at my face when we play." Heat began to creep up her neck.

"Just because you said that's a rule, doesn't make it a rule." Elara pushed the cards into a stack and shoved a bunch of twigs from the middle toward Romy.

Romy's pile of twigs was the biggest tonight. She smiled and felt the heat settle back down.

A booming knock sounded from the solid metal door at the front of the small room.

"It's Thrym," Elara and Phobos guessed in a chorus.

"Why does he knock so loud?" Romy asked, jolting with each crashing blow against the door.

The couple exchanged a smirk, watching her. "Because he doesn't want to walk in on you and Atlas getting your freak on," Elara said.

Romy's molars clicked as her mouth snapped shut. However, the comment had her hastily getting into her role.

Grabbing a few crackers from the plate in the middle of their game, she crunched them together, lay on her back, and sprinkled the crumbs over her torso.

The knocking stopped and the door creaked open an inch. "Hello, I'm coming in," shouted Thrym on the other side. Romy rolled her eyes at the muffled snorting coming from Elara and Phobos. The door cracked an inch further. "It's Thrym and I'm about to enter." One more inch. "If I shouldn't come in, now is a good time to let me know." Another inch and he muttered, "Here goes nothing."

As Thrym grew a pair and flung the door open, Romy let out a massive belch.

Thrym's nose wrinkled as he looked at her. "Uh, hey. Tina

said you guys would be in here. What's up?" He closed the door behind him.

Romy sniffed loudly and rubbed her nose on the back of her hand, wiping it on her blue coveralls. "Playin' poker," she said in a deep voice.

"What's wrong with them?" He jerked his thumb at Phobos and Elara.

Her eyes shifted to the couple. They were tangled around each other for support as their unsuccessfully stifled laughter echoed in the confines of the space. Atlas's room was larger than most—him being the commander-general's son—but it was still a rectangular and windowless underground bunker, with a sink, mirror and single bed.

"I just told a joke," Romy lied.

"Oh?"

"Yeah. . . ." *Please don't ask me what it is. I'm never funny on purpose.*

They stared at each other in silence and Romy's heart sank as the quiet extended. There was this tiny thing with Thrym where they were technically programmed to want each other. It didn't affect Romy anymore because, well, she'd gone a bit mental for a while. Her mind had obliterated the nano programming and controls placed inside her by the Mandate. Thrym, on the other hand, hadn't gone mental. The urge for him to engage in . . . coitus . . . with Romy was still very much there—and very one-sided. For a long time, he hadn't believed his feelings were fabricated by his nanos, and she strongly suspected he didn't now, though he'd hidden his feelings since they'd made a friendship pact a month ago. It hurt Romy that he hurt inside. Thrym was a member of her knot, and that meant he was her *family.* She didn't want him to be sad. That was why she sprinkled crumbs on herself and burped. It had to help, right?

"I got my injection," he said, holding out his arm.

Thrym was the last member of her knot to get the 'insanity cure'. Romy asked, "Charlee said everything was normal?"

When Houston betrayed the Amach and took the insanity cure with him, he hadn't counted on Dr Charlee switching files on him, or that she'd be able to replicate the cure.

"As normal as Elara and Phobos," Thrym announced.

His sky-blue eyes were piercing against his dark skin. Thrym was wide-shouldered, narrow-waisted, six foot, and everything a space soldier should be. He wore the same thing everyone here wore, dark blue coveralls with the word 'Amach' embroidered over the heart, but when Thrym wore it, he gave the impression the uniform meant more. Thrym had high standards, and expected everyone to strive for the same level. He'd always been ambitious, and sometimes that made him act like a jerk, but his heart was always in the right place underneath, and he wasn't allowed to act like a jerk for long, before Knot 27 slapped him back to normal. He spoke again. "I should be able to kill humans now without . . . uh. . ."

Phobos had recovered, but stayed tangled up with Elara on the floor. "Buying a one-way ticket to a padded cell?"

He was answered with a faintly reproving expression from Thrym.

Romy belched again and scratched her butt. "Charlee will be happy the shot worked." So was she. Now all of her knotmates were protected against the insanity trigger inserted in their nanos by the Mandate.

"Happy is an understatement," Thrym said, selecting a cracker. "She burst into joyful tears when I didn't—"

"Put the 'raz' in 'crazy'?" Elara piped up.

Romy scrunched her nose. "I don't think that one works. 'Raz' and 'crazy' sound different."

"It works if I say it works." Elara scowled.

Romy offered an indulgent smile and let her feisty sister have the win.

"We would've been in a pickle if Charlee hadn't been able to replicate Houston's work," Phobos said.

They trailed into silence.

The quiet in the room deepened and an almost tangible sorrow thrummed in the room.

Elara sighed heavily. "I wish Dei—"

"Who wants to play another round?" Romy asked loudly.

The others blinked at her. Heat crept up her neck again.

"I do," she announced, equally as loud. No way was she thinking about the ex-member of their knot. Traitorous meteor face, degenerate piece of poacher poop that he was. *Deimos.* She gritted her teeth, rolled over and knocked the plate of crackers aside, sending them scattering. Romy picked up the twigs. "Who wants a twig?" She glared at her knotmates. "I said, who wants a twig!"

Thrym started and quickly took a twig. Elara gave her a sad look with puppy-dog hazel eyes. Phobos avoided her gaze completely, but took a twig.

"Great," Romy huffed. "We all have twigs." She wouldn't talk about Deimos. She hadn't uttered his name since that night. The fifth member of Knot 27 made his choice when he tried to kidnap her on Houston's order. By force. He wasn't her brother any longer.

"What are you playing?" a voice asked behind them.

Phobos, who faced the door, was the only one who didn't jump.

Romy eyed the steel door, certain it creaked every other time someone entered. Just not for the person who opened it now, apparently. She didn't blame the door, though. Romy would stop creaking for the man there, too.

Atlas.

Her heart squeezed. The word meant so much to her. *Atlas.* There were a hundred different emotions it contained, and one hundred more experiences. It annoyed her to think when she said the word, no one else understood these complexities contained within. Atlas wasn't just a word to her, or a name. It signified so much more than she could articulate.

"Poker," Phobos answered as Romy continued to gape.

Atlas moved into the room and stood beside the spot where Romy sat. Elara was making faces at her from across the circle.

"What?" Romy mouthed at her.

Elara dropped her eyes to Romy's chest, pointedly.

Huh? She glanced down and jerked at the sea of crumbs covering her chest and lap. A suspicious snorting sound came from Elara's general direction as Romy did her best to get rid of the mess without Atlas noticing.

"Looks like you had trouble finding your mouth," he said, crouching beside her.

She stilled and craned her neck to meet his grey gaze. He brushed a hand through her bristly hair. A few crumbs fell to the floor. *Dammit.* She'd only put them on her shirt, she was sure of it.

They stared at each other.

He'd been gone all day. Atlas coordinated the Amach attacks for this quarter of the northern hemisphere. Since a third of the Amach ditched them to join Houston's new faction, he'd also been coordinating part of the southern hemisphere, too. Translation: She didn't see him enough. More than that, she didn't know when that would change. Things weren't exactly looking up. Or even left and right.

Phobos's dry voice interrupted their stare. "If she has any

trouble finding her mouth next time, I'm sure you can help point it out. You seem to know exactly where it is."

She shifted her eyes from Atlas's arms in time to catch him looking at her lips. She couldn't help giving a small smile, and glanced away to hide it, but was stopped by a finger on her chin. Atlas winked at her and bent down, placing his warm mouth on hers.

Bliss.

Her insides warmed as he lingered just a moment, then straightened. The kiss was bitterly short, but the perfect amount of sweet.

The eyes of her knot were fixed on them, and Romy gulped at their expressions. Happy, they were not.

"Something has happened," Thrym said, giving Atlas a searching look. "What is it?"

Atlas gave him a brief glance and crossed the room to the sink, turning on the tap. "Summons to the Mess," he said, splashing water on his face. Some ran down his neck and disappeared into the top of his black singlet. The black singlet and cargo pants were her favourite combination, though that was probably because that was all Atlas wore. He ran wet hands through his jet-black hair and over the nape of his neck.

"You're licking your lips." Elara's voice whispered in her ear. Romy bit her tongue in fright and whacked the smaller woman.

"Ow!" Elara said.

"You snuck up on me."

Her knotmate's eyes flickered to Atlas and gleamed. "Only because you were about to lick At—"

Romy launched herself at the woman and threw a hand over her mouth. "Don't say it," she hushed in her ear.

"What will you give me?"

Romy considered it for a moment. "I'll play with your hair two times, for ten minutes."

"Five times, one hour."

"Three times, half an hour," Romy said in her no-nonsense voice.

Elara pondered this, then jerked her head, tapping Romy's hand.

"What was that?" Atlas asked the boys behind them.

Thrym said, "From what we've observed in the past, it's a kind of code. It appears to have a set of indiscriminate regulations you must possess female parts to decipher."

Phobos grunted his agreement as Elara pulled him to his feet. "Yeah, yeah," she said. "Enough chit-chat. I swear that's all guys do—gossip about this, nag about that. Come on, we've got a meeting to attend."

Her knot filed out into the network of exposed-pipe concrete passageways that made up the Amach. Romy trailed behind, the warmth of Atlas at her back.

A tickling at her ear was all the alert she got before Atlas's low voice spoke. "I'd hoped to get a private moment to speak to you beforehand."

She half turned. "Why?"

He paused before replying, "Because there is about to be a big change."

Others joined them in the passage, and he fell quiet.

Though Romy could never agree with Houston's entire vision—to attain leadership of the world using whatever violence necessary—she could understand his frustration with the Amach's slow progress in overthrowing the Mandate. For a long time, the Amach hadn't made any real headway, and the time for something to happen was long overdue.

"Change is a good thing," she whispered back to Atlas. *Something* had to change.

Thrym looked back to check that they still followed. She smiled at him and he faced forward again. They continued down the dimly lit concrete passage.

Atlas took a deep breath. "Change in the *Amach*, yes."

"But?"

He replied, "What if it changes us?"

2

Romy squeezed through the two-thousand-strong crowd to stand between Thrym and Phobos near the front. People poured out of the asterisk of passages branching off the large mess room where they ate and gathered for announcements.

Thrym took one look at Romy's face. "What happened?"

Atlas had just whispered the news in her ear, that was what, and Romy still hadn't decided how she felt about it. She gave a terse shake of her head, ignoring the inquiring glances from Phobos and Elara. "You'll find out soon enough." There were too many people, and too close. The announcement had to be done properly.

The change was a good thing, a strategic move . . . but it felt like one more sacrifice on her part. *Let's take your memory, Romy. Let's take your sanity, Romy. Let's take someone you love, Romy.*

"Your attention." Gwenyth, Atlas' mother and commander-general of the Amach, spoke into a microphone. The Mess quietened, a few stragglers whispering with their comrades in hushed tones. The feeling that something big was about to happen hung heavy in the air.

"One month ago, the Amach was attacked from the inside," she started. "On the tail end of the most serious threat we'd ever faced, someone we thought we knew betrayed us, splitting off a large number of our force with false promises of change, welcoming in an army of alien invaders, and harming several of our own to get what he wanted." Her eyes fell on someone in the crowd and Romy stood on tiptoe, spotting Dr Charlee.

"Watch out. Coming through," someone said loudly at the back of the room. Gwenyth stopped talking. Voices rose in complaint at their backs.

"Move it!" the same person snarled.

A small, mahogany-haired woman shoved between two people in the row behind Knot 27 and gave Romy a scowling look. Romy returned the look with a smile.

"Tina," she greeted.

The woman dug an elbow into Romy's side to make her shift closer to Thrym and inserted herself in the gap. "Boy, it's crowded in here. Are they serving hot dogs again?"

Tina seemed small, but she was made entirely of muscle, and while Romy had heard the human body was sixty per cent water, she imagined Tina was sixty per cent tequila and venom, instead.

"Whenever you're ready, vice-commander," Gwenyth said into the microphone.

Tina pursed her lips and readjusted her sports bra underneath her coveralls. After another quick once-over she called out, "Okay, I'm ready."

"I'm so glad," Gwenyth said. A few people laughed nervously, but not too loud. No one wanted to incur the wrath of Tina.

Tina was Atlas's ex. She'd hated Romy's genetically enhanced guts for . . . most of their acquaintance, really, and their friendship shouldn't make sense, but it did. What they shared wasn't like her other friendships; it was sarcastic and often involved teeth and claws. Romy understood her now, and looked back on their prior interactions with different eyes. Before, Romy was untested and the woman treated her accordingly. Now, she was tested and Tina saw her as an equal. Or something in that vicinity. They had each other's backs, that was all Romy knew.

"Dr Houston's new faction, *the Renegades—*," Gwenyth started again.

"Stupid ass name," Tina muttered.

"If you have to name yourself that, you can't really be a renegade," Thrym agreed from the other side.

Phobos stood silent, staring at Gwenyth. Elara spoke to him in a hushed voice. Phobos had taken Deimos's betrayal extra hard, so any mention of the Renegades tended to put him on emotional lockdown. In her heart, Romy wasn't sure her knotmate believed Deimos betrayed them, which she couldn't understand.

"—have now taken over the southern part of New America and have based themselves in Florida. They've given the northern territories to the Critamal, and have mounted several attacks on cities throughout the world with large, unnecessary loss of urban life, the most recent of which was in New Melbourne. In addition, they are forcefully evacuating the rural settlements and taking these refugees back to their New America bases to swell their ranks."

The crowd shifted, murmuring in low voices.

"Many of you are from such settlements, and actively sought us out as a haven." Gwenyth scanned the crowd. "Yesterday, the Renegades took control of the Mandate's island prison in Madagascar, taking the prisoners back to their base in Florida. I assure you, if you had loved ones in this prison, everything possible will be done to get your friends and family back to the Amach. We are in contact with the Renegades already to negotiate their return."

A louder buzzing murmur overtook the room.

"Shoot," cursed Thrym, searching for someone in the crowd.

Romy followed his line of sight and spotted Nancy. The girl was younger than them by several years, around twenty now. Her skin was normally pale, a consequence of her carrot-coloured hair, but it had gone ghostly, making her beautiful violet eyes appear wide and haunted. The young woman had several friends in the Mandate prison, her friends from Jimboomba. Romy hated to think what might happen to Nancy if those friends hadn't made it. A year and a half after their capture, the woman still wasn't coping with their absence.

Thrym pushed through the crowd to reach Nancy. Her violet eyes were drawn to him immediately. Romy watched the pair, but backtracked as the violet eyes swung to her, flicking from haunted to beseeching to hatred in a second.

"She still pretending to hate you?" Tina asked above the still-buzzing crowd.

Romy hummed, turning to face the front as Thrym wrapped his arms around Nancy. The pair had been close since Jimboomba; Thrym was there for her after Nancy's friends were captured by the Mandate, but Romy had never seen him wrap his arms around the Australian woman like that. "Not sure her hate is pretend."

"It is," Tina said. "Easier to blame you than herself, remember."

Romy's reply was cut off as Gwenyth tapped the mic for attention.

She spoke. "You are here because you want a peaceful future. That is why our force is now as strong as ever. It is why our ranks continue to swell. We are here to protect your families. And the future of your families." Gwenyth cast a look behind her where Atlas stood, a silent support to his mother.

Not for much longer.

"However, we cannot ignore recent events," Gwenyth said softly. Her face was long and thin and the lines around her eyes weren't from laughter. More often than not, Romy expected the older woman to spit out chewed-up metal instead of words. She'd lost her husband, the previous Amach leader, to the Mandate when Atlas was young. In the tumultuous wake of that, she'd stepped into the leadership role, even sacrificing her son to infiltrate the Mandate's commanding ranks. There was nothing this woman hadn't given up for the Amach.

"One month ago, I failed you," she stated. Her grey eyes, so like her son's, were matter-of-fact. "I allowed a man too much power. I did not listen. I became complacent in our efforts to replace the Mandate."

The room was still, the occupants caught in her words.

"The Amach has been my life," she said, blinking a few times. "I have always done my utmost to support the best way forward for our people. That is no different now." She took a deep breath. "Which is why I'm stepping down."

"Oh shiiiiit," Elara whisper-screamed.

The three members of her knot turned to Romy to confirm the truth. She lifted both brows and nodded.

"The high command has voted and my replacement will be someone who has sacrificed more for this cause than most. He is highly qualified for the role and, indeed, has been my advisor since his return from Orbito Four. Please help me in welcoming my son, Atlas, into the position of commander-general."

"Oh shit," Elara said, her jaw dropping.

"I don't know how long this war will last," Atlas had said to

Romy earlier. *"If there is a choice between the Amach and you, it will be expected I choose the Amach. It's so much more than I can ask of you, Rosemary. We're only just starting to know each other. I can't ask you to put up with the expectations of this position."*

Time. That was what it came down to. Less time together, and a shifting of priorities. Was it really a shift, though? Was it really less time?

Romy stood, head tilted up as Gwenyth stepped back and Atlas took centre stage. She studied Atlas's concerns from a different point of view. The man wasn't afraid of telling her how he felt about their relationship. Atlas wanted her, and he'd made that abundantly clear since saving her from Orbito Four. His confidence in acknowledging that was a massive tick in his favour. Yet, he'd also displayed a deep-set worry over what she thought of him and his work on more than one occasion. He never mentioned what he'd been doing for the day, and he was close-lipped about his time aboard the orbitos as a spy-commander. Romy wondered if he constantly expected her to leave because of his responsibilities. The more she thought about it, the more she came to realise Atlas taking over was the absolute best course of action. He was made for the role, whether he liked it or not.

Her dismay with the change stemmed from him.

The crowd was quiet, watching Atlas. His eyes found Romy in the crowd and she gave him a brilliant smile. He blinked, mouth falling slightly ajar. He thought she wasn't sticking around? Romy would just need to change his mind. Not wasting any more time, she brought her hands together in applause that would leave her hands smarting. "Wooooo, Atlas!" she yelled.

Tina jerked, holding a hand to the ear closest to Romy. "Christ!"

Romy gave her knot a pointed look, and they hurriedly began to clap.

"Woooo," Phobos called, half-heartedly.

Their actions cracked the ice, and the Mess broke into applause.

She hadn't taken her eyes off Atlas who now had his lips pursed, giving her a wry look. Romy pursed her lips back at him. *Take that, Commander-general Atlas. . . .* That was a mouthful; maybe she'd just call him Cargos. Atlas couldn't possibly know, but there were going to be some big changes between them in the next few days. She hoped the poor man could handle all the goodness she was going to lay down.

He held up a hand after a minute of the noise. The crowd simmered down.

"My mother's shoes will be hard to fill, but I aim to do my best," he started in his low voice.

It reminded her of their nights in his single bed—torture. One, she tossed and turned all night wondering when he was going to come in from work. Two, when he did come in, he'd kiss her forehead and neck a few times, climb over her, pull her to him, and go to sleep. Was she the only one tied in knots over sleeping next to him? She'd gone through the puberty stuff, and she may have trouble figuring out exactly how old she was, but in mental and physical maturity she was around twenty-six, according to Char. There was more than kissing, she knew—despite Phobos's attempts to tell her otherwise.

She wanted to 'more than kiss' Atlas.

Atlas faltered over what he was saying, and Romy started when she saw his eyes on her once more. His grey eyes turned from cold to molten in a nanosecond.

Tina sniggered. "Did you eat this morning?"

With a frown, Romy asked. "Yes, why?"

Phobos spoke in her ear. "Atlas isn't food, that's why."

Yikes. She cleared her throat and crossed her hands.

"There will be a few changes within high command," Atlas continued, with a final intrigued glance at Romy. "But the alterations will be smooth and the transition, painless. Which brings me to my first announcement. I am pleased to tell you our technical team has successfully installed the transmission communication project worldwide. This means we are able to communicate with our other bases and with those out on mission in real time."

A loud cheer followed his words. That was huge. The Amach had been operating with the Morse code systems for decades. Romy glanced overhead. She hated when everyone clapped and stamped their feet and kind of regretted starting the applause. They *were* in a cave system, after all.

He held up a hand. "In the next week, a tribunal system will be established, in order to bring your thoughts and questions to the attention of high command. Each level will have a representative, and the voting of your rep will be coordinated by Vice-commander Tina, for interrupting earlier—"

"Bitch." Tina glared at him. "I hate exes, don't you?" She turned to Romy for support and scowled at her lack of agreement.

"—I would like to increase all missions. A small, specialised portion of our force will remain focused on garnering information on the movements of the Mandate, the Critamal, and the Renegades."

Atlas clenched his jaw and Romy knew he was remembering his last interaction with Houston. They'd aimed their guns to kill, and Atlas's last words to his best friend had been, 'You're dead, my friend. Dead'. Romy wasn't hopeful for a joyful reunion. If she saw Houston again, she'd be putting a bullet in his head, too. Depending how worked up she got. When things got . . . intense, Romy tended to get angry—a leftover symptom from everything she'd been through. Let's just say one poker game ended in violence.

But it was okay when she won. And she'd won every game since.

Wait a minute. . . . Her eyes narrowed.

"The remainder of our force not allocated to security will be focusing completely on making contact with the settlements. They have no way to get to us; the Mandate has abandoned them to close off the cities and their supplies. These settlements are now prey for the Critamal." His jaw tightened. "We can help them." He shook his head and amended, "We're going to help them."

Excitement jolted through the Mess and a hopeful fever ricocheted, unchecked, through the long, table-filled space. There was a surge toward Atlas, people clamouring for his attention.

"I'm just gonna go check Nancy is okay," murmured Phobos. He moved off to where Nancy still stood in Thrym's arms. Was there something going on there?

Romy allowed herself to be ushered to one side with Elara and Tina, not taking her eyes off the dark head of hair belonging to Atlas as he descended the stairs to join the masses of his people.

In five minutes, he'd shown everyone his promotion was the right choice.

Romy heard somewhere once, or read on her nano, that certain times called for a certain leader; that in times of peace, the people needed one type of leader, and that in times of war, they needed another type entirely.

They were definitely in a war, *that* much was beyond question.

And now they'd found their leader.

3

The bed shifted and woke Romy from a beautiful dream. She and Atlas had been trekking up Machu Picchu with summer heat beating down on them.

She cracked open an eye. "Where're you going?"

Atlas let out a husky chuckle and crouched down by the bed at her head. He kissed her temple, saying, "To work."

To work? She let out a jaw-cracking yawn and kicked off the blanket, swinging her legs to the ground.

"What are you doing?" Atlas stood. "You should sleep a little longer. You'll be going out with one of the teams to a settlement tomorrow."

"Tomorrow, Atlas. That's a whole day away. Where am I going for it?"

He gave her a playful grin. "I thought you might like to go to Rome."

Did she what! "Like Vatican, Rome?"

He pursed his lips. "I'll need to pull some strings. . . ."

She pushed to her feet, giving him a kiss on the cheek. His eyes dragged over her bare thighs where the oversized T-shirt she wore ended.

"What were we talking about again?" he asked in a low voice.

"You don't remember?"

"I don't remember anything when you're in the room."

She hovered her lips in front of his. "You seemed to do pretty well during your speech yesterday."

He didn't reply. Typical. Oh well, Operation 'Worm Your Way into Atlas's Work Life' was in full swing. She pressed her lips to his, not content with the peck on the cheek. He felt for each side of her hips, drawing her in, and groaned deep in his chest. A higher breathless sound worked its way up her throat. His lips were the most magical feeling on this earth, and his eucalyptus scent made her dizzy. She'd been using his body wash since moving in with him.

After Houston and Deimos tried to kidnap her a month ago, Atlas hadn't wanted her to be alone. Honestly, neither had she.

Plus, she wanted more of Atlas. Always more.

Romy retreated, evading Atlas as he lunged to pull her back to him. Approaching the single set of drawers—the top two drawers were hers—she took out some fresh underwear and coveralls. "I'm coming to work with you today," she announced.

"You . . . are?"

Romy wrenched open the door. The showers were just down the hall. She glanced over her shoulder. "Close your mouth, Atlas. It's not a big deal."

ROMY SPUN IN THE OFFICE CHAIR. "YOU JUST DO THIS ALL day?"

A throat cleared. "Uh, commander-general, sir? There's someone at the door."

Romy glanced at the assistant in the doorway. Atlas didn't; he watched her like she was about to explode. He even had his hands slightly raised. One day, she'd laugh at him for being so worried about what she thought of him, but not now when his past still traumatized him so much.

"This is my first day," Atlas admitted.

His first day commanding an army on *Earth*. Romy wasn't sure that this still counted as a first day just because he wasn't commanding an army in space.

"I'll gather reports throughout the day," he mumbled.

"Who does your old role now?"

"I promoted Tina to commander, but she will still go out with your team on mission."

Romy nodded. "Good choice. She's perfect for it."

Atlas rounded the desk, eyeing her. "That's what I thought. From here, I'll confer with the commanders of the other Amachs—"

"How many Amachs?"

"Just under four hundred."

Romy whistled. "That's a few. You sure you don't need another assistant? I could do that."

Atlas paled.

"I'd probably be in here most days," she shrugged, in internal hysterics at his horrified expression. She shouldn't tease him, but Romy was sure about one thing. "I'm determined to have a thorough understanding of what you do each day."

If the six-foot-something Atlas had ever looked ready to faint, it was now. Romy pushed down another wave of amusement and glanced down at a map with various red marks on the desk. "Are these the people we're killing today?"

He paled further.

The assistant choked. "Uh, sorry, sir, but the person at the door—"

Romy glanced at the flustered assistant again.

"I don't kill unless I need to," Atlas said, ignoring the man. The look in his eyes was at utter odds with his firm words. Romy uncrossed her legs and stood, placing a hand on his chest. "I know you don't. Not when the orders are your own. I have utter faith in the decisions you make."

He sucked in a breath.

"The thing is, sir," the person tried again, "he says his name is Commander Cronus."

"*What?*" Atlas rounded on the man. "Why didn't you say something?"

The man by the door shifted on the spot. "Sorry, sir." Atlas dismissed him with a nod and wave.

"Commander Cronus?" she asked, heart thudding. The Orbito One commander. "Here? Is that possible?"

"Apparently," Atlas said with a grim look. "He's one person I never thought to see again." He circled the desk, opened a panel on the right side, and pushed a series of buttons imbedded inside. The screens on the opposite wall lit up. "The question is: Why has he come here?"

Romy faced the screen, her booted feet set in a comfortable stance. The outside camera showed a black-and-white view of the trapdoor exit. Currently, an older man was waiting there. He was military, that much was unmistakeable. Even wearing a floral shirt and carrying a tattered briefcase, he stood with his spine snapped into place.

Her mouth dried. "It *is* him." The man who'd commanded Orbito One, and Knot 27. The man who lied to them, who let knot after knot be slaughtered. Red filled her vision.

"Rosemary," Atlas said, rubbing her arms. "I'm going to let him in, but you should know I have strong suspicions

Cronus never knew the Mandate had the weaponry to defeat the Critamal all that time."

Some of the red receded. "You're sure?"

He ran a hand through his jet-black hair. "No, but I mean to find out." He leaned over and pushed a buzzer. "Josie, Rory, take three others with you and bring Commander Cronus in from exit three as per usual procedure. I'll see him in meeting room one."

"Roger that, commander-general, sir."

Romy spoke. "What do we do?"

His eyes glinted as he looked up, showing why he was the person in charge. This situation tied her in knots, but Atlas looked forward to this the way she looked forward to loading her gun. He smirked. "We get answers out of one of the Mandate's commanders, that's what."

He pulled a handgun from a drawer in the desk and inspected it before handing the weapon to her. "Want to shoot him in the kneecap if he gets violent?"

"It would be my pleasure."

Atlas pressed a hand against Romy's lower back as they walked out of his office. The adjoining general command space was full of screens and beeping. Messages crackled through various speakers around the large room. Eight or nine of the people there joined them, and Tina gave a distracted wave from where she was hunched over a map with a large team. Romy expected taking Atlas's old job would keep the woman busier than usual.

Their group filed into the meeting room a few minutes later, and Romy selected a seat in the front right corner of the room, assuming the chair pulled into the middle front was for Cronus. Perfect kneecap angle. The other members of the command took seats around the rectangular table, Gwenyth included. Romy smiled at her and got a blank look in return.

She'd take blank from Gwenyth any day. Atlas's mother made no secret of the fact she thought Romy's crazy self was no good for her beloved son.

Gwenyth shared a look with Atlas at that moment, and they both pursed their lips. *Ugh*, they were both excited about this meeting. That was why Romy couldn't dislike Gwenyth in peace. There was so much of Atlas in her face and actions, but on Atlas the traits were irresistible. On Gwenyth . . . not so much.

Commander Cronus marched into the meeting room a few minutes later, and Romy tensed, trying to control her breathing. One member of his supposed security escort party was carrying his suitcase. The others looked like they'd been hung upside-down and shaken. Cronus already had them dancing to his tune, it appeared. Just like he'd done to countless space soldiers. She gritted her teeth.

"Cronus," Atlas said, not budging from the front of the room.

"Julius," the commander greeted.

Huh?

It didn't register to anyone else as odd.

"My name is Atlas," he corrected the commander.

That was his orbito name? *Julius.* Julius seemed so foreign.

Cronus took the middle front seat without prompt, owning the role of potential foe. "You're wondering why I'm here."

Atlas rested against the front of the table. "You didn't know."

"No."

"You want them gone."

"Yes."

Atlas studied the older man for a long while, then gave a

jerk of his head. "I'd welcome your expertise on the command team."

Several jaws fell open.

"What happened to me kneecapping him?" Romy blurted, bursting to her feet. She'd come in here to fight.

Cronus's eyes came to rest on her. "Rosemary, Knot 27," he said softly.

She didn't reply, seething. Her fingers twitched where they were wrapped around the butt of the gun.

"Knot 27 were my pride and glory for many years, until. . ." He trailed off.

Romy rolled her eyes and took the bait. "Until what?"

He glanced around at the listening ears. "Remind me, and I'll tell you sometime." The commander slapped his hands down on his thighs and gave the room an assessing look, pausing on Gwenyth for a moment. "How long until I can eradicate every trace of those soulless Critamal from the planet?"

"WEIRD," STATED ELARA.

"Weird," Romy agreed, sipping her water as Phobos dealt the cards.

Phobos whistled. "Weird."

Charlee peered around the group. "Should I say weird as well?"

None of them were sure what to think about Cronus's presence here. As a cadet, Romy looked up to the commander. She'd taken comfort from his solid presence aboard Orbito One and the sacrifice he made, staying alive year after year while the rest of them were recycled. Since crash-landing here, he'd become one of the faces that represented everything she detested about the governing world powers: the lies, their brutality, the fact they felt they could decide who should live and die.

"So, he didn't know the Mandate had the cannons to get rid of the aliens?" Charlee asked.

"Apparently not. But he did know humankind survived. He knew the Mandate was lying to everyone to keep us up there." She wasn't sure if that was forgivable, but Romy knew now that choices weren't always easy.

Charlee, the Irish doctor, leaned back against the concrete, shivering at the cold. "That's a tough one, to be sure."

Phobos placed the rest of the cards on the ground and they picked up their small stacks. "I can't like the man, but if what he says is true, he wants rid of the Critamal as much as we do—enough to lie on the Mandate's behalf for all that time to get rid of them. We could use his expertise." He sighed heavily.

"You all right, Pho?" Romy asked. She glanced at her cards and inhaled sharply. Her hand *sucked*. But she wouldn't crumple the cards; that was poor sportsmanship.

He forced a smile. "Yes, mother hen. I'm fine."

Heat flushed her cheeks. "Don't call me mother hen."

Elara made some chicken noises. "But you are a mother hen. Charlee said it's our knot model."

Wisely, Charlee remained silent.

"Don't," Romy said, curling her fists.

"Mother hen."

"Stop it!"

"Mother hen."

Atlas stepped into the room. "Who's a mother hen?"

"Romy," Elara said, poking out her tongue.

She waited until Atlas wasn't looking and returned the gesture. Phobos continued staring at his cards. Something was totally up with him.

"What do you think about Cronus being here?" Phobos asked Atlas.

Atlas went to the sink and did his washing-the-face routine. Romy watched him with a small smile, ignoring Charlee and Elara's sniggers.

Atlas dried his face and took a seat on the floor next to Romy, saying, "He has intel on the Mandate unlike anything we have. We'll protect ourselves, regardless, in case he's a double agent. But I trust him. In fact," he licked his lips, glancing at Romy. "I've made him my direct assistant."

She gave him a look. "Atlas, I was joking about becoming your assistant. I'd much rather go out on mission."

His brow cleared, and the right side of his mouth tugged up in a half smile. He pulled her to his side.

Elara pouted at Phobos, who gave her a secret smile and drew her into his side, too.

Charlee looked between the two couples. "Jaysus, I gotta get me some."

Someone shouted down the hall, and clanging echoed toward them.

"Next time it will be your head hitting the pipes!" a woman roared.

This was followed by several screams and the frantic patter of running footsteps.

Romy grinned. "Tina's coming."

There were more screams before the small woman strode into the room and grabbed a handful of jerky from the middle of their circle, stuffing it into her mouth. "Shit day."

She spotted Atlas and stopped chewing. "What's he doing here?"

"This is my room," he answered, lips pursed.

Her face screwed up. "Not sure how I feel about him being here." She chewed a little more. "Jerky tastes good." Her swallow was audible. "I think I'm okay."

She took a seat as Thrym and Nancy entered the room. Thrym led the young Australian woman to a spot across the room, smiling at something she said.

Shoot. Romy reached for some food to sprinkle over herself, but then remembered Atlas.

"Ro," Phobos said in undertones, "don't bother. That thing you've been doing doesn't work, trust me."

"What? I'm not doing anything?" She was burningly aware of Atlas listening. His head was tilted.

"You're not doing your best to make yourself unattractive when Thrym is around?" Phobos asked quietly, brows raised.

Her cheeks burned.

Phobos tucked away his grin. Mostly. "When you like a girl, Ro, anything she does is cute. It. Is. Not. Working."

Face falling, she asked, "Really?"

"I'm afraid so, sis."

"Poacher poop." She let the crackers she'd grabbed fall back on the plate and resumed her spot snuggled into Atlas's side. Honestly, Romy had the suspicion she may not need to do the cracker thing for much longer anyway—not with the way Thrym was looking at Nancy.

"You've really been doing that?" Atlas's chest rumbled with supressed laughter.

"Shh." Romy reached up and pushed a finger against his lips.

"What kind of—"

"I can't believe you gave my assistant job away," she said. Peeking up, she saw alarm cross his face a second before his gaze narrowed. He gave her a suspicious look and she bit her lip.

Thrym and Nancy took a seat near the door. Nancy smiled at everyone in the room, even Romy, though it was noticeably tighter.

"Tell her you like her hair," Tina whispered with an

encouraging look.

"Don't do that, Ro," Charlee blurted. "Maybe just offer her a bit of jerky."

"Quit whispering," Romy whispered. Louder, she said, "Hey, Nancy, want some jerky?" She got up and took the younger girl the plate.

"Sure." Nancy picked some up with careful fingers and Romy returned to her seat.

Awkward.

Atlas kissed her temple. "What is this game, anyway?"

Romy relaxed as the tension in the room dissipated.

"Poker," Elara answered. "You can't tell me you haven't played poker before."

The large man shrugged, and Romy's stomach twisted. In many ways, Atlas was getting to know himself as much as Knot 27. Except he didn't have the excuse of being cultivated in space. Everyone expected him to know what he was doing, and to be in control, and to be confident. But he'd never really had a childhood, or time to explore hobbies. Having been groomed to infiltrate the orbitos from a young age, Atlas had missed out on a lot.

Romy sniffed. "He's never played these card games before." The words came out a mite more ferocious than intended.

The occupants of the room stared and she gritted her teeth, temper rising.

"No, I haven't," Atlas said, calmly, taking her hand. "Maybe you could all show me?"

Romy kicked the cards towards Phobos. "You heard him, Phobos. Deal." She glared at everyone, spending extra time on Elara, who looked like she was going to make a comment.

Romy settled back beside Atlas again, and gave him a large smile, patting his hand. "You just wait. You're going to love this game."

4

Romy came slowly awake, smiling. Extending a hand back, she searched the bed, but Atlas had managed to slip off without waking her. She'd have to get better at waking when he did. Whether he liked it or not, every day Romy wasn't on mission, she'd be spending getting to know the side of him he was determined to keep hidden. He'd probably thought it best to sneak out after he won every single poker game last night. Romy had lost her temper a little.

The metal door crashed against the concrete wall. Romy tried to sit upright, but got tangled in the sheets and fell back onto the bed.

She lifted her head, body trapped, to peer at the doorway. Elara's face was awash with tears, and her eyes were huge with panic.

"Romy," she choked, crumbling half on the bed, half on her.

"Ellie," Romy said, frantically trying to untangle herself. "What's the matter? What's happened? Where's Phobos?"

She'd witnessed this woman fly battlers into the midst of fights with the poachers. What on earth had happened? Elara tried to talk, her chest heaving in stuttering gasps. Her words were incoherent through her sobs, but she thrust a piece of paper at Romy, who'd managed to free herself.

The note was written in Pho's hand, and Romy's world fell away as she read the four words there.

I'm going after him.

"He's gone after D-d-d—" A wail rose up in Elara's chest, blocking the rest of her words.

Romy took her knotmate into her arms. "Shh, Ellie. Deep breaths. Come on, let's settle down so we can talk about this." Not for a second did Romy think Phobos agreed with Houston's violent ideals. His motive in leaving was as simple as the four words on the note.

He was going after him.

Phobos thought Deimos needed him, more so than the other three needed him right now. He loved Deimos. The bond between them was different from the bond between the rest of the knot. In many ways, they were the same person split in two. They'd always been referred to as twins for that reason, though they looked nothing alike—aside from their green eyes. Romy may have thought Phobos was a fool, that Deimos wasn't worth wasting his time over, but she knew his heart was in the right place . . . and it was broken. That was why he'd done this.

Romy rocked her knotmate, shushing her at intervals, and after several minutes Ellie calmed enough to pull away.

"Ro," she whispered.

"He'll be okay." If anyone harmed Phobos, she'd hunt them across the galaxy and choke them with her bare hands.

"Ro," Elara said again. "I'm pregnant."

Romy froze.

"I'm pregnant," her knotmate repeated. "With a baby."

Forcing her lips to move, Romy said, "You're pregnant."

"Oh no, I shouldn't have said anything," Elara fretted.

Romy blinked and a fierce heat swept through her. "You're pregnant? With a baby! You're going to have a baby?" She covered her mouth with a closed fist.

Large tears squeezed from Elara's hazel eyes.

Romy shoved down the 'I'm going to be an aunt' and the 'I'll kill anyone who looks at this baby wrong' thoughts and gripped Elara's upper arms, saying, "Phobos wouldn't have left if he had known."

"Y-yes he would. He doesn't even like me." Elara flopped back onto the bed and threw her arms over her face.

That seemed . . . irrational. "Of course he does."

"No, he doesn't! Don't tell me what I know."

Yikes. "Okay," Romy drew out. "Right now, we need to get you stuff." She paused with a frown. "Do you know what you need?"

Elara lowered her arms and they exchanged a baffled look.

"I'll get Charlee," Romy decided.

"No." Elara clutched her arm in a death grip. "Earth humans aren't allowed to have children. They'll make me get rid of him."

Him? A nephew? Love swelled in her chest as she wondered how Elara knew the gender—a mother thing, most likely. Romy stood and marched to the mirror. She fogged up the mirror and then wrote words with her forefinger, eliciting a loud squeak from the mirror as she did so.

Elara shuffled up beside her and read the words aloud, "I, Romy of Knot 27, say Elara can have a baby." She crumpled onto the floor, wailing again. "Th-th-s-so-n-nice."

Her mirror contract wasn't nice, Romy thought, stiffening. It was a promise. Over her dead body would *anyone* ever hurt Elara and their baby. She'd make what Feral Romy did to that room of people look like a Christmas lunch. Romy had an inherent protective streak—she assumed because of the whole 'mother hen' part of her genetic makeup. But this? This was a whole new level of 'look at that baby wrong and I'll end you'.

"Ellie," Romy said, crouching. "I'm going to get Phobos back for you. Just let me figure out how. But we need to go see Char right now. You know we can trust her. I don't know what pregnant humans need. What if you're supposed to be in an incubator right now?"

"I didn't think about that."

They exchanged a serious look.

"You worry about keeping my nephew healthy," Romy said. "And let me worry about getting the father back."

Elara kicked the wall. "I'm going to kill him when he gets back." She began to cry again. "I'll kiss him first, though."

THE CLINIC DOOR CRACKED OPEN. "ROMY," THRYM HISSED from outside.

She glanced toward where Elara spoke in hushed tones with Charlee. "Be back in a second."

"Don't tell Thrym yet," Elara whispered low.

"You got it, Ellie," she replied. Romy pushed the door fully open, slipping through before shutting it, and for the second time that day, words failed her.

Thrym's face was as crumpled as his usually pristine uniform.

"Ro," he croaked.

This day had only just begun, apparently. Romy checked her watch. There was around one hour until they were supposed to leave on mission. Elara wasn't going in her half-hysterical state. Which meant Romy had to talk to Atlas before they went.

"What's wrong, Thrym?" Romy scanned him for injury. She'd never seen him like this, ever. Thrym didn't . . . do *this*. He looked nothing like the professional, tidy soldier he was.

"She's gone," he whispered with a furtive look down the passages each side of the clinic. "I've covered for her all day, but she hasn't come back. I think she's serious."

"Who? Let's start there."

"Sorry," he said. His hands clenched. God, he was completely losing it.

"Nancy," he breathed. "She's gone to the Renegades."

Nancy too? "Crap." Phobos's disappearing act after the meeting in the Mess to 'go check on Nancy' suddenly made sense.

He leaned in. "She'll be labelled a traitor. She won't be able to return. I'll need to join the Renegades."

Romy's mouth dried. Did he hear himself? Thrym *never* broke the rules. Even at Romy's craziest he'd barely been able to bend the rules to allow for her insanity, and now he wasn't giving a single thought to the consequences to save Nancy. Romy's jaw dropped as she realised what that meant. "She's gone to check that her friends are alive," she said as Thrym took rapid, shallow breaths.

He gripped her arm. "I know that. But Atlas won't."

"Thrym." Romy tried to hug him, but he backed away, hands raised. He was a *mess.* He was acting like Atlas when Romy was in danger. "They will understand. Phobos has gone as well."

"What?" he roared.

Romy meant it as a consolation that Nancy wasn't alone, but it didn't have that effect.

"That spoiled little—"

Romy winced as Thrym cursed long and hard. Phobos and Deimos had run away. Elara was knocked up. She suddenly snorted. "Thrym, we make terrible parents."

He broke off his cussing and an unwilling sound, part laughter and part sob, escaped him. "We do."

The situation terrified her; it was the only reason tears began to pour down her cheeks. Thrym joined her with body-wracking laughter, and finally—more from needing each other to stay standing—they ended up hugging and gasping and crying all at once.

Romy spoke once they'd simmered down. They were now leaning against the wall side-by-side. It felt . . . like it used to, and maybe there was a reason why. "Thrym, I think you have feelings for her." Not just feelings—Romy was pretty sure he loved Nancy and had no idea.

"Who?"

She arched a brow.

"Nancy?" he scoffed. "No, I don't. I. . . ."

This was what she'd missed out on with Phobos and Elara, watching this moment. But Romy had front-row seats as Thrym connected the dots.

"You're breaking rules for her," she added. "I never thought I'd see the day. The way you look at her. . . . Thrym, are you sure you don't love her?"

His mouth bobbed open and shut. "I. . . ."

"You literally just said you'd join the Renegades for her."

He inhaled sharply. "Yes, I would."

"You've been smiling around 500 per cent more than usual, just saying."

Thrym frowned at the floor, shaking his head.

She watched her knotmate sort through his feelings, exploring all the options, as he tended to do, and witnessing his expression as every possible pathway led him back to one answer.

"Holy crap," he said in amazement. "You're right." Shifting, he stared at Romy like she had all the answers, a wide grin spreading across his face.

"Yes," she said, pushing off the wall. "So, let's figure out how to get her back."

"ARE YOU OKAY?" ATLAS ASKED. HE SAT AT HIS DESK, A BLUE screen from a nanopad projected in a semi-circle before him. The graphs and numbers hovered forgotten after the news she'd just imparted.

Romy nodded. "It's not like with . . . the *other* one."

"Deimos," he supplied.

"Him, yes. It's not like it was with him. Phobos went because he felt he had to."

"And Nancy?"

"Her friends are there."

Atlas didn't look particularly accepting of either of them deserting, judging by the coldness in his grey eyes, but whatever he was thinking, he kept it to himself, seeing her distress. He ran a hand through his hair. "What is the likelihood of you charging off after them?"

Busted. "Moderately to highly probable."

He shut the screens off and stood. "That's what I thought. Before you do anything, I would like you to consider your importance as a player in this war."

"Houston already has the cure."

"Your face is known to all, Rosemary. To everyone on Earth. It's not about you giving us the cure anymore. You and the rest of your knot are figureheads, symbols. In some ways, that holds more importance. Not only that, they know of our relationship, especially Houston. They could use you against me."

"I know. But I've got to get them back." Romy stayed still as he came closer and rubbed his thumb over the top of her cheekbone.

"Will you let me handle it?" he asked. "Work with me, watch my every move, I don't care. But please don't let me wake up and see you've left in the night."

A refusal halted on Romy's lips. Her nearly overwhelming need to fly to Houston's front door, kick it in with her cool boots, and unleash the space fury was hard to rein in. But a question crept through that protective urge. *Do I need to do everything?* Really, Atlas was much better qualified for negotiations to have them returned. "As long as Thrym and I can be involved, yes, I'd be thankful if you'll get them back for us."

He pressed his lips against her hairline and inhaled. "Thank you."

Romy would hate to wake and find him gone, and she trusted him to shift cities to get her knotmate back. "Oh, Elara can't go to Rome today."

Atlas took his seat again. "She's sick?"

"Uh, she is pretty uh, not well after finding Phobos gone." Romy fidgeted under his look. "She probably won't be able to do missions for a while." She recalled the number Charlee gave them. "For nine months."

Atlas's eyes widened. "She's pregnant?"

What the—? "How did you guess that?"

His laughter filled the room and he swept her to him and pressed his lips down on her tenderly, then harder. Nothing existed for Romy but him. His lips. His kiss. His tongue entered her mouth and she met the action. He'd done this before. The first time Romy had burst into laughter, but now she saw the appeal of it. She gripped his hair and pulled his face down, and he lifted her onto his desk, pulling her hips closer.

"Atlas," Romy murmured and reached under his shoulder to pull him closer.

"I love you so much," he breathed.

They separated and she gave him a small smile that he kissed into a full-blown one.

"You're going to be an aunty," he said, watching her closely.

"Yes," she said, matter-of-fact. "Elara said it's a boy. I'll have a nephew."

"Oh?"

She narrowed her eyes at the neutral reply, but didn't quite know what to make of it. "For the record, I didn't tell you the news. You guessed. You need to pretend you don't know around Ellie."

"I can do that. Can I recommend that you don't tell others Elara won't be working for nine months?"

Romy shrugged. "Okay."

"I'll put Elara on non-combat duties for the duration of the pregnancy."

She glanced at her watch. Time to head to the hangar. "Thanks. I'd best be off."

"Be careful, Rosemary."

The words floated after her out the door, and she weaved her way through the chaotic command room and to the outer passage where Thrym waited.

He danced from foot to foot. "What's he going to do to her? I know you like him, Ro, but I'll probably need to kill him. Maybe you could do it as he slept."

"Jaysus, Thrym," Romy scolded, borrowing some of Char's Irish talk. "I don't just like Atlas, I *love* him. He makes me melt inside, do you hear me? And you can bet that if either he or you ask me to kill the other, I'll be killing the person who did the asking."

A speaker clicked on overhead. *'Thank you, Rosemary.'*

Thrym yelped, leaping off the ground.

The speaker clicked off, taking Atlas's voice with it.

Romy's heart hammered double time. What did she just say? Oh no, she'd definitely said embarrassing stuff.

"That is *not* a nice trick." She turned in a circle, glaring. There had to be a camera somewhere.

The speaker clicked on. *'You make me melt, too.'*

The speaker clicked off.

"Well then," Romy huffed, feeling her ears burning. She huffed again. "Right. Well then, okay."

Thrym watched her, nose wrinkling. "Your happy is leaking out."

"I'm not happy, I'm focused." Romy shoved past him. "There's a job to be done and you two are fooling around." She strode down the hall to the hangar, ranting to a silent Thrym about how she had to do everything.

5

"Where's Ellie?"

That Thrym hadn't noticed their knotmate's absence until now spoke for his state of mind. They were nearly in Rome. Perhaps she should've left him behind as well.

"Uh, she. . . ." Romy tried to remember her lie. "Oh. She's upset about Pho."

"You're lying."

"That is extremely insulting."

"What's happening?" he prompted.

"I'm not allowed to tell," Romy said. "But she's okay." She held Thrym's gaze for a beat before he played nice and let it go.

They descended ten minutes later and the craft bounced on its four legs, absorbing the shock of the landing.

"Wanna ride with me?" Thrym asked, rolling out a motorbike. The refugees they were contacting were in a settlement ten kilometres away.

"Nuh-uh, you handsome liquorice man. She's my motorbike buddy." Tina appeared and hauled Romy to a bike and chucked her a helmet.

Romy snorted, saying, "I know you only grabbed me because I'm tall." Tina had trouble propping motorbikes up with her shorter legs.

"Shut it, space Barbie. Where's Lazy, anyway?"

"She's sick," Romy said smoothly.

"Wow, you're a terrible liar."

"She is. I swear."

"What's she sick with?"

Romy brightened. "Certain foods are making her ill in the mornings, and she's irrational about small things."

Tina twisted to look back. "She's pregnant?"

"How do you people keep guessing this?" Romy exploded.

"Stick to something general next time, like diarrhoea."

Romy sighed. "Can you please not tell anyone else?"

Tina revved the engine. It didn't make much noise; these motorbikes were unsatisfactorily quiet. The smaller woman took off, not bothering to answer the question. The other members of their team followed suit, falling into line on their own bikes.

"Routine refugee mission," Tina's voice crackled through their helmets five minutes later. "The base is thirty minutes out of Rome and contains 150 civilians."

They'd completed ten of these missions in the last month. Other Amach teams were doing the same, methodically making their way through each country. Progress was slower than anyone would like—considering they had to get to as many of the settlements before the Renegades as possible.

So far, Houston's forces hadn't ambushed any of the Amach teams. He'd been 'recruiting' refugees in other areas, and had only attacked the Mandate's cities. That he considered the Mandate to be the bigger, more immediate threat was obvious, but eventually the Renegades and the Amach would meet. Their clash was inevitable. The doctor made no secret of what he ultimately wanted—to become the governing power of Earth. That meant the Mandate *and* the Amach were in his way.

Romy once thought she knew Houston.

Once, she'd found him entertaining and respected the power of his intelligence. That was before he tested an insanity cure on space soldiers and, when it didn't work, left them to die and refroze them, so no one knew what he was doing. And before he'd betrayed the Amach and his best friend to form the Renegades.

"Are we going into Rome?" Romy asked when Tina was done debriefing them. "Like, the Vatican?"

"No."

"Colosseum?"

"No."

"Why do I like you again?"

Tina's snort crackled in her ears. "Beats me."

"Where was the Renegades' last reported movement?" Thrym asked.

Tina replied, "In Greece, two hours south of Athens."

"Isn't that close?" Romy asked.

"Sure is," Tina said. "We'll be on guard, but he hasn't given us any reason to suppose he'll interfere just yet."

Romy couldn't imagine Houston *would* give any warning before he attacked.

She sighed and turned her attention to the passing country. Rome was warm, but not the same beating, relentless heat she'd experienced in Egypt. That blew her mind—that Earth wasn't one temperature. Orbito One had always been maintained at a steady 23.8 degrees Celsius.

She took in the different trees and tumbled mud-brick houses covered in creeping vines, thinking about all the places she'd go in New Italy if she ever got the chance. There was so much of the world she wanted to see, Romy wasn't sure it could be done in a single lifetime.

Tina pulled off the cracked tarseal road after another twenty minutes, and the team clambered off the bikes, ditching their helmets. They'd cover the rest of the distance on foot.

"—this one doesn't have sentry posts—"

"—Roger that. Makes it easier—"

Less fun, though, she thought, listening to the others talk as they walked. Romy quite enjoyed shooting people with tranquilisers from a hundred metres away.

The good thing about the settlements was each one had the same layout and the same routine. There were three to five official buildings depending on the size of the camp. This one, being smaller, would have three. The thing about the layout being the same was that the Amach—and everyone else—knew exactly where the official people slept: the bungalow directly behind the middle official building.

Their team crept through the settlement half an hour later, sticking to the weak shadows of the bungalows. These places never failed to remind her of Jimboomba, the first settlement she'd seen.

They beelined for the bungalow where the settlement commander would be sleeping, and Thrym raised a hand and knocked on the door.

He stepped back behind the sides of the bungalow where the rest of them were spread out. These folks tended to come out waving guns.

Romy waited for the creaking door, the inching footsteps, the click of a safety release.

Ping.

"Fire!" she shouted. She grabbed Thrym and shoved him around the back of the bungalow as two more shots rang out. "They're shooting from the medical wing."

"Anyone hit?" Tina asked, crouching.

The ten team members did a quick search and each gave a negative answer.

"Bolt for the trees, then work our way out?" Tina consulted Thrym. He eyed the distance and shifted in his crouch.

"They've chosen a good spot," he said. "The space all around the official buildings is pretty open. They only fired three bullets, though . . . and they had us in the open. Maybe they don't know who we are. I say we talk to them."

Tina's gaze narrowed. "I'm not a fan of talking. But okay, we'll try. Leroy?"

"Got it," he said. The team translator dropped his case and rifled through it before pulling out a megaphone.

"Eyes sharp," Tina said to Romy. "The civilians may be creeping up through the trees. Fan out while Leroy works," she said in a louder voice to the others.

They crouched in an outward-facing semi-circle, guns raised, scanning the treeline.

A string of rhythmic words that Romy assumed to be Italian blared out of the megaphone behind her.

By the time the settlement responded, her knees ached from kneeling on the sun-dried ground.

The blaring comments went back and forth behind her.

"Do you think we'll be back in time for dinner?" Romy asked Thrym. He didn't answer. He wasn't paying any attention to his area of the trees. She whacked him with the butt of her gun. "You're no use to her if you can't keep yourself alive."

He sighed. "I'm really worried about her."

"I can tell." Romy paused. "I hadn't realised you'd spent that much time with Nancy."

"Yeah, well . . . less in recent months with all the stuff happening in the knot. But before that, tonnes. And after Houston and Deimos, we began hanging again, and it was a bit different from before, I knew, but I was too. . . ."

Occupied with thoughts of me? "I got you." Romy covered his slip. "Your feelings for her crept up on you." She sniggered as a dark flush reddened his cheeks.

Leroy repacked the megaphone. "A group of them are coming over to talk." He glanced at Romy. "They saw the 'crazy one' and thought she was part of the Renegades, so they decided to hide."

"She's not crazy," Thrym said with a frown.

Leroy held up his hands. "Their words. They only know what they saw on the screen a month ago."

In other words, they saw Feral Romy kill a room of Mandate soldiers, and then Houston telling the world she was with their new faction.

A small group emerged from the trees on Romy's side. She scanned their body language and hands, then lowered her rifle to the ground, close enough to whip it up if any of them got violent. Some peered her way, and she attempted to look pleasant and peaceful to put them at ease. One of the Italian civilians blanched when she smiled at him.

Leroy took over once again, and soon Tina and the settlement commander were shaking hands.

"Thrym," Tina said, approaching, "call in the crafts. We have three hours to get their possessions loaded in the crafts, nothing unnecessary. Make sure they know not to bring snakes and shit like that," she called back at Leroy.

Romy and Thrym left for the hospital building to raid the medicines and equipment there. Their team took whatever they could back to the Amach. When you were bringing 150 more mouths to feed, you had to take whatever you could get your hands on.

She and Thrym worked in silence, moving on to raid the weaponry room afterward. Like her, he was caught up in worrying about Phobos and Nancy. They would've reached the Renegades at their main base in Florida long ago.

Romy hated to think about either of them in danger, especially Phobos. But traitor though Deimos was, he wouldn't harm his twin.

A heaviness weighed in her chest as she took a break and peered about the windowless room.

The monotony of tasks like this made dwelling on the despair of their situation too easy. There was too much time to tally the number of enemies the Amach faced in this war and wonder how they could possibly get out of this fight without losing countless lives. The Amach had around six thousand spread throughout their bases—six thousand against *tens* of thousands.

"That everything?" the pilot, Deanna, called as they brought the last cache of rifles to the craft.

They heaved it into place and Thrym moved to speak with the other pilots.

"As much as we'll get in," Romy replied. This craft was jam-packed, and the rest were filled with refugees. "Any problems?"

Deanna chuckled. "One of the elderly ladies tried to bring her bed. Said it was the only one that didn't make her back hurt."

A hand closed around Romy's upper arm.

"Thrym?" she asked at his drawn face.

"A message just came in from Atlas," he said.

She searched his face, heart giving a strong thud. "What happened?"

Thrym shook his head. "Nancy and Phobos are back."

Romy gasped. "That's great."

Why didn't he look happy?

He gave her a veiled look. "They're not alone."

6

"Ro, it will be okay," Thrym said, taking her clenched fist in his warm hand.

The slight jolt as their craft landed in the Amach hangar barely registered. Neither did Thrym's whispers until he ducked to get her attention.

She narrowed her eyes at his expression. "Spit it out."

His blue eyes darkened and his jaw set. "I'm worried about your temper."

"I don't have a temper," she protested.

"Every poker game," he retorted.

Okay. Maybe she had a bit of a temper after everything. "Do you blame me? Deimos has the nerve to show his face here. After what he did?"

He wormed his fingers between hers and squeezed her hand as he pondered the situation. "No, I don't blame you. You felt the betrayal most out of all of us. The rest of us have heard your story, and seen him on the screen a few times—"

"You don't believe me?"

Thrym shook his head. "Of course we believe you, but we weren't there, Ro. That's the difference. You looked into his eyes as he did that stuff. For the rest of us, there's an emotional distance. Anyway, it's not Deimos I'm worried about."

Romy met his gaze.

"Phobos," he finished. "Phobos felt strongly enough to leave Elara and try to convince him to come back. If we go in there and lose our tempers—" He grinned at Romy's wry smile. "Fine. If *you* go in there and lose your temper, you risk alienating Phobos too, and through him, Elara."

"And if I don't, we'll all stay the same as we've been?" she asked, untangling their fingers to take off her harness belt. "We'll be a big happy knot again?"

"No," he said, doing the same. "But you won't be the bad guy. He'll still be the bad guy, and it won't confuse the issue. No one expects you to be okay with this. Phobos knows that as surely as the rest of us, and hopefully has been smart enough to keep Deimos away, but if you see him, don't shoot him in the kneecap, okay?"

"You're good at this . . . Dad."

Thrym winced. "I really wish Dr Charlee never told you that mother-father stuff."

"I dunno." Romy gave him a speculative glance. "I think you're pretty good at it."

The cargo door lowered with a groan and Romy mimicked Thrym as he took a deep breath. His chat had achieved its intended purpose. It distracted her from the simmering anger she'd sat in on the flight back from Rome. Enough for her to see the merit of his argument. She didn't want to upset the newfound stability between her knotmates. That stability had been hard won and was more precious than her own life. A tiny part of her acknowledged that shooting Deimos in the kneecap *would* make her the bad guy. She wanted Deimos to suffer for what he'd done and remain the person who made the mistake. Damn Thrym for making sense.

As the cargo door thudded to the ground, Romy kept her eyes on concrete, unsure how she'd respond if she saw his face.

That was her intention.

What she saw undid that.

The hangar was full of people. They milled between the crafts and the stacked rows of crates around the outer piped wall. "Holy crap," Thrym said in awe. "How did they do it?"

Romy stared. The last time she'd seen these people, some were in crates, and the rest had been freshly saved from the orbitos. Even though they wore mismatched civilian clothing now, the straight set of their backs and the slight bewildered innocence of their faces made it crystal clear just who they were.

"They brought the space soldiers back." She blinked and began to walk down the ramp off the craft. "How?"

The hangar was a frenzy of activity, with the arrival of their refugees and the onslaught of space soldiers, plus the usual bustle of the place. Romy spotted Gwenyth squeezing through the crowd and it occurred to her to hide too late. Grey eyes found her. "Poacher poop," she muttered.

"The commander-general would like to see the both of you, immediately," she said tersely.

"Hi, Gwenyth. How are you?" Romy asked.

The thin lines on the woman's face deepened and with a glance around the hangar that said, 'Are you still crazy?', Gwenyth wound back between the horde without a word.

Still tense in case Deimos was around somewhere and could see her, Romy followed Atlas's mother back through the crowd, feeling Thrym close behind. One of the space soldiers on her left elbowed another, and muttered something in a hushed tone. She ignored it.

. . . The second time, too.

By the fourth time, it was getting hard to pretend the soldiers weren't gawking at her. "What's happening?" she mumbled to Thrym out the corner of her mouth.

"Uh, not too sure," he said with false calm that made her grin because he was obviously still worried about her shooting Deimos. "Hold on, they're saying something," he said.

She strained to hear and caught two words. . . . *That can't be right.*

One of the soldiers, dressed in flip-flops and a Hawaiian shirt, shuffled closer to her. "Mother hen," he said in a reverent voice.

Thrym choked behind her.

"Hell no." Romy picked up her pace, borderline rude as she wove through the crowd. "Excuse me. Nope, no hen here. Can you move, please? *Not a mother hen.*"

The passages were just as packed. All the way to the Mess, which was *also* packed. There were several thousand space soldiers here. The repercussions of so many new soldiers would have a massive impact on the Amach.

"Mother hen."

"Mother hen."

"Mother hen."

A strangled sound came from Thrym again, and heat began to rise up Romy's neck. "Cut it out. It's not funny."

A deep laugh escaped him. "Are you serious? You were just calling me Dad. This is karma at its finest."

He continued laughing and she spoke over him. "Why are they doing it?" Romy asked.

The mother hen thing was a personal joke amongst their knot and close friends, but how the heck had these space soldiers heard about it?

"Deimos's idea of a joke, you think?" Thrym asked.

Deimos. Of course. Romy clenched her jaw. Hard.

"I hope they never stop," Thrym said.

An evil thread wormed to the surface. "I wonder where Nancy is. The message said she returned as well," Romy said.

That shut him up.

"This crowd is seriously pissing me off," Romy snarled. The Mess was packed, and she had to get to the other side to reach Atlas.

Of course, that was when *he* decided to appear.

Romy glanced up and stumbled over her feet.

She heard Phobos hiss, "Don't."

Deimos clearly had no mind to listen. He stopped three metres in front of her, like they were in a standoff. Or perhaps because he, despite who he was now, knew her well, and knew physical proximity to the object of her anger heightened her fury. It had before, and certainly would with her new temper.

Three metres didn't seem far enough at the moment.

Deimos possessed the same green eyes as Phobos, but where Pho was blond and golden-skinned, Deimos's skin was olive and his hair a wavy black. He was the standard six foot height of most space soldiers and stood in a long-sleeved grey T-shirt and black cargo pants, watching her, lips pressed together.

Romy let her eyes glaze over him as though no one stood there, and forced her feet to move again, hopefully in the direction she'd been heading before. She did her utmost to ignore his existence. Her temper wouldn't allow more right now. To talk to him would snap the fragile hold she had.

Phobos hovered nervously by Deimos's side.

She gave him a warm smile and pulled him in to a hug. "Pho, I'm glad you're back. Have you seen Elara?"

"Yes. It . . . didn't go well."

"Romy, I—," Deimos began.

"She'll be fine." Romy spoke again to Phobos. "You just scared her, but you might want to kiss butt for the foreseeable future."

Phobos's eyes slid from Romy to Deimos and back. "Yeah."

Going on tiptoes, she gave him another kiss. "Please don't leave like that again, Pho. You really worried us. You know it would kill us if you were hurt." Maybe not literally kill them anymore, but Romy didn't know how she'd go on without Phobos.

His green eyes softened. "I know, Ro. I'm sorry."

She heard the 'but' in his voice and gave him the ghost of a smile, which he returned.

"Romy, can I please talk to you?" Deimos asked.

She ignored him and continued squeezing through the thick crowd toward Atlas, knowing if she stayed a second longer and felt those green eyes on her one moment more, she'd forget Thrym's words of advice and do something she really wanted to do.

"THAT WENT AS WELL AS COULD BE EXPECTED," THRYM SAID IN a long exhale as they stepped into the debriefing room.

Atlas glanced up from the table and made his way toward her.

Romy looked back at her knotmate. "Thank you for not speaking to him either."

"I'm angry at Deimos, too," he said quietly. "He shouldn't expect any less."

Romy couldn't see how that would ever change. How could you trust someone again when they'd broken it so decisively? "What are you going to say to Nancy?"

"I thought about sulking," he admitted with a smile. "But I guess we need to have a talk about . . . stuff."

"Yes, tell her you love her. Don't waste any time."

"You think? I don't want to scare her off."

I do," said Romy with a smile. Nancy had adored Thrym since Jimboomba. There was no way she didn't return his feelings. They were in the middle of a world war. If you couldn't tell someone you loved them now, you didn't love them enough.

Strong arms enveloped her and the scent of eucalyptus washed over her. Romy rested her head back on Atlas's shoulder.

"You okay?" he asked.

"I love you," she said.

The air stuttered in his throat. "My favourite words. I love you too," he said, holding her tighter. "And?"

"I'm angry. Let's get this over with."

He kissed the space behind her ear. "You got it. As long as you're okay to be here. There are a few developments that may shock you and I realise you've gone through—"

Trying to protect her again. Romy's chest tightened. "Atlas, I'm okay. I can handle it, I swear," she said, twisting to look at him. Romy brought a hand up and pushed back a few strands of his jet-black hair. The silky locks never failed to fall over his forehead, though it appeared as though he'd been running his hands through them frequently today—a sure sign he wasn't as calm as he wanted others to believe.

He kissed her hand, and Romy took a seat next to Tina and Thrym and listened as Atlas closed the door and moved to the front of the room.

"Two days ago, two of our force left this base for Florida. Their reason, in the notes they left, was to retrieve loved ones in the company of the Renegades."

"Why wasn't this made known?" a captain at the front asked.

"Because I didn't wish you to know," Atlas answered, giving him a flat look.

The captain fell silent.

"Tonight, these two members returned, and with them they brought 3,600 of the soldiers freed from the orbitos, and someone we have recently seen at Houston's right-hand side: Deimos."

Angry mutterings rose within the room. Charlee gave Romy a grim glance from across the table, and Romy returned it. What was Char feeling about this? The doctor and Deimos had been close for a night or two before he left.

"How did they get out?" Thrym asked. "Houston wouldn't have been happy."

Romy shivered at the thought of Houston's reaction.

"The better part of four thousand soldiers with guns are hard to say no to, especially when they have a reason to leave. Which brings me to the point of most concern." He gave Romy a cursory glance. Enough to warn her this was something that might affect her.

She held her breath.

"They've returned because the insanity cure Houston gave them wore off."

"What?" Romy said. Her exclamation was lost amongst the din of thirty voices demanding to know the same thing.

Atlas leaned onto the table where he stood at the front. "It began wearing off two weeks ago. The first to receive the injection were engaged in a skirmish with the Mandate's forces and shots were fired. It turned into a frenzy. Not only did the space soldiers lose their minds, they became extremely violent. Fifty of the Renegades were lost trying to fight them, and the last space soldier killed himself last week by running into a wall repeatedly."

"Was this change only triggered when they killed again after the cure had worn off?" Charlee asked. She was as pale as Romy had ever seen her. Charlee hadn't created the cure, but she had administered it recently . . . to Knot 27.

Romy swallowed, thinking of one of her knotmates running into a wall until it was over. What had Thrym said earlier about the difference between experiencing something first-hand, and not? Romy could still remember how it had felt to be standing on shattered glass. She could understand why the space soldier did that to himself—to get rid of the itch under his skin.

"The others have not shown any sign of instability," Atlas replied. She lifted her head in time to see his eyes move away from her. "Houston confided in Deimos five days ago that he believed the answer lay in there being too low a percentage of Rosemary's blood in the injection to ensure a permanent hold." His voice tightened. "Synthesising her blood proved ineffective. A further ten space soldiers were lost to these tests."

Thrym shifted beside her, the only sign of his anger. "That's why Deimos brought them back? To use Romy?"

"He maintains it was to protect the space soldiers from further testing, but he could have taken them to any of our bases and instead brought them to where Romy is, so your theory shouldn't be discounted, Captain."

"Why do we always get them when they're big, vulnerable babies?" Tina complained, then tipped her head back to look at the ceiling. "Are all of the surviving space soldiers here, then?"

Atlas sighed. "Unfortunately not. According to Deimos, there were several hundred in the labs in deep freeze that were unreachable when their plan was set in motion."

Houston still had some of the soldiers? "We have to save them," Romy said. "Who knows what he's doing to them."

"We're not in a position to do so," Atlas countered. "I understand your sense of urgency, but unless a window opens to negotiate their return, a rescue attempt would harm more of our people than it would save."

Easy to say when they weren't being tested on. Though Romy felt bad for the thought as soon as she had it. Atlas knew better than most what she'd gone through. "The Amach will help the other space soldiers as soon as an opportunity arises?" she asked. Atlas could be counted on to help, but the question was made to the other occupants in the room.

She waited until everyone had nodded or murmured their assent.

"Dr Charlee," Atlas said. "Can we count on you to put your team to finding a lasting cure?"

She appeared bewildered. "I'm not sure about counting on me. I only replicated the cure, remember." Her eyes cut to Romy. "If it is a matter of taking blood from Romy and it can't be synthesised, then it will take a long, long time to cure upwards of three and a half thousand, especially if we need to leave the tests for extended periods of time to see if it holds. It could take years."

"Please let Commander Gwenyth know if you require anything." Atlas nodded. "I won't need to remind you Romy is to be treated with respect, and if I find she has been taken advantage of, you won't like the consequences."

Romy coloured. "Atlas, Char wouldn't—"

"If I ever take advantage of any of my patients, I hope I won't like the consequences," Charlee replied. Standing, she nodded to two of the other medical team and made for the door. "I'll send one of my registrars with a daily report to your office, commander-general."

Atlas nodded before lifting a brow in response to Romy's loaded look.

"This changes the game," mused Cronus from a seat up the front. "That is a massive blow to Houston's numbers, and to the Renegades' morality. The populace loves the space soldiers, even more so after the Mandate's lies were revealed." He grinned around the table. "We are now a player in this game."

Tina rolled her eyes.

"I agree," Atlas said. "My next point of order might make us a larger player still."

There's more? Romy straightened, sharing a surprised look with Thrym.

"I received a message one hour ago from the Mandate. Considering our new numbers, they are interested in an alliance with us."

"You're joking?" Gwenyth asked. "They must be absolutely desperate. How is their intelligence so good?"

"I leaked it," Atlas said simply.

The resulting uproar was impressive. He pursed his lips and waited it out.

The Renegades still held all the cards overall. Not only did they have an alliance with the Critamal, and a third of the Amach, they had the high-powered laser cannons. Really, the Mandate and the Amach hardly registered on the playing board alone, but together. . . . The Mandate had access to the latest technology, and had their own forces as well.

"They'll turn on us the moment they can," Romy said.

The room quieted and several hummed their agreement.

Tina perked up. "We march the space soldiers in front of the city dwellers. We use the alliance to our later advantage. It is a chance to change their opinion of us."

Cronus spoke. "I don't like it; the Mandate are slimy bastards. They used me for years up there. Do you know how many thousands died because of them?"

"No one is denying what the Mandate is, or isn't," Atlas

said. "The Amach has lived underground for one hundred years, Cronus. We will not forget what the Mandate is capable of anytime soon. For now, I believe this offers the best course of action."

"What barriers will be in place to ensure they don't take advantage?" Thrym asked.

Atlas tipped his head to him. "I have several ideas I wish to put to the commanders and captains. We will need a clear strategy before I open negotiations with them."

Cronus grumbled. "I have no doubt in your abilities, commander-general. Neither does the Mandate. That, more than anything else, will keep them on the straight and narrow."

"Are there any objections to pursuing alliance talks with the Mandate?" Atlas asked, scanning the room.

No one objected.

A corner of Atlas's mouth lifted. Romy wasn't fooled for a second to believe this was chance. Atlas had been waiting for an ace to fall into his lap before leaking word to the Mandate. He'd wanted this alliance the whole time.

"I wonder what Houston will think when he finds out?" Thrym whispered to her.

"I wonder what he'll *do*," Romy replied.

7

Charlee glided around the lab in a different kind of frenzy from how Houston used to, but in a frenzy nonetheless. "I'm not a genius and people are treating me like I am one," she said.

"I believe in you," Romy said, watching her own blood flowing through the tube into a small plastic bag.

"Please don't believe in me. I want someone to underestimate me, so when I fail, I'll know one person isn't disappointed and we can get drunk together."

"I've never been drunk," Romy answered. "I was always too crazy for it."

"Well, then. I'll fail, we'll lose the war, and then you can do it."

"Sounds good to me."

The two young women grinned at each other.

Charlee checked the full bag and clicked an empty one in its place. "Last one."

"Tina's demanded a girls' night tonight. She's sick of being single in a room of couples."

"Hallelujah to that," the doctor muttered. "It's been dry as the Sahara in this place."

"Thousands of men arrived three days ago."

"They're like puppies, though. They need more time here to not look so bewildered. And the mother hen thing is kind of off-putting."

"Tell me about it."

Charlee snorted. "But frickin' hilarious, don't get me wrong. I'm so glad I originally started that, even if I never meant it to catch on." She hit the area above Romy's arm to get the blood moving. "You feeling all right?"

"A little lightheaded," Romy confessed.

The doctor had laid the bed flat and now lifted the bottom panel higher, so her patient's legs were elevated. She removed the cannula, ignoring Romy's muttered 'I'm fine'.

"If I harm a hair on your head, Atlas will murder me. I'd rather stop here," Char said.

Romy wrinkled her nose, replying, "Sorry about that. He's—"

"Hot," Char interrupted. "He's hot, is what he is. Futuristic caveman hot. You should've seen him when you and Thrym were looking at each other in the meeting."

"What?"

"Oh yeah, he totally noticed. I bet he's trying to play it cool."

Romy laughed. "Whatever. He's always upfront about relationship stuff, asking whether I have feelings for Thrym and if I'm comfortable." She frowned. "Though I do wish he'd do something more than kiss me. I've been waiting for him to make a move."

"I bet he'd never expect you to be upfront about that stuff. It will totally give him a kick up the butt," Char said, then continued at Romy's confused look. "You complained he's standoffish. I'm just giving you advice. You're like a little sister who is the same age as me, yet because you're not related to me, I feel no hesitation in leading you astray. Ask Atlas about the look he gave Thrym, and then ask him if he plans on taking your clothes off anytime soon."

Romy laughed again. "You want me to turn the tables on him? Will that work?"

"I know men, Ro. I may be extremely picky, still in the rebound stage, and a little angry at those with male body parts, but I grew up with four brothers. Trust me."

"I'm going to Tina's for a girls-only night," Romy said to Atlas.

"Dare I ask?" he replied, standing from his desk chair. She'd had to wait in queue to speak to him.

"Just snacks and cards, and Elara will eat the snacks, so just cards, really. What are you working on?"

"The Mandate wishes us to split any numbers we can spare between their largest cities."

Her brows rose of their own accord. "We go into their cities?"

"Yes. You see my problem."

"I think it sounds like a great way to split us up and murder us."

"I agree. Cronus believes we should ask half of the Mandate members here to be our guests in exchange."

She surveyed the flicker in his grey eyes. "You don't?"

"No," he said. "I don't trust what they'd see, and I also don't trust that the other Mandate members wouldn't hesitate to sacrifice their colleagues for the greater good."

"That's . . . barbaric."

"That is their mentality."

She placed her hands on his arms. "Their families? Children?"

Atlas grimaced. "I considered it, but it is against what we stand for, and it would change public perception. With families still seeking us out, it would be harmful, so says Tina. I'll think on it," he said.

Romy stepped into his arms. "You'll do great."

"To what do I owe the pleasure of this visit?" He tilted her chin and kissed her deeply. Romy pressed herself against him, melding her lips to his. When her breath was gone, she pulled back with a gasp. "Maybe I came for that."

He nuzzled the side of her neck and whispered in her ear, "Did you?"

"No, actually." *Big-girl pants.* She looked him in the eye. "I saw you watching Thrym and me yesterday, and I wanted to assure you there's nothing going on there. I love you, and Thrym has finally come around. In fact, I think we're returning to what we used to be."

Atlas swallowed. "You realise this is the third time you've assured me Thrym doesn't have feelings for you."

She kissed the side of his jaw. "I'll keep doing it until you believe me."

"I believe you. I'm afraid it's the general male population I have a problem with."

"That's a big problem."

He smiled against her forehead. "I'm working on it. You don't help matters by looking so beautiful."

"It's the coveralls, isn't it? They do something for you."

"They do. I don't know what it is."

"Is that why you haven't tried to take them off me yet?" she asked.

Atlas choked on his breath, and she stood back as he coughed, trying to clear his airway.

She turned at a knock on the office door. "Cronus," Romy said politely. "How are you?"

"Still alive," he barked. "What's wrong with him?"

She glanced over her shoulder at Atlas and widened her eyes dramatically. "You know, I'm not sure." Moving past him before letting her grin loose, she strode out of the office.

"You did what?" Charlee asked. "Christ on a bike, I wish I'd seen it."

"His reaction was funny at the time, but I'm a little worried about going back to the room tonight," Romy admitted.

Tina groaned. "This conversation is gross."

Elara entered the room and slammed the door behind her. She went directly for the bed and face-planted on the mattress. The others shared a look.

"How're you doing, Ellie?" Romy ventured after a beat.

"He doesn't deserve to know." Her voice was muffled against the mattress. "He left, so he doesn't get to know."

"About the baby?" Romy had confessed about accidentally telling a bunch of people. Phobos and Thrym were still in the dark. "Are you sure? He is the father."

"He doesn't deserve to know until he shows he won't just follow Deimos wherever he goes."

Romy clamped her mouth shut upon hearing Deimos's name.

"Well," Charlee said slowly, "that's your decision." She shrugged helplessly at the other two.

"Are those salt crackers?" Elara asked, turning her head.

Carefully, Romy pushed a cracker toward her knotmate, jumping when Elara snaked out a hand to snatch it away.

"So, Deimos," Tina said. Charlee whacked her. "What?"

Tina asked defensively. "The elephant in the room is so big, there's hardly any space for me."

"What about him?" Romy said, eyes narrowed. She'd been avoiding Deimos for the last two days. It seemed to be working so far.

"Have you spoken to him?"

She glanced away. "Why would I do that? I said it then and I say it now, I'll never forgive him for that night."

Elara sat up. "I'm considering forgiving him."

The words were like a slap across Romy's face. Was she serious? Elara fidgeted under her knotmate's heavy gaze. "I've talked to him."

Blood poured into Romy's cheeks. "When was this?"

"A few times."

"You didn't tell me?" Romy got to her feet.

"I didn't realise I needed your permission."

Her voice rose. "And I thought we were in this together. He did this to all of us, not just me."

Elara glanced away, jaw clenching, "Yes, but he's our knotmate, Ro. I can't forget that. He's part of me."

"He threw that away, not us."

Romy's knotmate leapt to her feet. "What if someone judged you by one moment in your life? What if someone judged you by the day you killed an entire room of people and never gave you another chance? How would that feel?"

A buzzing filled her ears and Romy took a step back, staring at Elara.

Elara's face crumbled. "Romy, I—"

Shaking, Romy strode to the door. She ignored the calling voices and left, walking as quickly as she could down the passageway.

In an ideal world, Atlas's room would've been empty when she got back.

Atlas was in front of the mirror laying out his shaving

razor and soap when she threw their door open, calmly closed it, and burst into tears. He dropped the towel and crossed to her in three long steps. "What's happened?"

Her heart was in two pieces.

"Tell me." He gripped her shoulders.

Why did he do it to her?

"Darling," Atlas said in desperate concern, pulling her into his arms. "Please talk to me."

Assembling herself would have been easier without his eyes looking into hers. Romy spoke between her sobs. "Do you think I'm overreacting about Deimos?"

"Ah," he said.

Ah? What did that mean?

Atlas led her to the bed. He tugged her down, so they were laying facing each other. "Who said something? Wait, don't tell me, it was Elara."

Romy nodded and repeated the conversation. A flash of anger crossed his face when he heard Elara's final comment. Considering he was the one she woke up next to, drenched in sweat remembering the screening of the moment she'd turned into Feral Romy and taken all those lives, Atlas would be well aware of what those words had done to her.

He rested his head against his arm—also a pillow for her head—and stared at the ceiling. "If anyone else had done what Deimos did, you would have written them off without a problem. Take Houston, for instance."

"He wasn't my knotmate."

"Exactly. You didn't love him, and so it was easy to sever the ties."

Romy looked at him through wet lashes. "I don't understand."

"A part of you wants to forgive him, or you'd already have accepted there was no future relationship possible between you, as I have with Houston."

She frowned. "I can't forgive Deimos, though. Not after what he did. I don't even know if I do feel anything else. All I can feel is . . . anger."

"You wouldn't feel anger if you didn't care."

Her throat tightened. "I don't want to care about him anymore."

"Come here." Atlas shushed her and held her as she submitted to a fresh, quieter bout of crying. A while went by before he spoke again. Long enough for Romy to feel bad because he probably was putting off saving the world to hug her.

"Have you considered hearing him out?" he asked.

Talking to Deimos was all she'd thought about for the last two days. Mainly that there was no way she would, but that everyone expected her to had been constantly on her mind.

"Maybe you need to listen. And if the talk doesn't go well, it might help you move on, but either way you'll know where you stand afterward, instead of being in limbo like this."

"I'm not sure how to talk to him."

He cleared his throat. "I don't think you'll have much of a choice, in the end. Phobos has been giving you time to adjust, but it won't last forever. He didn't drag Deimos back here for nothing."

Romy gave a wet chuckle. "No, I don't suppose he did." She paused. "I'm okay now; you can go back to your work. I didn't know you'd be in here." She trailed off.

"I've got nowhere to be," he said, tucking her closer.

Spotting her reply in her eyes, he added in a firmer voice, "Nowhere, Rosemary."

8

Tina lurched back, barely evading Romy's fist. She twisted her body, dropping down to a squat, then popped up on the other side, jabbing Romy in the side. A blow like that might have ended the game once, but now it was second nature to keep her stomach tensed. She felt it, but it didn't slow her.

Feinting, Romy swung her right foot out low. Tina jumped over it, but as soon as she landed, Romy swung out her other leg and swept Tina's feet from under her.

"Dirty trick," the redhead spat from the ground.

Romy grinned, but backed away out of reach. "I learned from the best."

The woman paused, head tilted. "So you did. Good job. You're almost fun to spar with now."

"I hope to one day be worthy of you," Romy answered in a dry voice. Turning, Romy began unwrapping her wrists. Her feet jerked to a halt at the crowd they'd gathered.

Of space soldiers. Whispering space soldiers.

"Mother hen."

"Mother hen."

"Mother hen."

"What the heck is wrong with them?" Romy whispered to Tina, who looked to be hanging onto her calm by a thread.

"I'm not sure, but do you realise there are over three thousand space soldiers going through puberty right now?"

Romy's lips quivered. "You are so mean. Leave them alone. They don't know any better."

"It's kind of endearing, though, right? They have no idea what to do. Like real chickens."

"They're not chickens," Romy said, clenching her teeth. "They've been thrown into this situation and then used by Houston and now they're floundering."

"I guess they're looking for a leader," Tina said.

She narrowed her eyes. "Are you manipulating me?"

"Yes."

"I just want them to stop calling me mother hen."

Tina finished unwrapping her wrists and wound the sweaty material into a ball. "Tell them, then. Or at least speak to them."

"And I'm sure that won't pull me into your plans whatsoever," Romy said, crossing her arms.

"The space soldiers need more leaders, and leaders they can trust. Deimos isn't enough to provide support for over three thousand, and you have celebrity space soldier status, being *The Space Soldier Who Resisted Insanity*."

Oh brother. But she knew Tina was right. Mentally pulling up her big-girl pants, Romy approached the closest group of soldiers. Their mismatched clothing had been exchanged for the Amach coveralls, and there wasn't a wrinkle to be seen on any of them. Their hair was neat and professional, and their expressions neutral, just with rounded eyes.

They stood to attention as she neared. *Why am I doing this?* She could care for them from afar, like she'd been doing this entire time. "Hello," she said awkwardly, feeling blood rush into her cheeks.

"Soldier Rosemary, ma'am!" they chanted.

The faint peals of Tina's laughter reached her ears from across the gym. Romy glared after her but, turning to face the soldiers again, wondered if others in the Amach had been laughing at the space soldiers' expense, like Tina. Not so long ago, Romy probably wore the exact same expression on her face. If not for her knot and new friends, she'd still look that way.

"You know," she said with a small smile, "on Earth, they aren't as rigid with greetings. You don't have to refer to the Amach civilians as 'soldier'. When on mission, you may refer to the team leader as captain, or commander, depending on their status, and to Atlas as commander-general. Otherwise, just call everyone by their first name."

The group exchanged confused glances. The sheer thought of calling anyone by their first name was an act riddled with rebellion.

"You can call me Romy," she pressed.

A cadet glanced at her shyly. "Romy."

"Lovely to meet you. What do you like to be called?"

The group in front of her announced their names in an orderly line. All the names stemmed from Roman and Greek mythology as per Orbito custom. Afterward, they fell quiet again and watched her expectantly. More had gathered. As much as Romy didn't want to put stock in Tina's chicken comment. . . .

"Tell me what you've gone through since the Amach freed you from the Orbitos," she said, taking a seat on the edge of the padded fighting area.

The same cadet spoke up. By this time the whole crowd of them were there. "It took us a long time to believe humankind had been here the whole time."

Sympathy broke inside of her. "Yes, I remember that very clearly myself."

"And Knot 27 crash-landed here, by yourselves," the girl stressed.

Romy redirected the topic back to the space soldiers, pulling the details out of what they'd been through, and the conversation began to flow steadily, the soldiers dropping down to sit on the floor in front of her.

She glanced at her watch and blinked at the time. A whole hour had passed.

The soldiers were peering over her head when Romy looked up. She twisted to see Gwenyth bearing down on her.

"Atlas wants you," Gwenyth said in a clipped voice.

"Then of course I will come," Romy said, standing. Smiling at the group, she said, "We will talk again soon." Romy had plans for them. Damn Tina.

"You know," Gwenyth said with a sniff as they walked out of the gym, "there are more important things to do than talk all day—"

"More to do than ensure over three thousand people learn they are safe here, give us their loyalty, and fight for us?" Romy asked her.

Gwenyth ignored her as they walked to the meeting.

Romy stopped just outside of the debriefing room, moving to the right so others could enter the room before her. "Gwenyth, I may be in a relationship with your son, but don't mistake that to mean I am your child. I understand in times gone by I haven't always treated you with the respect your position warranted, but I was rarely in my right mind back then. I would appreciate you giving me the courtesy of starting afresh, and in return, I will do the same for you."

"You call your behaviour disrespectful?"

"I call it rude." Romy gave her a flat look. "Yet you were just as bad and I'm sure you were *quite* sane at the time. Let's start again, Gwenyth. For Atlas's sake."

She stared at Romy's outstretched hand and gave another

sniff, shifting past her to move inside the debriefing room. Romy's cheeks flushed, but she wouldn't attack Atlas's mother. That would be a bad thing . . . wouldn't it?

"That seemed like it went well," Charlee whispered in Romy's ear.

Romy plastered on a smile for Atlas's sake as she walked into the room, and didn't drop it as she replied in a falsely happy voice. "About what I expected. Is there any option to date Atlas and not his mother?"

"That is a mother who will be in your life. She missed out on too much of his life, and now wants to be in every part of it, but I wouldn't worry." Charlee took the seat next to her. "You have the trump card."

"What's that?"

"Grandchildren."

Romy glanced at her stomach.

"Grandparents go nuts for them. Anyway, someone has a crush on her. Might distract her for a bit." The doctor jerked her head to where Cronus had pulled out Gwenyth's chair for her.

Romy laughed loudly and clamped a hand over her mouth. "Sorry," she said to the people across the table, then bent her head to Charlee's. "Oh my god."

"I know."

Romy grinned at her and then set her eyes around the room. There weren't many people here. Her gaze swung to the door and she tensed as Phobos and Deimos entered. Her fists curled on her lap.

"Easy, Ro," Char said. "This is a meeting to decide how to facilitate the space soldiers' transition here. Apparently, Deimos demanded to be here."

"Great," Romy said. She stared to the front of the room, ignoring the *person* who had walked in.

Elara and Thrym entered five minutes later and Atlas

started. "Just a quick meeting to set a plan in motion for our new arrivals. I want them settled in as quickly as possible."

"We are currently working on getting them all in uniform," Gwenyth said. "About half have coveralls so far. Three shipments from international bases are expected later today."

Romy leaned forward, drumming her fingers on the table. "Earth lessons would help. I spoke to them today and they still have very little idea of how to behave here."

"You have someone in mind?" Atlas said, giving a nod to a young man up front, another assistant. He bent his head over his device and began to type furiously.

She'd had about five minutes to think about it. "Yes, I do. Phobos, obviously, to handle their physical training, but I believe Nancy would be great at the job. She helped me a lot when I first landed here."

Romy gave Thrym a questioning look and he beamed at her, flashing white teeth. She truly did think Nancy would be perfect for the job, and Thrym's relationship with Nancy was also looking serious. Romy had to mend bridges with Nancy for her knotmate to be happy in the long run.

"Captain?" Atlas asked Thrym.

"Nancy is passionate about the wrong that has befallen those on the orbitos. One of her newly returned friends, Freya, may be of help too."

"Did Nancy find all of her friends?" Romy asked Charlee quietly. Only one had been killed before capture.

"Yes, I believe so."

"Eddie?"

"He's already been put to work with our other engineers."

Relief swept through her, and a fair amount of guilt she'd carried since learning of their capture eased. She'd been absorbed in her own problems lately. She bumped going to visit the Jimboomba crew to the top of her list.

"This Nancy is one of the females who deserted to retrieve her friends?" Cronus interrupted.

Thrym began to stand, face murderous.

"She is," Atlas confirmed. "She is also a Tait."

"*The* Taits?" Cronus said. Atlas nodded.

Thrym slowly lowered, glaring around the table.

"They had a lot to do with anti-global warming back in the day," Charlee whispered in Romy's ear.

The room fell quiet, and a few things Romy had heard others say in reference to Nancy suddenly made sense.

A voice spoke up. "The space soldiers want Romy at the moment."

Romy didn't look. She was the only one.

"Tina has plans for Rosemary," Atlas said. "She wants to take her into the cities once it's deemed safe."

"Let me put it another way," Deimos said. "They no longer believe anyone. They will only believe her."

Elara scrunched her small nose. "Why?"

The people in the room waited for Deimos's explanation.

He hesitated, and Romy finally gave in to look at him up the table.

His green eyes were on her, cheeks a dark pink. "Well, I told them stories of her from the start, when they were scared. I told them about what she'd done for them. That she was the mother of our knot, and kind of their mother, too."

"You did start the mother hen thing!" Romy exploded.

He rubbed the back of his head. "By accident. That story kind of caught their fancy."

Romy scraped her chair back and everyone jumped.

Phobos began to rise. "Romy—"

"I'm outta here," she muttered, blinking furiously. She turned to address Atlas. "I'll do whatever I can to help them around Tina's plans."

He gave her curt dip, his grey eyes speaking volumes as

they searched her face. She gave him as much of a smile as she could muster.

Making sure not to run, Romy made for the door.

Elara lurched to her feet and joined her.

"Here to tell me I'm a horrible person?" Romy asked bitterly once they were in the piped passageway.

Deimos had told them stories about her? Bet he didn't tell them the one about trying to subdue her and force her onto Houston's craft.

"I wanted to say that I'm sorry for the other night," Elara said.

Romy stayed quiet. She didn't feel like having this talk right now. Her anger wasn't directed at Elara, it was directed at Deimos, but she was worried about lashing out.

"I was out of line. The situation is completely different. You didn't have a choice about what you did."

"That's not true," Romy replied. "I did. I knew what would happen if Feral Romy took control. And I made the choice to use my final time to help my knot, and to help free the space soldiers. What I didn't expect was to come back after and have to live with what I'd done."

"You never knew she'd do *that*, Ro. Don't be so hard on yourself."

Romy lifted a shoulder, eyes burning.

Elara's face tightened into fierceness. "If you hadn't done that, all of us would be dead. Atlas, Deimos, me, and Phobos. All of us. You killed those people, yes, but I've never seen anything like it in my life. I'm not even sure how you did it. The way you moved, your precision, your ruthlessness. . . ."

"Is this meant to make me feel better?"

Elara whacked her and Romy shut up. "You were what you needed to be that day, Ro. You fought to protect your family, and I know what scars it must've left you with, but don't forget what was able to happen because you did those things."

They wound through the passageways for a few minutes before Romy answered. "I'll try." She paused. "And there's nothing to forgive. You made your point the other night. I heard you."

"Will you hear what Deimos has to say?"

Romy shook her head. "I'm not there yet. Not even close."

9

"Why don't the settlements always behave like this?" Thrym said, resting between Romy and Nancy against a bungalow.

Romy had practically jumped at the chance to go on mission, and get away from the Amach and her Deimos headache. That was before she remembered how monotonous these missions were getting. In comparison to picking up space junk for twelve years, this was a party, but with the sun beating down and making her body all kinds of sweaty under her bulletproof vest, remembering she'd carried out far more tedious tasks during a different war was hard. At times like these, she wished Houston would just make a damn move. Then they could just be done, one way or another.

Nancy rested her head on Thrym's shoulder. "It'd be nice if we could skip the 'we've come to save you, no *really*' chat every time."

Thrym rested his head atop hers. "At least you're here."

Romy made a face, but smoothed out her expression before Nancy could see. That wouldn't help mend any bridges.

The refugees from Pisa filed in an orderly line into a row of crafts. Elara was back on mission, adamant she wasn't staying behind because she was 'knocked up'. Romy had asked Tina about pregnancy last night and wasn't so sure the juddering of the craft wouldn't hurt her nephew, but wisely remained silent on the matter—Elara scratched when she got mad.

"Thrym said you recommended me for looking after the space soldiers," Nancy said, straightening, and squinting into the distance.

Romy folded her arms. "Yeah, thought you'd be good at it." She inspected her nails. "Heard you got Eddie and the others back okay."

"Yeah."

"Cool."

"Cool," Nancy echoed.

Thrym cleared his throat between them. "Well, that—"

Nancy rested a hand on his arm. "Babe, don't stress. It's cool."

"It's cool," he repeated in a daze. Smiling, he dipped his head to kiss her, and then faced forward.

Nancy gave Romy an uncertain look and Romy did her best to seem completely accepting of their relationship, though she wasn't 100 per cent certain how to express that with just her face.

Someone screamed in the distance.

Romy pushed off the bungalow. "Did you hear that?"

The others straightened, too, joining her a few metres into the clearing between their crafts and the other bungalows.

"Critamal!" The screamed words shot like an arrow through the settlement toward them.

Critamal? Romy gasped, her face draining of blood.

Thrym barked a flurry of orders into the device on his chest and soon footsteps pounded up behind them.

Romy's feet were stuck to the ground. She couldn't move.

The poachers were here.

"Load up the crafts!" Tina roared. "Leroy, supervise."

The thought echoed in her mind like it was wading through mud. Terror rooted her to the spot. Her breath came fast and the hand shaking her barely registered for a moment. Romy fixed wide eyes on Nancy's face, right in front of her.

"You need to snap out of it, sky girl, you're our sharpshooter." Nancy shook her shoulder.

"Where do we shoot?" Tina roared at Thrym. "Houston has sent those alien fuckers after our refugees. We need at least five minutes to get the civilians clear."

The soldiers behind her were setting up in a line facing out from the official buildings. The Critamal were coming up through the bungalows. Had they landed somewhere on the other side of the settlement?

Romy ignored Nancy's shaking and turned to look, head spinning.

The sun glinted off the liquid black shells of the Critamal. They were huge—two heads taller than a space soldier, and twice the width. Their pincers snapped, the threatening clicks loud even from where Romy stood by the bungalow. The enemy's yellow eyes glowed, locked on their targets with single-minded focus as they covered the ground at a furious pace.

Thrym tapped her cheek. "Romy? I'm thinking we need to aim for the head, or between the armour. What do you think?"

He'd clearly asked the question a few times.

Romy forced her lips to work. "Not the head; their skulls are . . . are s-stronger than steel."

"Any shot to the torso should serve to slow them," Thrym said. "If we can aim between their plates of armour, that may kill them. Rifles only. I don't think anything less will puncture."

The Critamal would be on them before the crafts full of refugees could take off. She knew what the aliens did to their prisoners. *Guts strewn across space.* Their victims always took on their yellow eyes afterward. A crushing pressure weighed on Romy's chest. They were so fast.

"You heard him," Tina called, repeating Thrym's advice.

"You in control?" Nancy asked her.

No. Romy couldn't answer. She didn't know what was happening to her. She was frozen.

The first of the Critamal burst from behind the bungalows. Nancy leaped into action, dropping to one knee in the front row and bringing her rifle up. Romy stumbled to follow, and brought her rifle up with heavy arms.

"Just like firing at the targets in Jimboomba." Nancy's voice reached her. "Just way frickin' faster. Crickey, they can jump high."

Her hands were slippery with sweat, and Romy, who very rarely missed a shot, missed the huge black-shelled poacher she aimed for by several metres. Her breath caught in her throat as she stared at the alien's massive pincers.

Nancy whooped beside her.

There was a wave of the aliens darting between the bungalows. How many? Romy's chest tightened. Houston hadn't attacked the Amach forces until now.

"Get firing, soldier," Thrym shouted at her. "We need every gun."

She was meant to be protecting the people behind her. And her . . . her. . . . Romy's vision spotted and she blinked it away, firing again. Missed.

Tina hauled her up by the back of her bulletproof vest.

"Leroy needs help getting the civilians in the crafts," Tina said.

"I can help here," Romy protested, limbs weak.

Tina took her spot in the front line and didn't answer. Romy backed away from the Critamal, who were now taking shelter behind the bungalows to escape the gunfire aimed on them. The braver ones were making a break for it, and so far, Nancy was halting them in their tracks.

Romy backed away, tripping over her feet in her haste.

"What do you want me to do?" she muttered to Leroy.

"They're all in," he said, then jogged up to Tina.

Romy tore her eyes from the poachers, from Houston's alien army. The engines of the refugee crafts whined either side of her, and as the row of her team members began to retreat in formation, the first of the crafts took off.

Only their craft still remained. She moved into the open cargo door and didn't even bother raising her gun as the others filed in, four of them remaining outside to maintain fire as Elara leaped into the empty pilot seat and started the engines of their craft. *Useless.* Romy was useless.

"They're closing in!" Thrym shouted.

Was she really just going to stand here? After everything she'd been through? Resolutely, Romy raised her gun and marched to the edge of the cargo door. She hadn't come this far to be afraid of aliens. Despite this realisation, her rifle seemed to be made of stone as she lifted it. Romy locked onto the left breastplate of the closest poacher. There were gaps between the panels of their shells.

She squeezed the trigger.

The Critamal fell backward.

"You got it, Ro!" Thrym called.

Romy panted, blinking cold sweat out of her eyes, and fired again, clipping another on the upper thigh. Nancy was right, these things jumped—something Romy had never seen when fighting them in space. She shifted her attention to another.

"Everyone in," Tina roared over the climbing engines.

The soldiers next to her fell back in a scrambling mess. The poachers were a hundred metres back, but with the speed they ran. . . . Those inside the craft encouraged them in a shouting mess, and Romy dove inside the cargo door as it began to close.

"Get us out of here!" The command flew over her head.

The craft slowly lifted.

Romy glanced back as the poachers closed in. "Faster," she yelled.

The cargo door gradually shut as they took off. The door got to forty-five degrees, and the soldiers who had been behind Romy's line lowered their weapons.

Romy sighed.

The craft jolted and Thrym shouted at the black-shelled monster clawing itself over the cargo door. It hissed at them, yellow eyes blazing. Tina reacted, unleashing a flurry of bullets that embedded in the alien's torso like bugs on a windscreen. The creature contorted in silent pain and fell to the ground, curling into a writhing corpse as the life drained from it.

Romy stared at the alien. She'd never been that close to a living one. Not face-to-face.

Thrym crossed to Nancy, hugging her close, his eyes squeezed tight.

"What was that?" Elara exploded from the front. "Houston's sending poachers after us now?"

"He's making his move against the Amach," Tina answered. She sat down with a thump. "Shit. This is really happening."

The others threw comments overhead, but Romy didn't join in.

Shame swept through her.

"Should I open the door and chuck it out?" Leroy asked, pointing his rifle at the alien.

"Keep it," Nancy said, shaking her head. "It can be studied."

Romy blinked back the burning behind her eyes, knowing it was the aftermath of an intense surge of adrenaline. Partly. What had happened to her back there? She'd known how scared she was of the aliens, but she'd fought them for *years*. She knew more about them than almost everyone here, barring Thrym and Elara.

Why had fear seized her like that?

She turned away from Thrym and Tina's probing gaze, placed her rifle in the rack, and joined Elara in the co-pilot seat. Romy put on the headphones and blocked out the energised chatter in the craft.

What the hell just happened to her?

ELARA HADN'T PROBED HER ON THE WAY BACK, AND ROMY WAS never more grateful to experience one of her knotmate's infrequent tactful moments.

The craft landed at the Amach with a jolt. Theirs was the only craft to come back to Ireland. Their Amach was near full now, so the other crafts had landed on one of their bases in Aberdeen.

She swung the door up and slid down to the ground with a sigh. Finding Atlas sounded really good about now.

"Hey, Ro." Phobos stood there, hands behind his back.

She gave him a tired smile. "Hey."

"Jeez, you look like you need chocolate cake."

Her stomach rumbled. "That'd be the day." The Amach didn't do chocolate cake. She'd need to have a word with Atlas about that.

"Today is that day," Phobos countered.

"No way! Where did you get your hands on that?"

He lifted a shoulder. "I've got connections. Anyway, you want some?"

Romy unclipped her vest and slipped out of the bulletproof garment, giving a groan of relief to be free of it. "That's a silly question."

A muffled noise had her looking back to where Elara was visible. Her eyes were wide on Phobos in a pointed look Romy couldn't decipher. He gave her a nonplussed look in return and wound an arm around Romy's shoulders, leading her out of the hangar.

Suspicion flared within her. "Where is this cake?"

"I hid it in our room. Where else?"

"Okay," she drew out. Her stomach gurgled again.

Five minutes later, he pushed open the door to the room and ushered her inside.

"Phobos," Elara called from down the hall. She arrived on the threshold, puffing from jogging. Romy eyed her. Why was she running? Elara didn't run.

"Can I have a word?" Elara panted.

"Like . . . right now?" he strained.

She gave him the same pointed look.

Romy held up her hands. A glance around the untidy room had told her there wasn't any chocolate cake here. "Okay, what's happening?"

"Hey," a voice said in the hall. "I got a note telling me to meet you here."

Her insides froze.

Deimos appeared in the doorway next to Phobos.

"You are kidding me," Romy said through clenched teeth. "That's why I'm here?" She made to push past Phobos, but he barred her way with an arm.

"It's time to listen to him, Ro."

"It's time to *move*," she said, kneeing him in the upper thigh and punching him in the solar plexus.

"Shoot." He coughed.

Thrym arrived behind Phobos, blocking the doorway. "I thought we were postponing it after . . . today." He frowned at Elara.

"I tried," she protested. "But Phobos ignored my looks in the hangar."

Thrym deliberated, taking a look at Romy's mutinous face and then at the gathered members of Knot 27. She saw the moment he decided to commit and tensed to bowl him out of the way.

"We've shown our hand," he shouted. "Grab her!"

Romy dove for Thrym, the weak link. Thrym was too nice to hurt her.

. . . So she'd thought.

"I'm not doing this!" she snapped at them as he threw her onto the single bed in the room.

"You are," he said, shrivelling under the force of her glare.

"It's *my* decision, Thrym." Romy bounced to the edge of the bed. "Mine. I hate him." She glanced around the knot, noting Deimos's violent flinch with savage pleasure. "I won't *ever* forgive him for what he did. He's not part of my knot."

"Romy, that puts us all in a crap position," Phobos countered. "If you're not going to give *him* the courtesy of listening, do it for the rest of us. I know what it's like to be caught between two of my knotmates, and I won't be repeating it again." He glanced at Deimos. "I love Ellie. I want to be with her for the rest of my life and have little Ellies. I came to save you because you are my brother and I believe you're not a selfish prick, though you've made mistakes. But if you can't support Ellie and how I feel about her, we're going to have a problem. We share something no one else understands, Dei. And that will never change." He stared at the knotmate they'd always referred to as his twin. "That is where I stand."

Deimos nodded and looked at Elara. "I was a dick."

She blinked furiously. "Yeah, you were. But you were right about some things, too. I didn't give your friendship space, and when I should have tried to understand what you were going through, I got angry instead because you'd turned your back on me." Large tears fell over her delicate features. "I'm the reason you left."

Deimos's eyes widened. "That's not. . . ." He moved to Elara and wrapped his arms around her. "That's not the case *at all*. I was jealous of what you guys had, and yeah, I felt left out, but it was no excuse for acting the way I did. Phobos is my brother, but I love you just as much. Even if you are annoying sometimes."

"You're annoying," she said in a watery voice.

"You are," he said gently.

They shared a soft smile.

Thrym was watching Romy and she refused to look at him. That was great and she was glad for Elara's sake that she was rid of that guilt.

"Stop looking at me like that," she said to Thrym.

"You see it."

"I can't believe you did this to me," Romy whispered, wanting to join Elara—and now Phobos—in shedding a few tears. "You know how I feel about this."

"I know what you *think* you need to feel about it. And I know what will give you the most happiness in time. I'm your best friend, am I not?"

"You want the honest answer?" Her cheeks began to burn.

He winced. "No, I don't guess I do."

Phobos strode to the door and planted himself in the exit. "You're staying here until you listen to Deimos, Ro. This is a knot intervention."

10

Romy tested her restraints. She was now tied to a chair with the bed sheets in the middle of the room. She tried to keep her breathing even, but she really didn't like being restrained.

Her temper was only partly to blame for the recent battle that had torn through the tiny room.

She felt utterly, *completely* betrayed by her knot for entertaining Deimos's lies after what he did to her. The worst part was, she felt sick because a part of her was beginning to doubt whether her stubbornness was warranted—and it *was* warranted. She knew that. Before her knotmate had left with Houston, Romy wanted nothing more than to heal the rift between Deimos and Elara. Her heart yearned for what they'd had as a knot before crash-landing on Earth. Her stomach roiled to think of Phobos, Elara, and Thrym having that with Deimos and excluding her.

"Make it fast," she said, glaring at Deimos with angry eyes. She gave some of it to the others afterwards. "I want it noted that you guys have seriously fucked me off."

Elara folded her arms.

Deimos cleared his throat and perched on the edge of the bed. "I'm not sure where to start."

"Just like you told me," Phobos said.

His twin shook his head. "It was different with Romy. What I did to her was worse."

Damn right it was.

He sighed, peering at his hands. "I wasn't in a good place after the crash-landing," he said in a curious voice. "The rest of you coped with what had been done to us, but I never seemed to get over it as well. I let the injustice get to me . . . change me." His green eyes lifted.

Romy rolled her eyes. So that was his game.

"It wasn't long after Phobos and Elara got together. I . . . didn't like your relationship, but not for the reasons I told you, or realised. There was a wrongness inside of myself, and the more that grew, the more distant I felt from who I'd been. When you guys got together, it was another change. I mean, the Mandate had taken Romy. My little sister," his voice broke, "*taken* by the people who enslaved us. I didn't know what they'd do to her or if they'd kill her while I was surrounded by people who didn't appear to give a damn. I was slowly being driven mad." He swallowed. "That's what split our knot apart," he said. "That worry. I cleaved away because I thought you didn't care enough about finding Ro. Looking back, I see that we were each drowning in our grief and too self-absorbed to do anything else." He shook himself. "Houston began to talk with me. I liked him—his intelligence, his quirkiness. He was the only person who understood. As time went on, he introduced me to other people. These people were just as angry as I was with what wasn't being done. In this way, I became involved in the plans to overthrow Gwenyth."

Romy stared at the far wall, listening and hating that she was doing so.

"You came back, Ro," Deimos whispered. "Your platinum hair was just the same, your blue eyes as soft as ever. But they'd hurt you." His fist clenched. "I saw the burn marks at your temples. Houston showed me the file of what they'd put you through up on Orbito Four. How they'd scrubbed you of your memories, tried to change your personality. My hate grew when it should have lessened. And briefly, fleetingly, it did," he said. "Until your mind began to crack." Deimos looked at her. "You didn't see yourself then, but I did. I saw you brought to your knees, made to crawl by a force you couldn't even see. I saw you smiling through the pain and it made me angrier than I'd ever been in my life." His knuckles turned white. "The Mandate was doing this to you, I convinced myself."

"If they started it, Houston finished it," she interjected bitterly. Her chest was tighter than she would have liked.

Deimos gave a sad nod. "The attempt to overthrow Gwenyth flopped, but the discontent within us surged. To that point, the meetings with Houston had seemed like a game of sorts. It's like that thought of leaving you all pierced through where nothing else had. Houston sensed my new hesitation. He gave me a front seat in the decision-making, by his side. He reminded me how it would look to go back, with what I'd done. Not in so many words, but . . . I understood his implication; I was in too deep. I gave up the thought of backing out. I knew I'd screwed up by now. I'd had a moment of clarity, but like all the moments before it, I then made the wrong choice. I convinced myself the rest of you didn't want me around. Thrym didn't trust us with information, Elara was taking my best friend, and my best friend was letting her." He closed his eyes. "Do you know what my favourite moments were?"

The others didn't move. Romy slid her eyes toward him against her will.

"When we were out on mission together. I was happiest when there was an excuse to be in your company. All of you seemed so far away, but my mind wouldn't accept that of Romy for some reason. Possibly because she hadn't been here and I had a chance to right myself in her eyes."

Romy dug her nails into her palms.

"The night of our mutiny came," he continued, "and Houston told me we were taking Romy. We were surrounded by his people and I had to go along with it. I told myself if I didn't go, I couldn't be assured of her safety. So instead of taking Houston out, I helped him wheel her to the hangar. She looked like a bruised and battered angel that night," he told the others. "Hair shaved, cuts and marks all over her. Shattered, yet still somehow as she's always been. You've seen the strength she has. When Romy woke and discovered what we intended to do, that strength came out." He chuckled without humour. "I hadn't expected the hold over me could snap so abruptly."

"When did it happen?" Elara asked in a low voice.

He focused his bright green eyes on Romy. "About the time Romy punched me in the face and knocked me out."

Romy blinked.

"I have an unfailing belief in the integrity of your character, sister," he said. "You possess a softness of heart that I only ever see harden when your family is threatened. As your fist swung toward me, I couldn't move through the shock. Because I knew what it meant that you would strike me. You saw *me* as the threat. My knotmate was afraid of me. She was protecting herself against me. I was the monster now."

A tear slid down Romy's cheek.

The breath shuddered in her chest, wanting to escape, but Romy wouldn't let it. The emotion in Deimos's words was unmistakeable. But they were words. "You betrayed us," she said hoarsely. "All of us."

His eyes were moist. "I know."

A lump rose in her throat and she broke away from his look.

"Keep going," Phobos encouraged.

Deimos craned his neck to look at the ceiling. "I woke up at the base in Florida. I went straight to Houston to tell him the game was off. Before I could figure out how to do it without him losing it, he took me to see the space soldiers he'd woken up." He struggled for words. "You've seen them, but back then, it was ten times worse. They had *no* idea, and where I'd suddenly seen my mistake, I then understood why it happened. They needed me, so they didn't become *like* me. That's why I volunteered to take the injection first."

He broke off and glanced around the room. "I had to get them away from Houston, so he couldn't manipulate them. When he began testing on them again, I accelerated the plans." He threw a glare at Phobos. "And when Pho turned up—"

"— he helped you set the plans in motion," Phobos challenged. Deimos scowled at him.

"How did you get all the space soldiers out?" Thrym asked.

The twins shared a grin and Elara snickered.

"You do realise who you're talking to, right?" Phobos said, bumping knuckles with Deimos. "We contaminated the guard's food with norovirus, and Houston's. Gave him a really good batch."

"You didn't?" Thrym said, aghast.

"Symptoms may include nausea, vomiting, diarrhoea, and cramps," Deimos rattled off, counting on his fingers. "We gave Houston the shits, in other words."

Well, that explained . . . that.

As for the rest, Romy refused to give Deimos an easy out. She'd listened, and now she needed time to talk about what she'd heard with someone she trusted. "Untie me, please," she said.

Thrym and Phobos scrambled to do so, probably well aware they were in her bad books.

Freed from her bed-sheet restraints, Romy's heartbeat settled and she straightened her coveralls, not looking at anyone. "Have a good evening," she said.

And walked out.

11

"Houston has definitely thrown down the glove," Tina whispered in Romy's ear as they stood around a huge map with the commanding officers. She'd come to find Atlas after the 'knot intervention', and located him in the middle of a frantic group of commanders and captains.

"Twenty of our teams have encountered Critamal today," Tina added.

Romy's eyes rounded. "Really? Any casualties?"

"Yes. Nine killed, forty-seven wounded, and five in critical condition."

"I didn't expect the poachers to do Houston's bidding like this. I mean, I know he gave them the means to land on Earth, but how is he controlling them so tightly?"

Tina sighed. "With the same trump card he's holding over the rest of us."

"The cannons?" Romy asked. Tina nodded.

A woman jogged up to Atlas. "Sir, there is a large host of Critamal within range of a group of battlers over Japan. The aliens are nearly in contact with a settlement there, but there are human Renegades members with the Critamal, too."

Atlas crossed his arms over his chest, staring at a projected image the woman pulled up on a nano. "How many in the settlement?" he asked.

"Six hundred fifty-six, sir."

"How many humans with the Critamal?" he asked.

"Eighteen, according to the crafts above them."

His focus turned inward, and Romy squeezed through the waiting crowd to reach him. She placed a hand on his and he jerked, fixing his grey eyes on her.

"Houston's trying to back me into a corner by sending humans along. He knows I don't want to kill them," he said in a low voice.

"Six hundred fifty-six refugees," she said in an undertone. "You know he'll force them to join the Renegades."

Atlas gave a tight nod, saying to the gathered group, "When the Critamal charge, they'll leave the Renegade humans behind. The aliens are faster. Instruct our air force to wait for that moment to open fire on the aliens. Tell them to avoid killing the Renegades, but none of Houston's force are to make contact with the settlement."

"Yes, sir." The woman hurried away.

"Cronus," Atlas said. "Deploy our forces to the area immediately for refugee pickup."

Cronus grunted and turned away, barking orders in his floral shirt.

"How did I do?" Atlas asked Romy, after speaking to a few people.

She answered without a shred of a lie. "I wouldn't have thought of that. You're great at this."

He exhaled and it baffled Romy anew that Atlas cared so much about how she saw him. "I have complete faith in the decisions you make," she added.

Red stole up his jaw.

She'd really hoped to tell him about what happened with

Deimos, but now wasn't the time, and Romy knew if she brought it up, he'd insist on dropping everything. "You're busy," she said. "I'll catch you later."

"I'll be back early tonight."

She smiled at him. "We'll talk then."

Romy started heading for their room, but when she got into the elevator, she pressed the button for level seven instead. She didn't want to be alone, and she didn't want to see anyone other than Atlas who might gauge her mood and pry.

The space soldiers were in the gym, the only space other than the Mess able to accommodate the majority of them. Some were on equipment working out, some had ventured into the shooting range running parallel to the gym, but most had congregated in their knots on the large fighting mats and talked quietly.

"Want an Earth lesson?" she called to them, crossing the gym.

Half an hour later, a huge group of space soldiers sat on the floor in front of Romy, who perched on a bench press.

"What happens if you have two of one kind of card, and three of another?" a space soldier called from the back of the gym near the treadmills.

Romy answered, "That's a full house, a pretty good hand, especially if you have three of the same picture cards."

"I do," the large man said, beaming.

"Great," she said. "But remember, you're not supposed to let anyone know what you have."

His face smoothed and he lost the 'Bambi' look. "I apologise, mother hen."

A few of the Amach members working out in the gym were sending her odd looks.

"Uhm, what are they doing?" Charlee asked, weaving between the sitting soldiers to reach Romy.

She smiled. "Playing poker." Or more accurately, practicing a poker face. The soldier's clueless expressions had to go, and this was a not-so-subtle way to achieve that.

"You're teaching them poker?" Charlee burst out laughing. "I needed that so much today." The woman placed her hands in the pockets of her pristine lab coat.

"Are you on a break? How're the tests going?"

"Uh, too early to tell. I've got a range with various percentages of your blood in them. But I don't feel like that's the answer. There's something I'm missing."

Romy glanced around. "Do you need me to help?"

"No, no. I was actually going to ask you about Deimos."

"The one I'm not sure if I'm forgiving yet?"

Charlee gave her a look. "Oh, I thought that was sorted now. I just spoke to Elara."

"No," Romy said hotly. "I listened to him but I haven't decided."

The Irish woman smoothed her already neat bun. "Okay, but when you do forgive him, do you think you could get a measure on what he thinks of me? You know?"

Romy winced. "Yes, I know. And ew, I've never spoken to any of my knot about that stuff, ever. Aside from listening to Elara. Unwillingly." Romy shuddered.

"Come on, help a girl out. You know my intelligence scares everyone off."

Romy glared at her. "What about one of these ones," she gestured around. "I fixed their faces."

The doctor peered around the gym. "You made them worse. I preferred the innocent look over the blank-faced soldier look."

The soldiers did look slightly creepy without any expression.

She sighed. "Okay, well, *if* I forgive Deimos, I *might* mention it."

Charlee kissed her on both cheeks. "Good biatch. Knew I could count on you."

"Is Japan okay?" Romy asked as Atlas entered their room that evening. It had been a long, emotional day, and she was glad it was finally at an end. She wanted to get into bed with Atlas and forget about everything.

"It is," he answered. "The crafts with the refugees landed at one of our bases an hour ago."

"What about the human casualties on the other side?"

"We suspect four or five."

"It's as good as we could have hoped," Romy noted.

"Tina told me you had a bit of trouble with the Critamal today yourself." He washed his hands at the sink.

Shame twisted her gut. "Yeah, I did. I don't know why; I've fought them all my life. I just couldn't operate. I freaked out."

"Fear doesn't make sense," he said, glancing back over his shoulder. "From Tina's report, you snapped out of it in the end. That's more than most are capable of in that headspace."

Romy shrugged. "I feel terrible about it, actually. Like I failed or something."

"I pissed myself on my first mission against the Critamal in space."

Her jaw dropped.

His eyes lit with amusement at her response. "True story, I swear. Don't sweat it over what happened. You've seen them face-to-face. Now you know what to expect."

"What if I freeze when it's some crucial moment?" she asked helplessly, trying to imagine the bravest person she'd ever met peeing their space suit.

He splashed water on his face and grabbed the drying

cloth. Watching him do this was one of her favourite times of the day. Atlas was a routine man, and for some reason she found that fiercely attractive.

"I like to imagine the worst thing that could happen if I don't overcome my fear," he said. "Some people like to envision themselves succeeding. You just need to find the thing that is more powerful than that fear."

She groaned. "You know, I thought my day couldn't get any worse after that, then my knot tied me to a chair so I'd listen to what Deimos had to say."

Atlas was pretty still most of the time, but always had a *tell* to show what he felt underneath the mask: a half smile, running his hands through his hair, a softening of his eyes.

When Atlas was angry he went completely still.

"They tied you to a chair?" he asked in a mild voice.

"Well," Romy backtracked, sensing this wasn't going to bode well for her knotmates, "I wasn't listening to them."

He unfroze and bent to unlace his heavy boots. "That's a yes then. What did Deimos have to say for himself?"

Romy wondered if she should ask whether he was going to do anything to her knot, but his face looked mostly calm, so she relayed what Deimos had said.

Atlas ran a hand through his hair when she was done. Back to normal. "Sounds like he was messed up and has a lot of regrets."

"Yeah." She clenched her hands together. "I do feel sorry for what he went through alone. I knew he was darker and angrier, but I didn't realise he was so . . . twisted up inside."

"What's holding you back from forgiving him, then?"

"I couldn't tell any of this was going through his head back then," Romy admitted. "How do I know he won't do it again? I don't want to trust him again because then he might hurt me a second time."

Atlas ran a thumb over her cheekbone as he sat next to

her. She was a little cold and the heat of his skin made her shiver. He smiled. "You would recognise the signs now," he said.

Would she? Romy wasn't so sure.

"You know," Atlas spoke again. "You were able to hide a lot of what you went through at Houston's hands." The words weren't condemning, though Romy knew it had hurt Atlas to hear she'd kept secrets from him during the testing on her brain.

"Have you considered the parallels between you and Deimos?" he asked.

She straightened. "You mean to say he was taken advantage of by Houston?"

Atlas's jaw clenched as it always did at talk of the doctor. They'd been best friends and each other's only support for years prior. "Yes. It seems that Houston's forte is making people conceal things from people they love."

The comment struck her dumb. She said quietly, "I hadn't thought about it that way."

"Might be some food for thought?"

Her stomach rumbled. "Have you considered putting chocolate cake on the menu here?"

He snorted, getting to his feet. "Can't say I have." Reaching to the back of his neck, Atlas drew his black T-shirt off over his head.

Holy meteor shower. Romy stared, blinked, and averted her eyes to the wall.

"Are you going out again?" she asked. There. That almost sounded normal.

"No."

"No?" What was he doing? Should she look? Romy didn't want him to think she was perving on him.

His face pressed into the crook of her neck and he rumbled against her skin in a low voice, "No."

"No?" she asked again, and hurried to add, "I mean, why?"

He brought his nose up to her ear and she giggled at the tickling sensation.

"Because two days ago a beautiful woman asked me why I hadn't taken off her clothes yet, and I haven't been able to think of anything else since."

Romy grinned. "Oh? Was she very beautiful?"

He pulled her onto his lap. "The most beautiful thing I've ever seen."

She let her eyes roam over his broad shoulders and sculpted arms before peeking up to his face. Grey eyes as soft as clouds looked down at her. "I can't think when you look at me like that," she said.

"Then we hold the same power over each other," he answered. "Would you like to join me?" He glanced down at his bare chest and back up at her with a playful grin.

She'd only been thinking about this since they'd started sharing a bed. "Yes, but I'm wearing coveralls."

"Don't I know it," he grumbled.

Romy laughed and drew the zipper in the middle down to just above her belly button. The cool air kissed her skin as she pulled her arms out of the long sleeves and pushed the coveralls down, avoiding his gaze.

He inhaled and put a finger under her chin to lift her mouth to his in a soft kiss. He reached for her hands and placed them on his chest. "You can touch me," he said, placing another kiss on her mouth.

She'd expected to feel embarrassed when this happened, but she should've known better. He was always so matter-of-fact, and Romy really had been waiting weeks for something more. Trying not to smile, Romy traced a finger across his collarbone, stomach erupting into butterflies when Atlas inhaled again. She glanced at him and saw he watched her with a heated gaze. Emboldened, she placed her palm above his heart and swept it slowly down his side over his taut stomach. He was perfect.

"You can touch me, too," she said in a husky voice.

He groaned. With obvious restraint, he did just that, mimicking what she'd done by brushing a warm finger over her collarbone and grazing her breasts to span both of his hands across her stomach on either side. His hands hovered above where her coveralls pooled around her hips. He swallowed audibly and, taking a breath, grabbed the ends of her sleeves and knotted the coveralls around her hips. "So I don't get tempted." He rested his forehead against hers.

"What if I want you to be tempted?" Romy wasn't cold any longer.

"I don't think you need to worry about that."

Atlas knelt on the bed. Sitting back on his heels, he slid his hands around the back of her hips and pulled her onto his lap, one of her knees either side of his thighs. They were at the same eye level now.

One of his hands held her pelvis close, and the other ran up her back. She sighed, and decided that touch wasn't enough. Romy pushed her lips against his in a hungry kiss.

Atlas's grin at her attack didn't last long. He melded his lips to hers with equal hunger, pulling her closer still. Romy rested her hands on the tops of his shoulders and gasped for breath, determined the kiss wouldn't end.

The need to keep her mouth on his was greater than any comfort air could bring. She smiled as the kiss continued and then grinned as his face widened into a smile as well. He was everything she wanted.

They broke apart, panting.

She held the back of his neck, staring into his wild grey eyes, her other hand on his arm melding their bodies together. His chest heaved and he watched her, unspeaking and almost unblinking as she did the same.

The door swung open. "I felt bad, so I actually brought you chocolate—"

Romy screamed as her knot filed in.

They wrenched to a halt on the threshold, frozen at the sight of her and Atlas wrapped around each other on the bed. The chocolate cake in Phobos's hand fell to the floor and splattered everywhere.

Thrym shouted, "What the f—"

"Get out." Atlas interrupted him. He lifted his brows, still as a rock underneath her. Romy tried to shift to pull her coveralls up, but his grip was like iron. "Get out. Now."

Her knotmates stared at him mutinously—except for Elara, who was fanning her face behind the boys and mouthing, 'Hawt'.

"Uh, could you guys give us a sec?" Romy said with a pointed look.

Phobos was on the verge of fainting. Elara tugged him backward.

"We'll be in the hall," Deimos said.

Thrym added, "Waiting to speak with Romy."

"Don't bother," Atlas called after them, silkily. "She'll be busy."

12

Romy covered her face with her hands. "That was embarrassing."

"Your knotmates need to learn how to knock," Atlas remarked. He stroked her back and a grin spread over his face. "They wanted to hurt me, you know?"

"Present tense," she corrected. "They want to hurt you."

Atlas took her wrists and lowered her hands from her face. "That was some kiss," he said, pursing his lips. Untying the knot around her hips, he brought the coveralls up for her to slide her arms through.

She climbed off his lap. "You're going to stay for this, right?"

One side of his mouth lifted as he rested back against the wall. "I wouldn't miss it for the world."

Spinning to locate his shirt, Romy picked it up and padded over to hand it to him. "Let's not antagonise."

As he put it on, she straightened up the room, shook her hands to get rid of a wave of nerves, and swung open the door.

"Finally," Elara said, pushing off the opposite wall. "Got any snacks?"

"I brought cards," Phobos said.

"Wait." Romy stopped them from entering. "What are you doing here?" Her eyes rested on Deimos, who lurked at the back.

"We gave you all day to think," Elara said.

Thrym interjected, "I tried to stop them."

From inside the room, Atlas called, "What if she decides not to forgive Deimos?"

This time four sets of eyes glared over her shoulder as Atlas came to stand behind Romy.

"Forcing a decision on her that isn't hers will fail. Where has the support gone for Rosemary?" he continued. "Are you taking advantage of her good nature? Is that what you're doing?"

"We would never. . ." Elara said in outrage.

"Looks that way to me."

Romy folded her arms. "I do feel a little betrayed that you've ganged up against me when you know how I feel about this. You tied me to a chair so I'd listen and you have no idea how that made me feel after being strapped to a medical table for months on end."

Phobos's face lost colour. "Ro, we never meant—"

She held up a hand. "Give me time to decide what I want to do. I'll come and find you myself when I know."

Elara's lip trembled. "Do you want to play poker?"

Her chest squeezed at the sight. *Crap.* But she'd made a stand already. "Not tonight, Ellie. Another time," Romy said, biting her lip.

"Come on, Ellie, we'll go get snacks somewhere else," Thrym said, pulling her down the passage.

Phobos muttered, "Sorry," and followed.

Deimos was last. He gazed at Romy across the hall. "I'll

understand if you don't forgive me," he said in a hollow voice. "I don't deserve it."

She watched, feeling like the worst person in the world as her knot walked off down the passageway without her.

"How're they doing?" Romy asked Phobos in the gym the next day.

Their team had been pulled from normal duties in light of the negotiations with the Mandate being finalised. Their knot would be going into the cities once that happened.

Houston had successfully conquered five cities in Europe, and now was headed west toward the Mandate's New Britain cities. The Mandate's desperation had to be climbing, and this was what Atlas had been waiting for to throw his weight around in negotiations with them. He'd only slept for a few hours the previous night before waking to go out again. Romy had barely slept herself, thinking about their kiss all night. Not one bit of her was glad the kiss had stopped where it had, and she had plans to rectify that as soon as everyone demanding Atlas's attention went away. She shuddered at the thought that might never happen.

Phobos observed the lines of space soldiers. "Great. They'd already started some training under Houston's orders. They are used to obeying commands and striving to do their best. It's their initiative that will be hardest to develop."

"Thrym said Nancy has plans to work on that, too."

"Already coordinated with her, mother hen?"

Romy groaned. "Please don't."

"They say it all day; it's kind of hard not to think of you that way after eight hours of constant 'mother hen' this, 'mother hen' that."

"Try," she said in a flat voice.

"We may as well train instead of standing here."

"Maybe in a bit; I want to hit the treadmill."

Romy laced her black sneakers tight and straightened the waistband of her black shorts before bounding up onto her favourite treadmill. The good thing about short hair was that she didn't need to tie it back. Though her hair was long enough to grip on to now.

Bumping the treadmill to a cruisy ten kilometres an hour, she settled into rhythm, feet pounding on the belt. Running always served to remind her of what she wanted in life. She wanted to run outside. She wanted to see the world. But first, she had to make sure everyone she loved was safe.

Wiping at her forehead with the back of her hand, she increased the speed.

Did she want to include Deimos in that future or not?

A huge part of her baulked at his explanation. How could he have even fallen far enough into that dark state to distance himself from his knot? Yet wasn't she doing the same right now because she believed so strongly he shouldn't be let off the hook? Would she continue distancing herself, unable to move past her deep hurt and anger?

Deimos hadn't been able to and look where it got him.

Ugh.

She increased the speed again, long legs now well warmed up and striding out in her regular pace, which was just shy of a sprint. The thing was, despite not wanting to for the last six weeks, Romy did love Deimos. Making that go away seemed like an insurmountable task, and one she wasn't sure she wanted to begin.

The future of their knot was in her hands. She could let them fall apart. Or she could do her best to move on.

The rest of her run passed in a zoned-out thudding bliss,

and Romy managed to evade Phobos's notice on the way out, so she didn't have to put on a show for the space soldiers.

She set out for the library.

She'd become a frequent visitor here since her brain had settled down and she could read again. The library wasn't a large room, only eight times larger than the rooms they slept in, but it was filled to the brim with sorted books.

There was one subject in particular she wanted to look at.

P . . . pe . . .po . . . pr . . . pra . . . pre . . . pregnancy!

"Five books on it," she mumbled to herself. Romy loaded the books into her arms and left the room, peeking over the top of the stack as she made her way down to the closest elevator.

She shoved her foot between the elevator's closing doors and squeezed inside. No way was she waiting—the elevators took ages.

"Rosemary," a stiff voice said.

Why me? "Hi, Gwenyth," she said in a pleasant voice. "How are you doing today?" Romy shifted the books away to look at Atlas's mother.

"Fine, I—" Gwenyth broke off, blinking at the books in Romy's arms.

"Are you okay?" Romy said, in real concern.

The older woman's mouth bobbed open and shut. "Y-yes, dear. Yes."

The elevator pinged and the doors retracted. Romy hovered in the doorway to her level. "Are you sure?" She'd heard of this kind of thing happening when people worked their bodies too hard and then retired and broke apart.

Gwenyth's grey eyes fell to Romy's arms and then raised again. Suddenly, her face split into a broad beam that transformed the harsh lines of her face into the carefree woman she might have been. "*Quite* sure, dear. You rest up now." She winked and Romy nodded in shock, stepping off the elevator and letting the waiting crowd on.

Weird. Had Gwenyth just called her 'dear'? Twice? Romy frowned. And what did she mean by rest up?

Shaking it off, Romy set off for their room and pushed the door open. Placing the pile of books on the small table next to the single bed, she kicked off her boots, slipped under the covers and grabbed the book on top.

Eventually, hours later, a flurry of knocks boomed at the door.

"Romy, are you doing it in there?"

She winced. "Come in, Elara!" *Before anyone else hears you.*

Elara burst in, Thrym in her wake, with Phobos not far behind.

"Hey, we didn't bring Deimos." Phobos's green eyes were sad. Damn, magical eyes.

"Is he in the passage, Phobos?" Romy asked patiently.

Phobos gave her a guilty look. "Well, I just thought if you did decide he could come in, it would be annoying to walk all the way to his room, so. . . ."

Here goes nothing. "Deimos can come in."

Her knotmate's smile was so big his ears lifted. "I'll get him."

Elara sniggered under her breath as whispers erupted in the hall. Twenty seconds later Deimos and Phobos trotted in, all innocent green eyes. Had Romy ever stood a chance resisting this? Maybe not.

She placed the third book back in the pile, having resolved to have a serious talk with Elara based on the information contained in the pages there. To say she was highly concerned about the baby was an understatement. She'd read some horrifying statistics about what an increase in body temperature could do to a foetus. Maybe they should move somewhere where it was winter.

"Hi," Deimos said with a small wave.

She nodded. "Hello, Deimos."

"I brought cards and twigs," Thrym announced. He began to set up a poker game.

Romy sat to pull on her boots again. The concrete floor was cold. She threw a pillow at Elara, who gave a grateful smile and shoved it under her butt.

"What are you reading?" Deimos asked. He swooped in and plucked a book before she could shove him away.

"Nothing," she blurted.

His eyes moved across the title *What Hole Will My Baby Come Out Of?* and the smile dropped from his face. Mouth open, he stared at her. "You're pregnant."

The room went quiet and Romy shot Elara a panicked look.

"What!" Phobos roared. "You're pregnant?"

He, Thrym, and Deimos crowded around her, waving their arms in a flurry and speaking over her head.

"No," she said.

"—she won't be going to Dublin, I tell you right now—"

"—I knew she was acting weird—"

Deimos reached out a hand and hovered it over her tummy. "But you're so little," he said, tears in his green eyes. "How is there a baby in there?"

"I'm not pregnant," she blurted, brushing their hands away.

"Romy." Thrym glanced at the books and back at her, brows raised. "Come on. You can tell us."

"We'll have a niece or nephew!" Phobos said. He and Deimos grabbed each other and jumped around in circles.

"You'll have a son, or daughter," Elara said from behind them.

The twins stopped jumping and stared at her.

"*I'm* pregnant," she added when they didn't make a peep.

"Stop staring at me like I'm diseased!" Elara stamped her foot.

Phobos let his hands fall. "*You're* pregnant? You?"

Do not screw this up. Romy held a finger up to her lips for Thrym's and Deimos's sake.

"Yes," shouted Elara, shoving him. "I found out the day after you ran off, you big, stupid meteor face."

"Why didn't you tell me?" he shouted back. "It's been nearly two weeks."

"Because I didn't want to," she snarled.

He paused. "How pregnant are you?"

"A month."

His mouth repeated the word silently. "With a baby?" he clarified. "Our baby?"

Her eyes narrowed. "What are you saying?"

Phobos stumbled toward her, shouting a short laugh. "We're having a baby girl," he said and swept her into his arms.

"A boy," she agreed.

The couple clutched each other tight as Thrym and Deimos looked on with the most joy she'd seen on their faces in . . . *on* Earth.

This was the moment to forget what had happened and what might have been and focus on what was happening now instead.

Romy would forgive Deimos for what their knot could have if she did, and because the love she had for him apparently couldn't be undone. Though he'd have to earn her trust back.

Romy picked up a second pillow and, winding back her arm, she hit Deimos around the face with it as hard as she could.

"What are you doing?" Thrym said, wrenching the pillow out of her grasp.

She ignored him, watching Deimos recover. A glint entered his green eyes as he straightened and picked up Elara's abandoned pillow.

"To the death?" he asked.

"To the death," she replied.

13

Atlas walked back in three hours later. Romy watched as he took in the room scattered with white pillow fluff, and the five members of Knot 27 sprawled over the concrete floor.

His eyes found Romy's, where she lay with her head on Phobos's legs. She smiled and his frown disappeared. The others turned to face him and the talk in the room came to a halt.

Thrym stood. "I guess we better get to sleep. Big day tomorrow."

"I don't know," Deimos said. "Maybe we should stay."

Atlas grinned.

"Yeah, maybe we should stay," Phobos agreed.

The twins fixed their eyes on Atlas, and his grin widened.

Romy stood, sweeping her hands down her front to dislodge the pillow fluff off of her thighs. "No, you should definitely go." Her voice was firm.

"Come on, guys." Elara gave her a slow wink, and Romy cringed.

The grumbling male members of Knot 27 made their way

out behind Elara, and Thrym shut the door behind them, leaving Romy and Atlas in silence.

Atlas made his way to the sink, and Romy watched through her peripheral vision.

"It's about to begin," he said.

"What?" Romy began picking up the bits of fluff, certain the pillows hadn't had this much in them to begin with.

"Your knot is going to start messing with me."

"No." Romy disregarded his remark. "They wouldn't do that." She trailed off at Atlas's half smile. "Well, not in the middle of a war."

He dried his face. "This war could go on for a long time."

"I'll speak to them." She sat on the bed.

"No, don't do that," he said, making his way over to her. "I knew it would happen eventually. Though I wondered if I'd gotten away with it when Deimos left." His grey eyes glinted.

"You're looking forward to it," she accused.

He shrugged, kicking off his boots. "I like chess."

Romy groaned at the excitement on his face. "I still think you're wrong."

"Wait and see," Atlas said. "Just wait and see."

Something else occurred to her. "Hey, your mother was acting really strange in the elevator today. I'm worried something is wrong with her."

He pursed his lips. "I had a visit from my mother, probably about three minutes after she saw you."

Romy bent to unlace her own boots, turning away as Atlas rose to change into his pyjamas—a fresh set of cargo pants. Perhaps it was a commander thing; Easiest to always be dressed when odds were someone would wake you up to deal with something. "What's the matter?" she asked. "Is your mum okay?"

"I would say it has something to do with those books you have on the nightstand."

She glanced to the right. "They're books for Elara." *Poacher poop!* Romy gasped and covered her mouth. "I was carrying them when I was talking to her. You don't think—"

"Yes, she did think."

Romy gasped again, mortified. A shrill laugh punched through. "But I can't be pregnant! e haven't. . . ."

He nodded. "I am painfully and daily aware of that fact."

Avert the eyes.

"I corrected my mother."

Another giggle escaped her, and then a full laugh. Gwenyth thought she was pregnant? That was why she'd been so nice? Char had been right about the grandchild thing. . . . Did that mean Gwenyth would go back to being mean to her? Maybe they could have kept the charade going a while longer.

Atlas's eyes were heavy on her. "I also told her that I want to have many children with you, if we get there one day."

Romy brightened. That might do the trick.

Then Atlas's words sank in. "W-what?" she asked.

"I want to have children with you one day."

Her eyes widened. "That's . . . a while off, isn't it?"

"Probably," he said.

"I want to travel the world first—if the war goes away."

"I don't think that's what happens to wars." He returned to the bed, moving over her to occupy the space closest to the wall.

"You know what I mean."

He ran a thumb over her cheek and pulled her against him. "I do." He kissed her gently. "I guess I better get busy making that war go away, then."

"ATLAS TOLD ME HE WANTS KIDS," ROMY SAID.

Elara's cupid mouth parted. "Please have kids. I want mini-Romys. They would be the cutest thing." Her face fell into a scowl. "I'll kill anyone who hurts them."

Her brows rose. "Well, I'm not into all that yet, or for a long, long time. But it's a good sign, don't you think?"

"A good—" Elara snorted. "A good sign? Do you have comets in your head or something? That man is head over freakin' heels for you. Sometimes I wonder if the only reason he's leading the Amach is because of you, to get the job done so he can multiply with you."

Romy blinked. Elara had a way of making love a little gross. "I did ask if he could make the war go away."

"What did he say?" Elara leaned forward, hazel eyes huge.

Deimos and Phobos entered, and Romy stilled as she saw the twins fist-pump, evil matching grins upon their faces.

"What have you been doing?" she demanded.

Their faces smoothed and they switched the innocent eyes on. *Oh, crap.*

"Nothing, Ro," Deimos said, blinking at her.

"Why do you always think we're doing something bad?" Phobos asked, giving her a sad look.

Romy's anger melted.

"How will we ever become better people if you always expect the worst?" Deimos added, sighing as though the world was on his shoulders.

She gave them each a pat on the hand. "I'm sorry. I do believe in both of you."

"*Oh brother,*" Elara muttered. "Every time."

Thrym jogged on-board last and shouted to the pilot they were good to leave.

There were twenty in their craft today. Atlas combined two teams together for added protection for the Dublin trip. The usual people were there, and ten of the top fighters and shooters in the Irish Amach. Romy hadn't said a word about it, sensing he needed to overdo her security detail for his own peace of mind.

Tina beckoned Romy from the front as soon as the craft was in the air. "You aren't wearing what I told you to wear."

"I didn't want to," Romy said. The clothing would make her stand out, and she'd already stand out enough where they were headed.

Tina threw her two coal-black garments. "Put it on, or you'll ruin my plan. You'll be in plain sight today, and I'm sure some of it will be screened. Quick, we'll be there in ten minutes."

Romy sighed. "I don't want to look different than everyone else."

"You are different. The sooner you get used to that, the better." Tina surveyed her. "Or, put another way. I could tell Atlas I don't believe you should be on active duty because of your Critamal problem. I can tell him you've come near death five times and begged me not to tell him."

"You wouldn't." Romy narrowed her eyes.

Tina cackled. "You know I would. On. Now."

"Pain in me 'ole." Romy borrowed Charlee's euphemism, and snatched the tight black garments from Tina. She joined Elara in the cockpit to change.

Five minutes and a lot of pulling and huffing later, Romy glanced down at the outfit. The clothing wasn't that much different from the navy coveralls they all wore. . . .

Elara whistled. "Whoa, that is way different from what we wear. I want a set. It looks like you have boobs."

"I don't."

"I know, but it looks like it."

The pants weren't so bad. They reminded her a little of Atlas's, actually. Black cargo pants, crisp and snug, but comfortable. The black top, however, was skin-tight. The shiny material tucked into the waistband of her cargo pants, and was taut across her toned stomach, chest, and arms.

At least she got to keep her black combat boots.

"You look totally badass," Elara said. "Kind of like a female Atlas. Cute."

Romy made a face at her.

Tina poked her head around. "Ready?"

"What exactly am I doing today?"

"What you do naturally," Tina said. "Walk with grace and elegance. Be kind. Smile, and make people feel extra super-duper great about themselves. And whatever else I tell you to do."

Yeah, right. "What might that include?"

"Shaking hands with a Mandate member on camera."

Romy folded her arms and stopped when Elara's eyes fell to her chest. "No way. I'm not doing that."

"Yes, you are. They specifically requested you do it."

"Why not Atlas? He's the boss," Romy said, cheeks heating.

Tina ignored her, asking Elara, "How long've we got?"

"Take your seat." Elara's voice crackled through the mic. "I'll be starting the descent soon."

Romy looked back to find Tina had disappeared into the back. *How convenient.* But seriously, Romy wasn't shaking hands with a Mandate member. She could barely manage a poker game without losing her temper.

The craft landed with a jolt, and Tina made herself unusually busy to avoid Romy. Then she opted to ride in a different vehicle to the city.

Clearing the Dublin gates and security took another hour. The Renegades hadn't attacked any Irish cities yet, but clearly the Mandate expected it. It was a strange feeling to drive through these heavily armed gates that not so long ago,

Knot 27 snuck through with ease . . . the night she shot Mandate Saavin.

"Keep your guns down." Tina's voice crackled through the walkie on Thrym's shoulder. "But do not drop your guard. Our priority is protection of Knot 27. They're our public VIPs. The objective is to get them in, put on a show, and get them out."

"Roger that," Thrym said, holding down the side of the device.

"Did you guys ever think we'd be VIPs when we crash-landed?" Elara asked.

Deimos grinned. *"Public* VIPs."

"Do you think that comes with foot massages?"

He shook his head. "I think that comes with an 'I'm going to smile so much today my face will hurt'."

As they drove between the sky-rises of white bubble houses into the centre of the city, Romy caught glimpses of many of their squads on the ground, often in mixed groups with the Mandate's forces. She hadn't known what to expect. City dwellers peered into the cars as they continued farther into the sparkling white heart of the city. The levitating rail system criss-crossed overhead, transporting the people here to their various leisurely pursuits and social engagements.

"What do you think?" Thrym asked.

With the Mandate by their side, the Amach might be able to win this war. From there, they would need to unify Earth's people, who, at this point, were massively divided. To Romy, Tina's plan to 'break the ice' with these city dwellers seemed like something the Amach should worry about after they'd won—*if* they won. Romy didn't understand how it would be possible to undo prejudice by walking around in someone else's city, and by shaking hands with someone everyone knew you hated. Romy blew a breath out. "I think that I have no idea if this will work or not, and whether we're wasting our time."

The cars pulled to a halt in the blinding white centre of New Dublin, the place they'd once watched Mandate Saavin make her speech about how the Amach were an evil rebellion.

"Smiles on," Tina crackled again.

They filed out of the huge bulletproof vehicles and walked toward the small greeting party. Romy was relieved to see none of the Mandate members were there waiting for them. Four were white-clad soldiers. High up, judging by the assortment of silver medals pinned to their chests. The rest she recognised as their people. Two were commanders from their Amach sent to Dublin a week ago to make sure the city was secure.

"Welcome," the most decorated Mandate soldier said. "I am General Kristoph."

They went through the introductions and Romy was uncomfortably aware of the glares from the enemy soldiers. They'd definitely seen the recordings from Cairo. The one of her killing a lot of them. She straightened and gave them a wide, disarming smile.

"I didn't bring you to antagonise," Tina hissed for her ears alone.

"You told me to smile."

"Not like a maniac. Do your normal 'marry me and I'll cook for you' smile."

"I don't know how to cook."

The general gave them a surreptitious glance. "Mandate Tony Debranc is flying in at 1500 hours for a public address. Until this time, we plan to show you around the city as per your commander-general's . . . request." He said the word like it was rotten.

Mandate Tony. The man who'd nearly pressed the button

that would've killed thousands of space soldiers? He was the Mandate Tina wanted her to shake hands with? Over Romy's dead body.

"Yes," Tina said, stepping forward. "That sounds great. I believe your civilians spend a great deal of the day in leisurely pursuits—"

"They do. However, I thought a rundown of—"

"I look forward to seeing the everyday life of a city dweller." Tina overrode him, a hint of venom entering her tone. "I'm sure it's vastly different to that of the Amach. It will be a solid step forward in ensuring a peaceful alliance between us. Understanding each other is key, wouldn't you say?"

The general's face turned faintly purple. "Of course, Tina."

"Commander Tina," she corrected. The red-haired woman glanced around. "Lead on, general. We aren't getting any younger."

MANDATE TONY.

Shaking his hand was all Romy could think about as they were paraded through a variety of classes. Pasta class, yoga, meditation—which Elara fell asleep in.

On a surface level, Romy could understand why the Amach had to give the alliance with the Mandate their full attention. An alliance was the only chance to beat Houston. The problem was, Romy hated the Mandate and what they represented, what they'd *done* to the space soldiers.

At least the request for Romy to be the one sealing their alliance now made sense. Tony had a personal vendetta against her. The Mandate member had one less finger after meeting with Feral Romy in Cairo. She'd literally shot a remote out of his hands, and everyone had seen it. Was Romy and everyone else supposed to forget that happened? Was the entire world supposed to believe things were okay because she shook hands with the guy?

None of the Dublin city dwellers had forgotten. They approached everyone else—aside from Deimos, whom they recognised as someone usually found by Houston's side. But the others. . . . The Dublin residents shared their carbonara with most of the Amach team, including the rest of Knot 27. Romy hadn't expected a warm welcome, but she hadn't expected a five-metre radius of fear. She found her smile coming out regularly over the day as she tried to put the people at ease, but what point was there, really, when they'd seen her slaughter all those people?

"They just need to see you're a person," Tina said for the twentieth time.

Mmmhmm, yep. "Sure." Romy smiled at a woman whose face went blank instantly. "This is why Thrym should shake hands with Tony."

"People know how much you hate the Mandate. They've seen evidence of it. You shaking Tony's hand means more. We need this alliance to work, Romy."

Romy rubbed at her temples. "I *know.*"

Deimos slid next to her. Tina had kept them separated for most of the day so their sheer unified presence didn't overwhelm anyone. "What I want to know is, are you going to shake his hand with four fingers, or five."

"I shot his left hand."

"Lucky. An awkward situation has been averted." His eyes cut to the simmering Tina. "How important is this handshake?"

"Don't be an ass, Deimos. If we don't seal this deal, Houston is going to steamroll us. It is crucial—"

"Making pasta?" he interjected.

"Yes, making pasta. Don't you understand how spending even one hour with someone of a different culture can alter your perception?"

"Honestly, no," he said, and Romy had to agree.

"Stupid space soldiers." Tina walked over to Thrym, who could clearly be trusted.

Deimos tossed an apple in the air. "That was rude."

"She is good at what she does. She's probably right about pasta being important," Romy said, tapping her lip. "How are you doing?"

He glanced around the packed kitchen. "No one's given me carbonara yet."

"Me neither."

A few beats passed. "How did we become the rebels of our group?" she asked, leaning on the stainless steel bench.

"Ro, honey, I was always a rebel. You, on the other hand, I can't explain."

She cleared her throat. "You know who doesn't mind your rebellious tendencies?"

"Doesn't mind as in respects them, or doesn't mind as in finds them sexy?"

Yuck. Romy scrunched her nose. "The second one."

"Do tell."

"Charlee."

He backed up next to her, gripping the apple tight. "Really? I thought she'd be well and truly pissed at me for running. She hasn't spoken to me since I've been back."

The fact he'd noticed was surprising. It told her he might return some of the doctor's feelings, which she hadn't expected. "Well, she wanted me to tell you . . . I'm not exactly sure, but I think the underlying message was she wouldn't be averse to sleeping with you again."

He gave her a speculative look. "Charlee's not like other girls I've met."

"She's smart," Romy said with fondness. "Sometimes she's crazy and Irish."

"Oh, I've met her crazy side." His green gaze grew heated.

Romy shuddered and peered over to Tina, who was herding everyone to the door. "Deimos, I can't do this. Too much rides on it. What if I lose my cool, and ruin things by shooting him and then Houston wins?"

Deimos quirked a brow. "Don't take a gun."

"I'm serious."

They trailed after the main group.

"Ro, you've done a lot of big things in a short time, and you've never failed to do what you had to do. This handshake is nothing in comparison, and, I suppose, much more in some ways. There's no *heat* to this moment, no adrenaline; you've had time to think beforehand. Believe me, you're not the only one who'd like to put an end to that guy. I've dreamed of doing it myself for a long, long time, but Romy, there's something bigger at play here. We have to put aside our anger to achieve what we really want. That's what I'm trying to remember. If you really can't do it, I guess we'll deal with that," Deimos said. "We've dealt with far worse, after all. Just . . . don't forget you were a soldier before you were anything else. One who has always preferred to run and read —but a soldier still."

14

"Tina, I'm serious," Romy said. "I'm not doing it. It's hypocritical. He is the epitome of everything I hate in the world."

The commander threw her hands in the air, cursing. "Talk some sense into her," she snarled at Thrym before stomping off.

Romy gave Thrym a flat look. They were in the wings of the stage, waiting for Mandate Tony to wrap up his speech— no doubt a meticulously put-together piece of propaganda.

"I'm not doing it," she repeated. "You do it."

"Let's discuss the pros and cons," Thrym offered.

Elara smirked. "He's going to try to talk her around."

Phobos shrugged. "I can see her point. She's had more direct interaction with that guy. I can see why she'd hate the thought of putting on a show that's nothing but lies. But, Romy, think of what happens if you don't."

"Thrym does it, and we go home," Romy said, crossing her arms.

"The people see someone who isn't the person they've

seen on the screens shaking Tony's hand. They then think about the woman in black they've seen walking around all day, and wonder why she wasn't the one to do it. . . . And if you *do* shake hands with him?"

"I stab him in the heart," Romy said viciously, cheeks flushing.

Her knot stared at her.

"Deep breaths, Ro,' Elara said. "That temper is just peeking out."

"*Just?*" Deimos muttered. Elara stood on his foot.

Romy took deep breaths.

"Maybe she's right," Thrym said shrewdly. "Maybe she can't handle it."

What? "That's not why I'm not doing it."

He turned away from her to address the rest of their knot. "We can't trust her temper after everything that's happened." He sighed. "It's a shame because this really was a crucial step in the eventual merging of Earth's civilians, but it has to be done right. We can't risk any . . ." He glanced back. ". . . tantrums onscreen."

Romy's mouth dropped open.

"Deimos," Tina called. "You're up."

With a tight nod, Deimos strode to the curtain and disappeared through it. The others watched him go.

"Did you guys know he was speaking?" Phobos asked.

Everyone shook their head in reply, and drew closer to the stage curtain.

Romy blanched at the thousands of people in attendance. All the usual city dwellers, plus a chunk of the Amach force. Romy tracked Deimos's progress to centre stage.

"Greeting to the people of New Dublin," Deimos said, voice booming out through the speakers in the audience. "I asked to speak to you today because I know my presence with the Amach must have you confused. When you last saw me, I was by someone else's side, the leader of the group who call themselves the Renegades." He stood tall, encased in his blue coveralls, handsome and sure. Though Romy knew the other members of Knot 27 could sense his nerves, as she could.

"I want you to know why I was there," he said, peering into the crowd. "I was a soldier aboard Orbito One. A year and a half ago, my knot crash-landed here after a battle with the Critamal. We survived, just. But I speak on behalf of all space soldiers when I say that learning humankind still existed and we'd been enslaved up there. . . . It broke me into pieces for a good, long time."

"What is he saying?" General Kristoph hissed.

Tina glared at Deimos. "Nothing I told him to say, I assure you. He will be disciplined."

Romy bit back a smile. *Liar.*

"I got angry, people of New Dublin, so very angry at the thought of what was happening to my friends. I sought to extract revenge by fighting fire with fire, and that was when I realised doing so wasn't helping my fellow space soldiers at all. I was simply thrusting them into even more danger than they'd been in before."

The general quieted beside Tina.

"I was wrong to side with Houston. The Renegades leader had been conducting cruel medical tests on my comrades," he admitted to a horrified collective gasp from the crowd. "So I escaped with the space soldiers in tow, and Commander-general Atlas allowed me to join the Amach ranks once more. On this point, there is one thing I want to make clear. My knotmate, Rosemary, was never with the Renegades." The crowd hushed to listen.

"Houston tested on her for weeks before he left to form the Renegades." He nodded sadly at the audience, green eyes operating at full tilt. "The person you saw in Cairo was the person he'd made her to be, not who she is." Deimos glanced toward Romy, with a wry smile. "People of Dublin, there is so much uncertainty right now, but of one thing I am absolutely certain: If we let the Renegades and Critamal win, no one will be safe. Not the space soldiers, not you, nor your leaders. *That* is why I wholeheartedly support our alliance with your people today."

"He didn't even choke on the words," Elara mused in Romy's ear.

To Romy it sounded as if Deimos believed every single thing he said.

"Tina must've threatened him with something," Phobos said.

"All right, Romy, get ready," Tina said, approaching her and fussing with her outfit.

Thrym wound through their group from the back. "I'll be doing it."

"No, you won't," Romy said, pushing in front of him. "*I* am." She sniffed. "Don't think I'm not aware of your reverse psychology tricks back there."

If Deimos was strong enough to speak just now, she could shake Mandate Tony's damn hand. As long as, at the end of this, he ended up getting what he deserved.

Mandate Tony took the stage again and Romy lifted her chin to peruse him. He was the same as ever. Brown hair and unyielding brown eyes. Mandate Tony was one of the six remaining Mandate members, but time spent in his company had informed her he was the mastermind within the Mandate. He pulled the majority of the strings. His was the face the people knew and adored.

She hated him.

He'd nearly killed her knot. He'd promised to torture her

for the remainder of her life. He'd been one push of a button away from killing thousands.

Blood rushed to her cheeks and she took deep breaths, trying to get a hold on her temper as the Mandate spoke.

"We are two very different peoples," Tony said, stressing the word 'different', "but we unite now under a common goal. We will take down the Renegades and Critamal together," he called.

The people roared.

"He's good," Tina said. "I'll give him that, but his hair sucks."

"I hope you will join me in welcoming our new allies to Dublin city." The crowd burst into wild applause, and he smiled at them indulgently, saying, "With a final handshake, I would like to make the alliance official on behalf of the other Mandate members, and planet Earth."

Tina shoved her forward and Romy trotted obediently onto the stage, dressed head to toe in black.

There was a weird few seconds where she remembered reading her nano on her cramped cot aboard Orbito One. That memory seemed like so long ago. . . . Equating this moment with that memory was impossible. She was about to seal an alliance that might prove crucial in winning this war. How was this happening to *her*?

Blood pounded in Romy's ears as she crossed the stage. Mandate Tony's amused face as she approached him didn't help any. They couldn't trust this man. He'd turn on them as soon as the job was done. In her eyes, the Mandate were just as bad as Houston—they just didn't have control over the cannons.

Whoever had control of the cannons, controlled the world, Romy realised in a blink of clarity.

As soon as the Renegades were out of the picture, *if* they

were ever out of the picture, the Mandate and the Amach would be left scrambling to seize the cannons.

"Rosemary," Mandate Tony said in greeting.

"Tony," she said demurely. "A pleasure."

". . . Likewise."

It came down to whether Romy trusted that the Amach could get to the cannons first. When it was put in those lines, then yes, she did believe that. Because she believed and trusted in Atlas.

Romy extended her hand. "To a peaceful alliance for the longevity of our people," she said.

He'd been speaking, but cut off at her words.

He didn't like that she'd stolen his thunder, so she continued. "I hope it may heal wounds we've caused each other in the past, and pave the way for a prosperous future for all." The people clapped and when Romy gave them a beaming smile, they shouted in approval.

Mandate Tony smiled and it etched into the lines of his face. He extended his hand. "Just as you say, Soldier Rosemary."

His hand was cold where hers was clammy, a fact that had the amusement coming back into his broad, impassive features. Romy let her gaze fall to his left hand. To her surprise he wasn't missing a finger anymore. A closer glance showed her a jagged scar at the base of one knuckle.

They turned away from the microphone, heading back to her knot together. "It's shorter than your other fingers," she said.

"You'll die, Rosemary," Tony said. "It's only a matter of time."

"Will you chop off my finger, Tony?" she replied, smiles plastered on for the cameras.

"Of course not," he said. "Someone else will do it."

Romy pursed her lips and turned slightly toward him.

"That's why you'll lose the war," she said, brow raised. "Because you don't get your hands dirty."

"I'm aware you have no problem with that."

Her stomach dropped, but hopefully it didn't show on her face. "No, I don't, when the situation calls for it." She paused. "And I do think your name is calling for it. Don't be too quick to point the finger, Tony." Romy glanced at his left hand again. "Just because you don't do it yourself, doesn't mean your hands aren't filthy."

She ducked behind the curtain and re-joined her knot.

Tina gave her a passing nod and joined the Mandate and his small contingency.

"You did it," Thrym said, squeezing her arm.

"Looked like it got intense at the end," Phobos said.

Romy gave a curt dip of her head. "Just a bit of friendly talk."

Deimos wrapped an arm around her shoulders. "That's my girl."

"You spoke well," Romy replied. "Did you mean it? About the alliance?"

"Yes. For now." His gaze grew far away. "I hope it helps."

"Has to be more effective than sharing carbonara."

Tina re-joined them. "Come on. Time to head back to base."

Finally. This top was slowly suffocating her.

They moved back through the exuberant crowds and Romy found herself smiling when the people edged closer to her than they had all day. Maybe coming here wasn't such a bad thing. It seemed to have done something to soften the strain between their factions. She said just as much to Tina, who replied, "I'm not worried about changing how the city dwellers perceive the Amach."

"You're not?"

"The *Amach* are the ones who have wholeheartedly hated

these civilians for one and a half centuries." Tina sighed. "Getting them to change is the bigger task here, and that's where we are most likely to fail in ensuring long-term peace."

"When will the first city dwellers come to the Amach?" Thrym asked.

Tina glanced at her watch. "For dinner. In about . . . two hours."

15

It was painful. The dinner reminded Romy of all the staring when Knot 27 first arrived at Jimboomba.

A group of one hundred city dwellers exchanged looks of disgust over the meal in front of them. Miscellaneous green slop, one of the worst dinners the kitchen had ever served. Romy knew it was on purpose, which angered her because she had to eat it, too.

Until this moment, their Dublin guests had been blissfully and, she suspected, purposefully unaware of the world outside their city walls. They were ignorant of how hard those in the rural settlements had to work to provide the cities with food. They'd been supposedly unaware of the enslavement of the space soldiers for 150 years. Some ignorance could be forgiven, but when ignorance hurt others it was hard to pardon, and harder still to believe the ignorance wasn't wilful on some level. If the Mandate had taken control for so long, so absolutely, it was because these people let them.

Yet, Tina's comment had taken root in her mind, and Romy knew the woman was right. How the Amach treated these people while they were here would prove incredibly important.

"Come on," Romy said to her knot. "We're going over there."

"Really?" Phobos complained. "I spent all day with them."

"Which is why we should go over there," she pressed.

With loud groans, even from Thrym, Knot 27 picked up their trays and distributed themselves throughout the long table of city dwellers.

Romy settled onto the bench seat between an overweight greying man and a slim brunette who looked like she went to the yoga thing each day.

"You're the one that killed all those soldiers." A city dweller's trembling voice reached her from across the table.

Why did I come here again? "Yes, I did. Mandate Tony was about to push a button that would've killed three and half thousand space soldiers." Romy dug a fork into her miscellaneous meal and shoved it in her mouth. Not too bad.

"He never told us that," the same person answered.

A man watched Romy eat another mouthful before loading his fork with some of the green slop. "There's a lot they haven't told us. Sometimes I think they only show us what they want to."

This was met with some uneasy fidgeting from the others.

"Do you know what you'll be doing while you're in the Amach?" Romy asked.

"Just living life like you guys," the man answered.

She held out her hand. "I'm Romy."

He cracked a smile. "I know who you are. I'm Dan."

"Well, Dan, just hope you don't get Tina for an instructor in combat classes."

A middle-aged woman spoke. "We'll be learning to fight?"

Her eyes rounded. "I've always wanted to punch someone. Right in the throat."

Chewing and swallowing another bite, Romy then answered, "Well, you probably won't be able to go for the throat, but you'll certainly be punching. Probably not each other at first."

"Will the food be like this every night?" another asked.

Romy shrugged. "We don't have the same luxuries you have in the cities. We can't afford them. But you'll get used to the food. This is one of the worst meals I've had here."

"Is there any heating?" another asked.

Her brows rose and she forced them down with difficulty. "No, I'm afraid not. We're in a cave system and all the energy goes toward lighting and dealing with the waste."

"You know," the man said, "you don't seem nearly as. . . ."

"Crazy?" Romy supplied.

The city dwellers nearest gave guilty laughs. The man gave her a sheepish look.

"I assure you, I'm normal . . . most of the time."

Someone tapped a microphone up front and everyone glanced over as Atlas came into view standing at the podium.

"Welcome to our guests," he started. "I am sure each and every person in the Amach will ensure you have a comfortable stay while here." The words were loaded.

"That's nice of him," a city female said, nodding to her friend.

They were kind of like the clueless space soldiers in a way.

Atlas gestured and the screens came on, replaying what happened in Dublin earlier that day. Romy watched her screen-self walk across the stage dressed in black. She almost looked graceful as she did it. Screen Romy extended her hand to Mandate Tony, and the crowd went wild when she smiled at them. You couldn't even tell that she and Tony had been exchanging death threats afterward. It looked as though they were discussing the weather.

. . . Tina had been right about wearing the black outfit. Romy's clothing was the exact liquid onyx opposite of Tony's pristine white.

"What's Mandate Tony like?" a male sighed dreamily.

Didn't you just hear me tell you he nearly killed over three thousand people? Romy hesitated. "What do you think of him?" she asked, trying to keep her expression neutral.

The person straightened. "What?"

"What do you think about what he does?" she said.

A warm hand landed on her shoulder. "Rosemary."

She glanced up into grey eyes and her stomach erupted in butterflies. "Atlas."

"Got a moment?" He dipped his head at the city dwellers in greeting.

She wiped her mouth with a napkin and loaded up her empty tray. He reached over and took it from the table, walking off to put it in the cleaning area.

"You're with him?" a woman asked.

"I am." Weird question.

"He is so into you."

"Sandra *never* does the dishes," another complained.

"Don't start with me, Robert. That's always how we've worked."

Robert sniffed. "Maybe it's time that changed."

With a hasty goodbye, Romy made her retreat, meeting Atlas at the door. "You just started a domestic dispute. Robert is angry at Sandra for never doing the dishes," she added in response to his inquiring look.

"How are the city dwellers tonight?" He led the way out of the Mess past a team coming in from mission.

"Unimpressed with the food. Clueless, but surprisingly open-minded otherwise."

He took her hand. "Good."

"What do you need me for?" she asked, intertwining her fingers through his.

"Because I haven't seen you all day, and I missed you." He pulled her behind a corner and kissed her until she forgot they were in a damp, dimly lit, pipe-lined concrete passage.

"And I want to show you something. Come on," he whispered.

She grinned and let him tug her down the hall. He was clearly excited about something. He very rarely acted in such a playful way.

They went through the commanding offices, to a room she hadn't been inside before. She watched as Atlas entered a code, and scanned his fingerprint, then his eye.

". . .What are you showing me?" Romy didn't know the Amach had such intense security.

They walked into a dark room and Atlas reached behind her to flick on the light switch.

"Wow." The word left her mouth as she was still registering the sight before her. A giant metallic sphere was suspended in the middle of a ring. The orb was enormous, filling the entire room and only allowing enough space for a single person to walk around it at a time. "What is it?" she asked in awe.

"This is our solution," he said. "This is how we ensure corruption no longer affects our world government. It is a computer."

"I didn't know," she said.

He nodded. "It's been top secret since the concept was first brainstormed."

"How does it work?" she asked, beginning to walk around it. An array of tiny lights flashed on it: blue, green, and red.

"We enter all the figures into it—the number of people in an area, the resources from an area, the particular needs of an area—and this computer calculates how the collective resources need to be distributed, so everyone has what they need."

Equality. "That's incredible. Is it foolproof?"

"We will need public figures to address the people," he said. "And we are currently discussing ideas for how data entry should be safeguarded. This computer won't be utilised until we are sure it is entirely unable to be used for personal advantage."

"I love it," Romy said, looking at the huge, flashing orb. "I absolutely love it. It's ingenious. Think of what this could mean for Earth."

His arms wrapped around her from behind. "Imagine what I'll be free to do once a computer takes over."

". . . THAT IS WHY SOMETIMES IT SEEMS LIKE A PERSON IS saying something more than just their words," Romy finished.

A space soldier with a five o'clock shadow raised his hand. "Could you give us an example of sarcasm?"

Romy glanced at the muesli bar in her hand. "This muesli bar is the best thing I've ever eaten."

A room of faces contemplated her like she was the greatest puzzle in the world.

"What you're saying is . . . it's *not* the best thing you've ever eaten?" the soldier said, then brightened. "It's bad."

Romy replied, "Correct."

The stares turned to beaming smiles and mutterings of excitement.

Pounding footsteps echoed outside of the gym, followed by shouting.

"Stay here," Romy said to them with a frown. "I'm going

to check that out."

"Do you need assistance, mother hen?"

She waved the woman back. "No, it's probably nothing."

Murmured whispering broke out behind her.

"—so, is she saying it *is* something—?"

"—I don't think they do sarcasm all the time—"

Pushing the doors open, Romy stuck out her head and reared away as a small unit of panicked soldiers sprinted past and almost collided into her. She caught sight of Atlas, not far behind them. He didn't slow his steps.

"What's wrong?" she called after him.

"Don't worry, I'm handling it," he shouted back.

Her stomach sunk. "Is it Deimos and Phobos?"

"Yup."

He disappeared down the next passage and Romy retreated back into the gym.

. . . Perhaps it was better not to know. A part of her was disappointed Atlas hadn't lasted long against the twins' pranks. She didn't know what they'd done to him specifically; all three of them had remained close-lipped. No one had ever beaten the twins, though. She returned to her seat, a workout bench, and faced the soldiers once more.

"Uhm, Miss Rosemary?"

Romy blew out a breath, glancing back at the gym door where the person had called from. A woman hovered there. "Just one moment. Practise being sarcastic to each other," she said to the space soldiers.

"—I like your hair—"

"—You're good at what you do—"

"—No one talks behind your back about how annoying your laugh is—"

"What is it, Bridget?" Romy asked, reaching the gym door again.

The woman held up an envelope, a perplexed look on her

face. "This was found for you. Taped to the trapdoor exit."

Outside the Amach? Romy took the black envelope. "Whoever left this wasn't seen?"

"It would take an atomic bomb to get through that door, ma'am. We have cameras on it, but it isn't guarded. I went to take it to the commander-general, but I couldn't find him."

Romy's name was written in a silver scrawl on the front. "Yes," she said, only partly paying attention to Bridget now. "Thank you. I will handle this from here. Could you ensure a guard is put on the trapdoor from now on?"

"Yes, ma'am."

"Thank you."

The woman bobbed her head and left, the gym door swinging shut behind her. Romy stared at the letter in her hand, already certain the contents weren't an invitation to a delightful evening abroad.

Remembering her pupils, she returned to them for the second time. "I'm afraid I'll need to cut class short today. Something has come up. Why don't you play poker instead?"

"I lost all my twigs yesterday," one said forlornly. "But I have a good feeling I'm gonna win big today." The soldier's eyes gleamed with unhealthy fervour. "Really big."

Romy left them and headed off to one side. Slipping her finger under the wax seal, she pried the flap open and extracted the letter.

My dearest Rosemary,
I must apologise at how our last meeting ended.
When one knows how something is to be done, but no one around them listens, it is easy to become frustrated. But I won't get into that.
I write to you today to appeal to your compassion and sense of duty because I know that, like myself, you want peace and prosperity for all.

I have in my possession three hundred of your fellow space soldiers, and they are very sick. Phrased another way, I guesstimate they have around three days to live.

Unless.

I'm sure you know what I'm going to say next.

Unless they get your blood.

This is bigger than you or I. You now have the chance to save three hundred lives. I don't claim friendship with you any longer. I know I have destroyed any semblance of the friendship I once had with Atlas, which I regret most deeply. However, now we must work together.

I propose this, Romy. Ten of your people meet ten of my people at the location where we landed outside of Cairo not long ago. If you are able to help, I would gratefully and humbly accept half a litre of your blood. If Dr Charlee is able to spare it from her testing schedule.

"How do you know about her tests?" Romy murmured to herself.

I ask that Charlee extract it from you either once you've landed in Cairo, or on the journey there to make sure the blood will still be viable for use by the time my team gets it back to our base.

I do not expect a return reply from you. If you wish to help your fellow comrades, my representatives will be in Cairo in twenty-four hours and I will be thankful you have seen past our enmity to grant my space soldiers aid.

Yours sincerely,

James Houston

P.S. Reports tell me you are doing exceptionally well, Rosemary. My wonderment at the power of your mind will never cease.

16

Atlas stalked across the debriefing room, Houston's letter clenched tightly in his grip. "When did security find this?" he said through clenched teeth.

"Bridget gave it to me two hours ago," Romy replied.

"Why am I only hearing of this now?" he seethed.

She met his gaze calmly. "Because I wanted to think about it."

"This isn't a decision you make on your own."

"I think it is."

The rest of the room, packed with captains, commanders, Cronus, and her knot, watched in tense silence.

Romy addressed them. "This is an opportunity to negotiate the space soldiers' return." She addressed Atlas. "You said you would do so at the first available opportunity."

"Houston won't give them up."

"He will give *some* up for the blood."

"You're aware it's a trap?" Cronus asked, taking the letter and scanning it.

Atlas closed his eyes. "Of course it's a trap."

"Just making sure."

Tina plucked it from Cronus's grasp and read it, shaking her head. "If we don't help, Houston won't hesitate to make it known to the public. Romy's right; we have some power here to get a portion of the soldiers back. We should open negotiations for two hundred and leave with no less than one hundred."

"Regardless of negotiations, if there are three hundred lives to save, we have to do it," Elara said, curling her fists. "It's our responsibility."

That was Romy's sentiment. If they could get some of the space soldiers back, great, but she'd be giving her blood to Houston regardless.

Atlas rubbed his temples. "Rosemary would have to go to have her blood drawn in-flight. It's too risky. He wants to lure her out."

"It's a risk. Just like any other." Gwenyth spoke. "We secure the perimeter in advance. We'll send out one team member with her blood."

Cronus hummed. "I'd personally like to make reparation to the space soldiers for all those years I did the Mandate's bidding."

"You didn't know, Cronus," Atlas said, clapping the man on the shoulder.

The older man was silent. Then he cleared his throat. "If we go ahead with this exchange and the ground teams pick up anything suspicious, we can turn the craft right around. We can make sure it's safe before landing."

Romy let her gaze fall to her hands. As bizarre as it was to be a player in this game, she knew by now she was. People associated her with power, and more than that—her blood was a hot commodity. If Houston took her, the space soldiers here would be bereft of further testing and would still be vulnerable.

On the other hand, Romy knew what a room full of dead

bodies looked like. Her mind had already multiplied what she'd done in Cairo by six to show her the devastation of three hundred dead space soldiers. To put their fate on her shoulders wasn't fair, but Romy had done so already.

Like Cronus, she felt this was a way for her to make up for past misdeeds. "It needs to be done," she said, interrupting someone.

"I disagree," Atlas said instantly.

They stared off. Romy's stomach tightened at the frantic edge to his voice.

"You don't think you might be biased?" Tina asked. "Are you sure the only reason you don't want her to go is because you love her?"

"Of course that's the reason," he said tightly. "But this is clearly a trap, and my feelings aside, Romy is wanted by every damn power on this planet."

Gwenyth sighed. "It's three hundred lives, son."

"I'm confident the ground teams can clear the area," Thrym said. "Commander Cronus is right. We don't have to land if something looks off."

"We?" Romy said. "You aren't coming."

Her knot stared at her with stony faces. "You aren't going without us," Phobos said.

Romy shook her head.

"It's okay for you to go out into danger, but not the rest of us? You don't get to decide that," Elara said. "We feel just as much responsibility to see the space soldiers safe."

Atlas contemplated Romy. "If you don't go, your knotmates won't go."

She narrowed her eyes. "Nice try, but I'm going." And she'd do her best to change her knotmates' minds after the meeting.

"He's unpredictable," Atlas said through clenched teeth.

Houston was a genius, no one was questioning that, and

a genius half out of his mind was a dangerous genius. She knew so little of the doctor, really. She didn't know anything about his life other than his medical career, which he'd told her about. "Where did Houston come from?" Romy asked.

"Aberdeen," Atlas muttered, not looking at her. She waited for him to meet her eyes, but he wouldn't.

"What do we know about him? Is there anything we can use?" Phobos said, picking up where Romy was going with her question.

Cronus waved at the assistant frantically typing up the meeting notes. "Have someone look into it."

"Yes, sir." The boy tapped furiously on his device. "I'll have a report for you in three hours."

"It looks like it will be a vote," Atlas said, glaring down every person in the room, arms behind his back and shoulders tensed. "Those in favour of meeting the Renegades in twenty hours?"

Only he left his arm down. . . .

The fire died from his eyes before flaring, and he pushed off the table. "Very well. If you wish to walk into this trap, so be it."

"Atlas," Romy called to him.

He didn't stop on his way out the door.

"I'm sorry, Ro," Deimos said for the fifth time as they all sat eating dinner in the Mess.

She shrugged. "It's not your fault you couldn't save all of the space soldiers, Dei. You brought back over three thousand of them. Stop apologising."

A force had already been deployed to ensure the meeting area in Cairo was secure. The backup would stay far back and out of detection, but would be there if they required help.

"Charlee gave us another injection," Thrym said. "One with higher blood percentage in it. She said the tests with twenty-five per cent of your blood have held past two weeks, too."

Elara shovelled food into her mouth. "Can I just say it's gross to be injected with your blood, Ro? Like, you're my knotmate, but it's still sick."

Romy forced a smile for her and Elara set down her fork. "Oh, Ro. It will be all right. He's not mad at you. Not really. He's angry that you'll be in danger's way, and that he got outvoted. Males hate that."

"He possibly wasn't in the best mood today, either," Phobos added with a guilty look.

"What did you guys do to him?" Thrym asked.

"Which time?"

Thrym's white teeth glinted. "Maybe I'll just ask how many times."

"Five in the last two days. Resetting the fusion waste system to a lower heat, so the waste turned to sludge instead of evaporating, was probably the best one."

"Our crowning glory." Deimos wiped a fake tear from his eye.

That explained the panicking people.

"How have you guys been going with him?" he asked Thrym and Elara.

What? Romy gave the other two a disapproving look— which bounced right off Elara. "I was counting on you to be the responsible one," Romy said to Thrym.

"It's going well," Thrym answered the twins cryptically, ignoring her.

Elara scraped her plate and shoved the last morsel in her mouth. "I've been nice to him for the most part. Sometimes I give him endless, boring advice. I snap at him at least once during our talks. Pretty sure he has no idea what to do with me." She cackled. "He brings food each time. Like that's going to win me over."

Phobos glanced at Ellie's empty plate.

"What are you doing to him?" Romy asked Thrym.

He shrugged. "Being in command can be a huge task when someone in the room won't stop asking questions."

The others snorted.

"You all realise I love Atlas?" she asked them.

Phobos answered, "You realise we won't stop until we're sure he's the man for you?"

"I thought that was my choice," she countered.

Elara patted her hand. "It is, Ro. It is. We're just making extra, quadruple sure for you."

"Thanks," Romy said drily. "So, about tomorrow. . . ."

"Save your breath. We're all coming," Thrym said.

There wasn't the slightest weakness in their resolution as Romy ran her eyes over her knot. With a heavy huff, she took her tray to the bin and scraped it, watching as the full bin disappeared below the floor and another bin took its place. Spotting Charlee, she hurried to intercept her.

"Char," she called.

The doctor tore her gaze away from where she'd been eyeing Deimos.

Romy scrunched her nose. "What were you just doing?"

"Foreplay."

Bile rose in her throat. "That is . . . never mind. I want you to take as much blood as you can from me before we leave for Cairo."

She shook her head. "You'll already be giving half a litre to Houston. It's not safe."

"How many can I give without dying?"

Charlee frowned at her. "Five. Maybe six with your nanotech, but I'm under strict orders not to risk you in any way." She held a hand up as Romy opened her mouth. "No, Romy. That's my final word. Space soldier maximum is half a litre every month because you heal more rapidly than other humans. You did that two weeks ago, and now you'll be doing it again. I'm not taking more from you."

"If I don't make it back, you might need the extra juice, though."

The doctor drew in closer. "I'm not so sure. I've returned to mapping your genetic discrepancies. Houston did this in the initial stages, but he didn't go back to it when your brain overrode your nanos. There may be something in there that helps the blood injection hold."

"Thrym said the twenty-five per cent tests are going well?"

"*Were*," Charlee said with a heavy sigh. "They lost hold an hour ago. The ones of stronger concentration are still viable, but I don't foster much hope of any of them holding. If one at twenty-five per cent doesn't, a fifty or ninety per cent won't either. No," her eyes shifted, "there is another answer. Or a combination of answers."

"I know you hate me saying so, but you're the right person for this job."

"I'll never be brilliant," Charlee said. "But I can be methodical. Let's hope that's enough."

"You're sure you won't take any more blood from me?"

The doctor pressed her lips together. "Absolutely sure. You'll just have to make sure you come back now, won't you?"

Romy grinned. "I guess so." She stepped in and hugged the doctor hard. "I'm so glad I met you, Char."

The doctor's arms came up around Romy and she gave a surprised chuckle. "Me too. Never been happier someone crash-landed on Earth."

"Deimos seemed surprised you'd give him a second chance. I think you're good to go on that," she whispered in the doctor's ear.

Charlee grinned as Romy pulled away. "Did he indeed?" She pushed back her hair, blew a kiss at Romy and wove over to an empty table, ignoring Deimos completely.

Five seconds later, Deimos joined the doctor at her table.

ROMY PUSHED OPEN THE DOOR WITH NO SMALL AMOUNT OF trepidation.

He was sitting there, on the bed they'd shared for the last six weeks.

"Hey," she said after a beat.

Atlas lifted his head. "Hey."

Unsure what to do, Romy hovered in the doorway. "If you want to be alone, I can leave."

He stood and frowned at the ground. "No, I don't want to be alone. I've been alone my whole life. That's the whole point."

Her breath stuttered in her throat in shock. "I'm not doing this to leave you, Atlas."

"I know that. That's not what I mean."

"Then what do you mean?" she asked softly. "Those space soldiers need our help."

He ran his hands through his hair, pacing on the spot. "But why does it always need to be you?" He crossed to her in long strides. "When will this world leave you alone?"

She couldn't watch his deep-rooted scars pushing to the surface. "I don't know. But it's not right now."

His hands shifted up her arms. "I hate that it's always you." He wiped his thumb under her eye, brushing away a tear. "Don't cry, darling. It's not you I'm mad at. I'm mad at everyone else for trying to take you away."

"I wish I hadn't had to hurt your feelings in the debriefing room. I'm sorry," Romy said.

He gave her a sad half smile. "Never be sorry for making the choices you have to. Isn't that what you told me?"

"I'm wise sometimes."

"It's Houston that worries me, his unpredictability."

"All you can count on is that he's a jerk," Romy said.

Atlas shook his head. "All I can count on is that he wants a show. He has always waited for the moment when most people can see his genius in action, and the second when he can make the largest bang. I can *count* on him wanting to bear witness to his triumph, to be unable to resist the temptation of front-row seats. It's why he will come to Cairo to meet you, instead of allowing others to take his place, you'll see. His arrogance is predictable in so many ways, but his mind is utterly *un*predictable."

Romy played over his words. "I've never seen him in exactly that way, but you're right." She smiled up at him. "That's why you're commander-general."

Atlas grazed over her cheekbone with his lips. "I would tear apart every inch of this world if something happened to you. I love you so much, Rosemary."

"I love you, Atlas," she managed to get out just before his lips touched hers.

The kiss was different from anything they'd shared before. The intensity and depth of the touch so endless it scared the comets out of her. A silent desperation dictated their movements. His hands moved to her zipper and he drew it slowly down, pushing the coveralls off of her shoulders. They fell to the ground around her feet.

Not pausing their kiss for a second, Romy reached for the bottom of his shirt and slid it up over his head.

He broke away, whipping the garment over his head and returning to her with new ferocity. "You're okay?" he asked, looking into her eyes.

If he stopped now, Romy would have a full-blown lady tantrum. "Don't stop," she said, closing the gap.

With a growl, he picked her up and covered the ground to their bed, tossing her onto it.

She gave a breathless laugh, and reached for him. . . .

. . . Pulling the man she loved down to join her.

17

"Everyone on-board?" Tina asked.

Thrym did a third head count. Always dotting his I's and crossing his T's. "Affirmative."

Their usual team of ten sat strapped into the cargo area of the craft, except Nancy had been switched out for Dr Charlee. Elara sat up in the pilot seat, with Phobos co-piloting.

The area behind them cleared of personnel, and as the cargo door began to close, Atlas stepped into the craft.

"Hold the door!" Tina shouted to the front. The door stopped. "What are you doing here?" she asked him incredulously.

As well as his usual cargos and black T-shirt, a black bulletproof vest was strapped in place, he had a handgun on each hip, a knife was strapped to his left calf, and he held a sleek rifle in his hands. Atlas walked to Don. "I'll be taking your place on this one."

Don, one of their regular team members, unstrapped his harness and walked off the craft without a word.

"Wait, wait, wait," Tina said, eyes flashing.

Atlas passed his rifle to Thrym to hold while he sat and fastened the harness in the vacated chair.

Tina got in his face. "We're not just giving Houston Romy, we're giving him the opportunity to take the commander-general, too? This isn't how you play chess, Atlas. Do you not trust the way I run things?"

His eyes cooled. "When it comes to her life, there's no one I trust more than myself."

Hurt slashed across Tina's face and she stared at him for a drawn-out moment.

"Take off," Atlas called to Elara.

The door closed. Tina smoothed her expression and took a seat.

As soon as they were in the air, Atlas unstrapped himself and stood in the centre of the cargo area. "Our forces have been in place for fifteen hours outside of Cairo. They have scanned the meeting point and set up a perimeter one kilometre back. We won't be going in until Houston's party have landed and our ground teams and eyes in the air say we are clear. We'll be landing close to their location, so the cannons cannot be used against us."

"Yes, sir," Romy chimed with the others.

She wasn't sure how to feel about his presence. A part of her was elated not to be parted from him for any length of time. She felt safer for him being here; she understood *why* he'd been unable to remain behind . . . but there was also intense worry over what might happen to him—which was ridiculous. Romy had seen Atlas in action several times. Where she'd had twenty or so missions to get used to the idea of her knot being in danger, there was a kind of reassurance to know there was someone she loved back at the Amach to return to.

All of her eggs were in one craft, and it was unsettling.

Atlas approached where she sat next to Deimos. He

addressed her knotmate. "I had some ideas I wanted to run by you."

"Already?" Deimos answered. "I'm impressed."

Atlas shrugged. "I have ground to make up. Can't say I had time for pranks in my childhood."

"Man, have you got a few things to learn," crowed Deimos.

What is going on?

"Do you mind if I have a word with Rosemary?" Atlas asked Deimos. Her knotmate gave a quick nod and moved across to sit next to Thrym.

She waited until he was out of earshot. "What the heck was that?"

"I had to readjust my strategy," Atlas said, pursing his lips. His eyes shifted to make sure no one was listening. "Keep your enemies close and all that. I said that they had permission to play pranks within the Amach as long as I could be involved."

"I'm not sure if that was . . . wise."

"No, which appealed to them. In the meantime, I get a glimpse into how they run their operations, which will make it easy to hamstring them later."

Romy winced.

"Thrym is easier, so I'll leave him until last."

She gave him a curious glance.

"His emotional weakness is Nancy," Atlas explained, eyes glinting. "I can make it very hard for her."

Laughter erupted from Romy's lips. "That's terrible."

"The gloves came off when I was covered in garbage sludge three days ago."

"Covered?"

"From head to toe."

Romy giggled.

"The person I can't figure out is Elara." His eyes narrowed.

"She's very deep," Romy said in mock seriousness.

Atlas's brows lifted. "I wouldn't have thought so before, but she's proving . . . elusive. I can't gather that she cares about anything much I can exploit. I thought to ply her with food or a new craft, but she takes the food and treats me just the same." He pursed his lips as Romy laughed again at the thought Elara was successfully psyching out a commander-general.

"Hey," Romy said after a few minutes of listening to the familiar whine of the engines. "Do you think Cronus is after your mum?"

Atlas's brows slammed together. "What?"

Oops. "Uh, nothing. Just thought. . . ."

"My mother and Commander Cronus?" His face twisted in disgust. "My mother and *anyone*." He shuddered.

Romy nudged him. "She's been alone for a long time, Atlas."

"Yes, but I'm back now."

"What if I had plans to keep you all to myself? Who would she have then?"

His jaw tightened. "When has this been happening?"

She shoved down a snort and replied, "Right in front of you. During debriefing. I'm not saying that's what is actually happening." *She was.* "But you can't begrudge your mother for moving on, can you?"

His face was still twisted in disgust and he shivered again. Clearly, it wasn't the moving-on part he objected to, it was the moving-on-with-another-human part which disturbed him. Space soldiers didn't have parents, but Romy gathered this subject was like her discussing sex with her knotmates—gross and awkward.

Thrym beckoned to her from across the craft. He and

Deimos were bent over a nano. She crossed to him and sat on his other side.

"Check this out," Thrym said, tilting the screen to her.

She took the device from him and read the title of the document. "This is Houston's file?"

Thrym nodded. "Atlas's assistant dug it up. The file was just sent to all the captains and command team."

Romy began to scan through the document—there were twenty pages of information. None of it seemed abnormal. He'd been born in Aberdeen, and both of his parents were in the medical field. He'd displayed ultra-intelligence from a young age and his career path was accelerated in response to it.

Her eyes fell on a paragraph on the twelfth page. "Wait, what's this?"

"That's what we found interesting," Deimos said.

"Parents, both deceased. Father, declared insane. Committed to a safe holding cell at thirty years old, died twenty years later from a carotid artery embolism. Mother, died from early onset dementia at age fifty-two." Her mouth dropped as she finished reading.

Thrym and Deimos met her gaze.

"I don't know what to think about that," she said, skimming through the pages again.

"If he inherited either of those illnesses from his parents. . . ." Thrym trailed off.

". . . It could explain his sudden change," Romy said in a low voice, thinking of the unhinged look in Houston's eyes in the weeks before he left the Amach.

"Exactly," Deimos said, staring at the nano where a picture of Houston's father was showing. There was a strong father-son resemblance. "Look at this part." He pointed to comments further down. "His father was locked up after attacking others in the base."

"Seems like he had a more personal reason to be working on the insanity cure than we ever realised," Thrym said, whistling low. "Do you think he has daddy issues?"

Romy lifted her head and looked across at Atlas, who was in talks with Tina. "When did you receive this, Thrym?"

"About thirty minutes ago."

Atlas had already read it. It explained his sudden decision to join their mission. Whatever he'd seen in Houston's file had concerned him enough to come along for Romy's personal protection. Not that he'd needed much of an excuse.

Romy handed Thrym's nano back to him, and listened to her knotmates discuss the information with half an ear, lost in troubled thoughts. For a long time, she'd believed Houston wanted to discover the insanity cure to leave behind a legacy. Then she'd decided he was power hungry, but was it possible his obsession with the cure stemmed from a fear of losing his *own* mind?

"Ready to be drained?" Charlee asked some time later.

Romy blinked, startled from her troubled thoughts. Charlee had already set up her medical instruments. They had to be nearing Cairo.

She beckoned to Romy when everything was laid out. Romy joined her in the middle of the cargo area, lying on the ground.

"Atlas," Tina called. "Ground force says Houston's group have arrived. Our people are running through security checks now."

"Roger that, Commander," Atlas said.

"Are there any Critamal there?" Romy asked.

Atlas quirked a brow at Tina and she shook her head. He shifted to stare at where Charlee was sliding a cannula into Romy's arm.

The doctor's hands shook and she murmured, "It would be helpful if he didn't stare."

"Good luck with that."

She placed tape over the cannula's end to hold it steady and set about connecting the first bag. "Speaking of luck, I got lucky last night."

"Oh?" Romy asked. "Did you win a poker game?"

Charlee grinned. "Of a sort, Ro. Of a sort."

The first trickle of blood landed in the bag. Atlas was focused entirely on it. "Atlas," Romy called. He started and looked at her face. "How long will it take for the ground force to give us the all-clear?" Best to distract him. He appeared more than a bit murderous at the moment.

He rose. "I'll go and check." She gave him a smile that he didn't return.

Charlee switched out one bag for another and whacked Romy's arm. "Jeez, it's coming slow today."

"Altitude?" she asked, already knowing perfectly well it was because she'd forced Thrym to take blood from her back in the Amach and leave it in a cooler for Charlee as a backup.

"Have you been drinking enough water?" the doctor mused.

"Five litres a day, like you said."

Atlas's voice boomed from the cockpit where he'd been talking to the ground force. "We are clear to land. How much longer do you need, Dr Charlee?"

Charlee had three bags now. "Another ten minutes."

He lifted the pilot's speaker to his mouth and spoke again to the ground forces, then handed it to Elara and addressed the rest of them. "We'll be landing in fifteen minutes. Arm up, but make sure no weapons are visible. Do not engage unless we are attacked. I want us in three tight rows with our backs to the craft, and Rosemary in the middle. Be ready for an ambush."

"Yes, sir," came the chorused answer.

The team set about readying themselves with practiced

hands, and an underlying tension that made it clear they all knew what would happen if this went haywire.

Charlee switched the last bag onto the IV. "Nearly done, Ro. How're ya feeling?"

"Your Irish is coming out," Romy teased. She *was* feeling a bit woozy, actually. But she'd cope once her feet were on solid ground again.

"I'm a wee bit nervous," Char admitted. With a last jiggle of the line, she announced, "All done."

Romy's head spun and she decided to stay still as the haze cleared. The doctor unhooked the line and removed the cannula.

"Char, I left something for you in your blood cooler," Romy confessed, now Houston's half a litre was out. "The one next to your desk."

Charlee stilled. "You didn't." She took in Romy's face. "You didn't! Romy, I told you not to. Who helped you?" Her eyes landed on Thrym and she cursed long and hard in Gaelic.

"It's done now."

The doctor glared at her. "And how do you feel? Ready to fight for your life?"

"A little dizzy," Romy admitted.

"Serves you right," she snapped, then sighed. "I know why you did it. But I told you no for a reason. You can't give all of yourself to these space soldiers, Ro. I know you feel an obligation, and guilt, and whatever else, but if there's none of you left, you're no help either."

Romy averted her eyes. "I'm sorry."

Charlee let out a derisive snort. "You're sorry, but you'd do it again. Don't you try that with me. It may work on Thrym, but I make sure elderly men take their medicine each day. I can sense a lie across a room."

Romy grinned, and the doctor glared at her again. "Do you need a hand up?"

With Atlas watching her like a hawk? "No thanks. I'll manage."

She slowly sat, careful to put an arm out and stabilise herself. That was all right. . . . Then she got to her knees. Not so good. Her head throbbed and the blood drained from her face. Romy cut her nails into her palm. No way was Atlas turning this craft around because she fainted. He'd take any excuse she gave him.

Inhaling a long, thin breath through her nose, Romy stood and walked with minimal stagger to the nearest seat.

Deimos gave her a look. "You're pale."

"Hey, could you do me a favour and stick close when we go outside? I'm not feeling the best, but I don't want Atlas to know in case he turns back. The space soldiers need this blood right now."

Deimos's green eyes surveyed her. "What if you need to run?"

"Buckle up, everyone," called Elara from the cockpit.

"Will you?" Romy pleaded.

He gave her a reluctant nod. "Yes. But you better not make me regret this."

She rested her head back on the seat and hung on to her harness feeling like a sack of flour. "I won't," she said. "I promise."

He hummed noncommittally.

Romy closed her eyes for the landing and felt a degree better as Atlas gave the order to disembark.

He gave her a look, laying a hand on her shoulder. "Are you okay, soldier?"

She gave him a firm smile. "Are you?"

Atlas cocked an eyebrow and moved to the front and she let out a breath of relief.

They got into position in three rows, with four at the front: Atlas, Thrym, Tina, and Phobos. She, Elara, and Deimos were in the middle, and Charlee, Deanna, and Leroy were at the back.

"Keep your eyes peeled," Atlas said, glancing behind him. "We'll be moving just outside of the cargo door to show we're upholding our end of the deal and don't have a craft filled with soldiers. Any sign of foul play and we retreat inside again, immediately. Phobos, keep Deimos blocked from sight as best you can. I'm not sure how strong Houston's grudge against him will be."

"Roger that," Phobos replied.

Atlas took a step forward and punched the door release. The cargo door slowly lowered and no one made a sound as the dry, hot wind swirled through their craft with a low whistle. Huge sand dunes came into view—the last time Romy had seen them it was night and she was sure she was about to die.

This time felt better, and worse.

She couldn't see over Atlas's head in front of her.

"Forward," he instructed.

Their rows made their way out, three seconds after each other, and resumed their formation at the bottom of the door.

"Atlas," someone called in cheerful greeting.

Atlas stood tall, completely blocking Romy from view. "Houston. We have the blood, but we would like to open negotiations for the return of two hundred of the space soldiers into our custody."

"Which means you are willing to accept one hundred," the voice called back. "Done. But you understand I won't be able to return them until after I've administered the blood?"

Atlas snorted. "And what assurance will you give us that the space soldiers will be put into our care?"

"I can leave one of my men as collateral."

Atlas paused.

Romy spoke under her breath to him. "You know he won't hesitate to sacrifice them."

Tina hissed back. "But if he does, it shows the rest of his faction his true colours. It's still a win."

"Not for the space soldiers."

"You will leave five of your men with us today. In addition, another two hundred and fifty millilitres of blood will be given to you once the soldiers are in our hands."

He was lying just as readily as Houston was.

"I want access to Dr Charlee's latest research."

"Done," Atlas lied again.

Nothing would come out of the talk. Romy deflated, but she was at a loss to see how Atlas could do any more. They could withhold the blood, but Houston would call that bluff, knowing the Amach wouldn't let the space soldiers die. If it came to a waiting game, they'd lose the three hundred space soldiers as well as their bargaining chip.

"Well then, enough of the boring talk." Houston clapped his hands. "Who have you brought to see me?"

Romy's insides chilled at the gleeful voice. She wished she could see his face. With that in mind, Romy shifted to peek between Atlas and Thrym's arms. Humorous hazel eyes caught hers across a gap of several metres and she gasped, rearing back.

"Oh, but there is little Rosemary in the middle. So nice to see you again, skyling," Houston called.

She didn't reply as Atlas shifted in front of her again.

Houston's force stood in a line, with him in the middle. They didn't appear to have any weapons. At least he seemed to have stuck to his word. Though their team was carrying hidden weapons, so it couldn't be discounted that Houston's men were, too.

"I see the strapping Thrym and Phobos, and Elara," he said. His voice tightened. "What about Deimos?"

Deimos answered, calling across the gap, "How are you, James?"

There was silence, aside from the low howl of wind scuttling across the large sandy dunes. Tiny granules hit Romy's face, even contained in the middle of the group as she was. The heat here was stifling, and her head gave a warning pang.

No way. Not here.

"You doing okay?" Deimos whispered to her.

She pressed her lips together, determined not to barf on Atlas, and gave Deimos a thumbs-up, sensing that nodding her head would undo the last thread of her control.

"Is that Dr Charlee's neat hair I spot in the back? I hear you've been able to replicate my cure. I hope you cited the founder."

"Aren't cures usually permanent?" Char called back. Deimos winked at her.

Romy grabbed onto her knotmate's arm, wavering on the spot, and inhaling strongly through her nose.

"Ro?" Elara asked, breaking away from her continuous scan of the area when she sensed movement.

"I'm okay," she managed.

"Houston," Atlas said in a bored voice. "We're not here to talk. We're here to help the space soldiers in your possession. We have half a litre of Romy's blood here. That's the last you'll be getting, so use it well. Next time, she won't have a choice in the matter."

"Oh, trouble in paradise?" Houston cackled. "I never thought I'd see the day. But then, our Rosemary isn't quite the same as she was, is she? She's stronger." His voice grew fevered. "She is *one of a kind.*"

"Hand me the blood," Atlas instructed their team.

Charlee walked to the front, but Tina snatched it before Atlas could take the cooler.

"I will," Tina said, moving to cross the gap before Atlas could respond.

Now that Tina was out of the line, Thrym, Phobos, and Atlas spread out and gave Romy a clear sight of the Renegades. There were ten of them, as agreed. Romy didn't recognise any faces, but the nine burly soldiers with Houston could be from other Amachs, or from settlements.

She dug her nails into Deimos's arm when she focused on Houston, completely. "What's happened to him?" she asked under her breath.

Great shadows marred the area under the doctor's crazed eyes. His clothes were as wrinkled and as stained as ever, but he'd shaved all his curly brown hair off.

"He was bad when I left him, but he looks terrible," Deimos answered. Freeing his arm, he wrapped it around Romy's waist and held her up.

She took a dragging inhale through her nose, blinking away some dizziness. He looked unwell, distracted, and like he hadn't been caring for himself.

Tina went all the way to the Renegades, passing a frowning Houston the cooler of blood bags. He crouched and cracked the bin open, saying, "I'd hoped you'd give us more than half a litre."

"That's all you asked for, and that's all you're getting," Tina said, one fist clenched.

A part of Romy hoped she'd let loose and punch him in the mouth. Houston had never been a fighter. His mind was his weapon, but one-on-one, he stood no chance. Unfortunately, the nine men he'd brought with him *did* seem like they knew a thing or five about taking a hit.

"Yes, yes," Houston said sadly. "It's just a shame." He

glanced away from Tina to look at Atlas. "I don't suppose you'd agree to letting Romy come with us?"

"As long as you agree to let me put a bullet in your head, I'd say that's fine," Atlas replied.

Houston sighed heavily, placing the lid back on the bin. He picked it up and retreated back into the line of his men, away from Tina and their team.

"I'm sorry to hear that, Atty boy. It leaves me no choice."

18

"Back to the craft!" Atlas roared.

Sand erupted around them in a swirling funnel. Deimos's hand was wrenched from Romy's arm. Disoriented on top of her current dizziness, Romy fell to her knees, shielding her eyes from the flying granules.

"Romy!" Elara screamed to her left.

Heart tightening, she glanced over and saw Elara flat on her back, a Critamal standing over her. Gunfire exploded to the right, and Romy rolled away from it, panting.

"Deimos," she shouted as the black-shelled Critamal advanced on Elara.

No answer.

Romy staggered to her feet, surging toward her knotmate. She made it two steps before she fell, and wasted no time getting to her feet again. Elara threw herself to the right, narrowly missing the stab of a pincer that would have gone straight through her stomach.

"No!" Romy shouted, a bolt of pure adrenaline shooting through her.

Surging to her feet, she covered the remaining ground

and threw herself at the poacher. The armoured alien was lean and at least eight feet tall. She clung to the alien's ridged back as it writhed trying to throw her off. Grunting, Romy reached around the Critamal's shelled shoulders and gripped the base of each of its pincers, her head pressed against the side of its huge bulbous head.

And pulled. The creature hissed, twisting in agony.

Her arms shook. "Run, Ellie!"

Elara rolled out from underneath. The ground bucked and surged, sand continuing to burst up in whirling chaos. *The Critamal hid in the sand before the meeting.* Houston had planned this from the start.

Two more Critamal crawled out of the sand behind Elara. Romy shoved away from the poacher she clung to, and stumbled to her knotmate. Pushing Elara behind her, Romy dragged out a knife she'd hidden in her boot as the three Critamal crowded them. Her knees trembled, and she knew in her current state, this wouldn't be much of a fight.

"Where's the craft?" she yelled over the tumult, breathing hard and blinking to keep the blurriness in her eyes at bay.

Elara twisted to look. "I don't know! I can't see through all the sand."

The Critamal took a step closer, caging them in. Romy tightened her grip on her knife, tensed for their attack, knowing her pitiful weapon and drained body wouldn't do anything against the alien's black armour.

The Critamal didn't attack, though.

The aliens parted and Houston walked between them, exclaiming, "Ah, here she is. And Elara, too." He deliberated. "I did always like you, Elara. If you come peacefully, you can remain alive for now." He nudged the closest Critamal. "Might not be a bad thing to have a bargaining chip along for the ride."

The Critamal snapped its pincers.

Houston smiled at Romy before turning away. "Take them."

ROMY GROANED, UNSTICKING HER TONGUE FROM THE ROOF OF her mouth. She felt awful: lethargic, thirsty, and there was a throbbing pain on the right side of her jaw.

She'd woken like this too many times to feel confused. She'd been knocked out.

Elara!

Jerking upright, Romy scanned the area for her knotmate, sagging in relief when she spotted her curled in a ball on a bed against the far wall. Romy waited for her heartbeat to settle again. What had happened? She rubbed her temples. It felt like a Critamal had battered her over the head, which was probably pretty near the truth.

A second, calmer search showed her Tina was in the stone-walled cell too, unconscious.

Her face had been bandaged, telling Romy the woman had put up a fight. Though Tina hadn't stood a chance, being separated from their group to start with. The Critamal had exploded out of the sand. She remembered Deimos's hand being ripped away from her arm. Bile swept up her throat and she swallowed. What about the rest of them—Phobos, Deimos, Thrym, Charlee . . . Atlas?

With a bone-weary sigh, Romy sat again and swung her legs over the side of the bed, the springs creaking as she did so. Were they in the Renegades' base in Florida? She rubbed her face with both hands. Standing, she wound around her bed to Elara's side.

There were four beds in the room, spaced out evenly around three concrete walls. The room was large, but the bulk of it was empty. On the fourth wall, there was a barred door that showed a glimpse of a passageway outside.

They were in a prison cell.

Romy crouched by her knotmate's side. "Ellie, baby," she hushed, stroking her knotmate's brown hair. "Wake up now."

It took some coaxing, which didn't overly concern her as this wasn't out of the ordinary for Elara.

"Ro?" croaked Elara. A small wrinkle appeared between her brows. "What happened?"

Romy lowered her voice. "We were taken. We're in one of the Renegades' bases. I think."

Elara jerked to life.

"Shh," Romy said, leaning to kiss her on the cheek. "You're okay. Do you feel all right?" She gave Elara a pointed look.

Her knotmate glanced down and blinked. "Yes, I think so. Do you think the b—"

Romy covered Elara's mouth. Putting her lips next to her knotmate's ear, she whispered, "He can't know that."

She heard Elara drag in a ragged breath. When Romy pulled back, Elara's hazel eyes were hardened and she dipped her head once.

Next was Tina.

"Don't get too close," Elara whispered.

I wasn't born yesterday. It had been at least five months since she was harvested from the tanks. This time. Romy held her head back and poked Tina in the side.

Sure enough, she came up punching and snarling. The red-haired woman staggered and sat heavily upon recognising her cellmates. "How much do we know?"

That *would* be her first question. "Nothing much," Romy replied. "No one's been in yet."

"The alien fuckers were under the sand." Tina's face contorted with fury. "Do we know if anyone else is here? Or if they got away?"

Elara sniffled behind her. "No." Her voice broke off. "What if Phobos was hurt?" Her voice shook. "What if he's—?"

Tina cut her off. "We don't think like that, soldier. We can't possibly know the answer. Snap out of it."

"O-okay."

A closer glance told Romy their commander might not be doing too well herself. Her eyes were darting around the cell and her chest showed her breath was shallow and quick.

. . . Tina had been a prisoner before, to the Mandate. Something that involved a large amount of torture.

"It will be all right," Romy said softly.

Tina's lips trembled before she pressed them together. "Why did he bring me and Elara along?"

"He said he was bringing Elara as a bargaining chip. I guess to make me do what he wants," Romy replied.

"And me?"

Houston's voice rang out through the barred door at the front. "You were brought because you're a part of my plan, Tina, and have been for a long time. I just need to convince you my side is the right side."

They all jumped.

Tina recovered first. "I'm not sure I enjoy your plans, H."

"You refer to the regrettable circumstances under which I left, I gather."

She gave him an incredulous look through the bars. "Are you serious? Try needless violence and inviting a horde of aliens into our midst, you freakin' lunatic."

His face darkened and it took him visible effort to regain his smile. "We shall have time to talk. I apologise for your sleeping quarters."

"James," Romy said to him, "could you cut the crap and tell us what you mean to do?" She was tired, worried and in no mood for his nonsensical conversation.

He gave her a genuine smile. "I plan to experiment with your blood, Rosemary. Which you knew. Elara is here to control you."

Romy waved a hand to cut him off. "What is the purpose of the experiments?"

"You know that, too," he said, eyes shifting around their cell.

"To find a permanent cure to the insanity trigger with the space soldiers?" she pressed.

"Yes," he answered.

"If there's a different motive, you know I'll refuse, with Elara's full support. We both know our lives aren't worth three hundred."

"When push comes to shove, you'll choose her over them."

"Then you don't know me, or Elara, James. You are judging our reaction by what you'd do."

"First," he narrowed his eyes, "I want to ascertain just how much our past procedures have altered you. Nothing too horrible, I assure you."

Great.

The bed creaked as Elara sat. "The rest of our team, did they make it?"

The three women waited with bated breath for his answer.

He assessed each of them in turn, his eyes growing hard then soft over and over again. Houston had always been a little 'off', but it was an off that, while eccentric, wasn't outside of societal bounds. This version of him was something else entirely. It wasn't the brand of insanity she'd experienced as Feral Romy. Judging by his eyes, he was volatile to the extreme, yet completely lucid between these moments. She had no idea how he was going to react from one moment to the next. He'd gone downhill *fast*. His father had been locked in a padded cell at age thirty, and Romy knew Houston was around that age.

"Everyone you love is fine, though others were lost in the struggle. You had a number of extra soldiers hidden not far away, which I had not counted on." He glanced at Romy. "I received a very angry message this morning from none other than my friend, Atty boy."

She gave him a look of pity. "James, your friendship with Atlas is over. He despises you. I can truly say there is no one he hates more—not the Mandate, not even the Critamal."

Houston's face clouded, his eyes turning to stone. "Never say I did not make my own sacrifices to see the world peaceful and prosperous, then. Though I know he'll forgive me one day. Hate and love are not so far away in the human mind. You forgave Deimos, by the looks of it." He blinked and the unfocused expression receded. "I will give you today to get settled in, my dears. Toodle pip!"

Romy crossed to the door and craned to see down the hall. Houston disappeared around the far corner. A glance the other way told her they were alone. That wasn't to say he didn't have microphones in the cell, or cameras.

"Wow," Tina said, sitting heavily. "I . . . did not expect that. He's absolutely bonkers. Did you see his eyes?"

Elara and Romy gave mute nods.

"Did you read the file before you left the Amach?" Romy asked Tina.

She nodded. Bending close, Romy related the contents to Elara.

After Romy finished, Elara said, "He was lying about his reasons for running tests on Romy. Did you notice? He has another agenda aside from the insanity cure."

"Really?" Romy asked. She'd missed that.

"I agree. He's covering for something else," Tina said with a sigh. "At least we know the others are alive."

"According to him," Romy countered. "I wouldn't put it past him to try to make us more compliant that way."

Elara paled. "Really?"

Hope was the best and worst thing in the world, in Romy's opinion. It could lift you up and it could crush you with a signal swoop. Hope was like having a knot. It made you strong, and it protected you, but it could also destroy you. "We need to be prepared if he is lying." She turned to Tina. "Do you know what his plans are for you? Any guesses?"

"Not a single clue," Tina answered, nonplussed. "I have so many skills it's hard to know which of them he plans to utilise."

The words would be laughable coming from anyone else, but with Tina they were true. There was a reason she'd been expected to become a Mandate member.

Romy sat on the bed. "Looks like we're hanging tight until Atlas gets us out of here."

Tina made a disbelieving sound.

"What?" she asked her.

"Nothing."

Romy groaned. "That's not allowed."

The woman flashed her a quick grin that faded. "Okay, I'm not sure we should hold our breath for a rescue. It would take all of our firepower to storm this base, in their territory, with the Critamal here, too. Likely, they'll need the Mandate's help."

"What are you saying?" Elara asked, eyes rounded.

"I'm saying that if Atlas comes here to get us back, it's going to be World War. . . . What one are we up to?"

"Five," Romy supplied.

Tina huffed. "God, humans are shit. Anyway, if he comes, it will mean a battle until someone wins this damn thing.

With the odds so even, we can't be sure it will be the Amach who comes out on top."

"So, you don't want him to come?" Elara asked.

The woman shrugged. "It's irrelevant what I want."

"Why do you say that?" Romy asked.

Tina smiled at her. "Because you're in here, my friend. Atlas will come."

"One plus one equals two," Elara said, as though that explained everything.

Romy, however, was less at ease than she had been five minutes ago. What was that she'd said about hope again?

Tina was right—the opposing powers were too similar in size. The Mandate and the Amach had united temporarily to take down the larger danger, but there were factors that still had their tentative alliance at a disadvantage, namely that they had little idea what Critamal could do and what their weaknesses were, aside from a few rifle shots to the thin parts in their armour. Houston also had the ever-powerful cannons, which he no doubt had plans for.

This battle was too even.

Which meant they'd better start thinking of a way to get themselves out.

19

This was familiar.

Romy lay strapped to a bed, covered in electrodes in a lab that mimicked all other Amach labs. A low current ran through her while a team of doctors monitored screens.

Day one of testing.

"Feeling okay there?" a doctor asked. Romy ignored him and he took the hint.

Guards had escorted her from the cell this morning, directly to this lab. The base used to belong to the Amach, before Houston took it over to house the Renegades, and this gave the three women a distinct advantage—all Amachs were set out in a similar way. This meant there would be four exits: one through the trap door at the top, one through the hangar exit where the crafts flew out—though this usually led out the side of a cliff or to the ocean—and emergency exits at each end of level one. Stairwells ran up the far ends of each level toward these exits, but the stairwells and level one exits required authorised approval to unseal them.

When Deimos and Phobos left this base, they took the space soldiers through the craft exit. Escaping via this route had the highest chance of success. They could theoretically steal a craft to escape in. The downside was Houston surely expected it, and Tina had raised the point that security had likely been tightened after the exodus of the space soldiers, the twins, and Nancy.

That left the trap door up through the hangar, or either of the level one options.

Escaping their cell and getting to any of these would be hard enough. What came after made escaping more dangerous. They'd climb out of the Amach and would then need to elude Houston on foot. They didn't know where the Critamal were. Reports said Houston gave them the northern territories of America. But were there poachers around this base? Would she, Tina, and Elara be walking directly into a Critamal encampment?

The electrical current increased through Romy's limbs.

"Oh, yeah. There we go," Houston said. "Look at her lateral septum. It just switched off." He laughed, and the surrounding doctors gasped, all looking at a screen over her head.

"The hypothalamus and hippocampus are working overtime, but they are nowhere near as effective as the lateral septum as an anger gatekeeper. Her brain is now at a distinct disadvantage with pushing down violence and aggression." Houston clapped his hand and pointed to a young male in a white lab coat. "Mark down the stimuli, Sawyer."

The current was increased several times before they unstrapped her, gave her a sickly-sweet drink, and moved her to the treadmill.

A headset with probes on it was fitted around her temples and the doctors started her on nine kilometres per hour. Just above a walk. Romy ended up reaching over and increasing the speed herself—may as well get an actual run in.

Someone tutted and came back to decrease it to nine

again. Romy simmered, woodenly shifting her legs to the slow pace. Running at this speed was almost harder.

A doctor finally came and increased the speed in increments, until Romy was flying at eighteen. The faster pace was much nicer on her legs, but the multitude of wires dangling off of her was concerning.

Another doctor decreased speed to nine again.

Comets, were they just going to do this over and over?

"Interesting," Houston mused. "She shows more tendency toward aggression at a slower speed."

She always had. Something about adrenaline and endorphins sharpened her mind.

Houston stared at the results while his minions hovered anxiously for his reaction. "It's perfect," he finally muttered. "A soldier who is in control during action, but excitable with low-level current. Imagine the possibilities."

"Doctor?" someone asked in confusion.

Houston blinked and looked up. A grin broke across his face. "Don't mind my mutterings." He gathered a bunch of papers together before saying, "That's enough for today. Make sure she gets enough fluids to recover for tomorrow."

Romy's stomach was still in knots about Houston's careless remarks a few seconds ago. What had he meant by that? It had sounded as though he wanted to . . . control her.

She was escorted back to the cell by six guards, which amused her. Feral Romy had been a magnificent fighter, but Romy was no longer insane. She was a better fighter in general, but there was no way she'd manage six armed guards by herself. If she was pissed off, she could manage two, maybe three if they were unskilled.

The guards didn't jostle her or sneer on the way down. They really did seem like the Amach guards. Probably because they had been Amach guards once. "You know," she said softly, "if you wanted to come back to the Amach, the commander-general would pardon you, and anyone who admitted they'd made a mistake."

The guard in front snorted. "Back to that peace-yapping place? No thanks. We're here for a reason, and that's because we plan to get something done about the Mandate."

"And become the Mandate by doing so?" Romy asked in genuine curiosity.

The relaxed demeanour of her escort disappeared, and she was glad to arrive at her cell a minute later and see the backs of the six men.

"Ro," Elara said in relief, coming to hug her. "Are you okay? What did they do to you?"

"Put an electrical current through me, and made me run on the treadmill." Romy beckoned them in, sitting cross-legged on her bed. They bowed their heads close. "I overheard Houston say something in there." Romy repeated the doctor's crazed mutterings.

Tina straightened. "That sounds. . . ."

"Like he's trying to create a certain kind of soldier?" Romy finished. "I agree. I can't decide if it's me he means to control, or a whole bunch of soldiers."

Elara whistled. "Poacher poop."

"Poacher poop, indeed," Romy said.

Tina bent her head in again. "Do you think he plans to tamper with the space soldiers he has? Maybe you should ask to see them tomorrow," she urged Romy. "Getting you away from him is our priority, but if there's a chance we can get the rest of the soldiers out, we need to know where they are and how many of them are alive."

Romy agreed. "Okay, I'll do that."

"Do what, little skyling?" Houston's voice slid through the bars.

She jerked, but managed not to squawk like Elara. How

much had he overheard? They had to set a watch at the door from now on.

Romy decided to go with the truth. "I want to see the space soldiers you have. Tomorrow."

"Why?" he asked, pressing his face against the bars.

"Are you actually crazy?" Romy asked, going on a tangent. "You were never normal, but you actually seem crazy now."

Tina sucked in a breath that needed no translation: Not a wise move. Romy pressed her lips together, stopping her question about his father in its tracks.

Houston smiled slowly. "I suggest you don't try to find out." His eyes unfocused and snapped back into awareness. "But I am happy to show you the space soldiers. Maybe that will . . . help your participation levels."

Romy raised her brows, saying in a firm voice, "I did everything you asked today."

"Ah, yes. I have no complaints . . . about today. You may find the coming days more trying." He shifted his gaze. "I am here for the beautiful and fearless leader, Tina Lyons."

"Save it," Tina sneered at him. Still, sensing an opportunity to obtain more information, she sauntered up to the bars.

Guards appeared behind Houston.

"A precaution, you understand?" the doctor said.

"I understand that I would definitely seize the chance to kick your cowardly ass if you didn't bring them, yes," Tina replied without batting an eyelash.

The guards approached and Tina didn't look back as she was led out of the cell.

"I MISS PHOBOS," ELARA SNIFFED INTO HER PILLOW.

Romy's heart squeezed and she threw off her blankets to

slide into bed with her knotmate. "I'm sure he misses you, too, Ellie. Be strong; you'll see him again."

"Do you believe that?"

Her reply was honest. "I can't not believe that, even if my brain tells me it's foolish to hope."

"This is so messed up."

"More or less messed up than me having three personalities two months ago?"

". . . Less." Elara giggled. "Much less. That was scary stuff. Crazy Romy was the shit, though."

Romy smiled. "There's still a bit of her around."

"That's for sure. Hey, did you and Atlas ever end up . . . ?"

She pretended to think. "Redecorating our room?"

Elara snickered. "You know what I mean. Did you, or did you not, engage in illicit activities with commander-general cargo hotness?"

"Can you call him that to his face?"

"I enjoy that you think I haven't."

Romy laughed under her breath. "What did he say?"

"Nothing. Just pursed his lips and walked off."

"That means he wanted to laugh, but he caught it before it escaped."

"Really?"

Romy nodded. "To answer your question, yes, we did. Just before the meeting in Cairo."

"Finally." Elara sighed and shifted closer, hugging Romy. "You know," she said in a sleepy voice, "you guys are a great couple. I hope you guys grow old together."

A tear trickled from Romy's eye. She cleared her throat of the thickness there. "I hope we all grow old," she said hoarsely. "I want it more than anything in the world."

The cell door creaked open and Tina was shoved through. She rolled across the concrete floor, but sprang up against the hastily closed door, screaming obscenities.

When the guards disappeared, she stopped and turned, searching the dark cell until she spotted her cellmates in Elara's bed.

"What'd you do to piss off the guards?" Romy asked. They hadn't treated her that way.

Tina panted. "I've been known to antagonise one or two people in my time."

The others waited.

"I punched Houston in the face. After I asked whether he was insane because of his mother, or his father."

Romy gasped, unable to hide her smile. "What did he do?"

Her white teeth gleamed in the dark. "That's what I wanted to find out. He had a full-blown, someone-stood-on-my-sandcastle tantrum, that's what. He threw papers, smashed beakers, kicked walls. Completely lost it. I might've hurt his feelings."

"Wow," Elara said.

"You had no idea what provoking him would do." Romy admonished her. "What if he'd decided he didn't need you anymore? Or did something while he was worked up?"

"Did you find out what he wants you for?" Elara piped up.

Tina sat on her bed and unlaced her boots. "Obviously I found that out before I pushed his buttons. I'm not stupid. He wants me to rule the world when he conquers it."

There was a moment of disbelieving silence.

"What?" Romy and Elara chorused.

"You heard me. He said I have a reputation of strength and fairness and all this other crap. Then he said, he worried that though he was a trailblazer, the public opinion was turned against him, that he was willing to bear that cross for the betterment of humankind, but that in the interest of lasting and prosperous peace, he wanted me to consider taking the figurehead position."

"Figurehead?" Romy asked.

"Exactly. He still means to be in full control of everything. That is about the time my fist had a disagreement with his face." She padded over to join them on the bed and threw herself on top of them, whispering, "I do mean to try to negotiate the position. I'm hoping I can get Elara out of here." Her emerald eyes shifted to Romy. "Not you; he'd never let you go. But Ellie, he might."

"No," Elara protested.

It would strengthen their position. One less person to get out, and one less person to force her compliance.

Romy held Tina's eyes. "Do it." She sat on the bed, a crease between her brows. "Do you think Houston has had a more personal agenda than we've thought? He told me this was all about leaving a legacy, but. . . ."

". . . His parents both lost their minds," Tina said, nodding.

"Wanting to prevent the same fate for himself seems more in line with his selfishness than the whole legacy idea," Elara added.

It seemed that way to Romy, too. "This whole time, he just wanted the cure for himself." Her eyes widened. "He must've been livid when he saw it didn't hold in the space soldiers."

Tina sighed. "Yes, but what is he planning now?" She tilted her head to Romy, eyes hardened. "That's what we need to find out."

20

The guards arrived the next morning and took Romy to the first level, instead of the lab.

It looked like Houston was keeping his promise to show her the soldiers after all.

The guards marched her to the far end of the passage on this level, and the head guard swiped his card to open a set of double doors.

Houston was standing inside. He didn't lift his head upon her arrival.

Romy glanced around when the guards fell back, and walked slowly around the room. Her heart grew heavy as she took in row upon row of upright sealed cases. Inside were space soldiers, frozen in time until Houston saw fit to release them. She did a rough count and gritted her teeth. Nearly three hundred.

She was glad more of the space soldiers were alive, but this wasn't living, being encased like this.

"They've all been given another injection," Houston called to her.

Romy spun. He still stood in the same spot. She looked

past him and saw he stared at an empty cultivation tank, like the ones the space soldiers grew up in.

She swallowed at the gleam in his eyes. "They'll live?"

"Yes." He tilted his chin up. "They'll live."

"Then why keep them frozen?"

A ghost of a smile flashed across his face. "Because the first thing they'll ask will be where their other comrades are. I need the others back first."

He had plans for the space soldiers, and after his mumbled words yesterday, Romy had a gut feeling that curing the soldiers of the insanity trigger was the least the Renegades leader planned to do. "I assume you don't mean to give the Amach the one hundred soldiers you promised. How shocking you didn't keep your word," Romy said sarcastically, but then she decided to prod. "Are you any closer to finding a permanent cure?"

Houston didn't answer. He raised a hand and rested it on the cultivation tank.

Romy held her breath. Why was he looking at it like that? The guards neared her and she tensed. "You plan to put me in there," she said, on the edge of panic.

Her comment startled a laugh out of the mad doctor. "You?" He laughed again, and dropped his hand. "No. Not you, skyling." He blinked, coming out of his daze. "I did want to show you something, however. Seeing as we're here."

Romy gave the cultivation tank a wide berth, the hairs on her neck rising as the guards crowded behind her. She'd never willingly go into one of those again.

Houston led her to a glass pane and gestured for a guard to turn on the light.

She gasped as the other side came into view. "What have you done?"

On the other side were five cages, and each one held a space soldier. But they weren't space soldiers anymore.

Romy shied back as the . . . creatures began throwing themselves against the bars in response to the light. Their white orbito fatigues were stained with blood and yellowed with the soldier's waste. Their eyes were bloodshot, and wide with madness. Saliva trickled from their mouths, and even through the thick glass, Romy could hear their snarling screams.

Her chest tightened as her own past hit her with enough force to give her whiplash.

"Not pleasant, are they?"

Romy curled her fists and turned on him. But she was surprised to find him completely serious. "No," she said shortly. "What happened to them?"

"You are looking at a space soldier who has had the injection, and then killed once it's worn off. It makes them incredibly violent. They make what your insane version did to those Mandate soldiers look like child's play. Ten of them killed one hundred of my soldiers before we managed to take them out."

"Why are you keeping them alive like this?" Romy said, looking back at the screeching space soldiers with burning eyes in the cages.

"To try to save them. Why else?" Houston replied.

Her eyes narrowed. Romy didn't believe that for a second. He wanted to save himself. How much testing would it take for Houston to find the actual cure?

Romy had to get the space soldiers out of here before any more ended up in cages.

BLUNTED NEEDLES PRICKED HER IN ACUPRESSURE POINTS WITH methodical order.

After three days, she knew this phase of testing was about

what made the anger inhibitors in her brain disappear—to find what made her volatile. Romy was certain Houston meant to replicate it somehow. But the other space soldiers hadn't gone through what she had, so how did the doctor mean to mimic her specific reaction?

She jolted as they dug the sharp end into her upper trapezius. *Ouch.*

"That was a good one," Houston murmured. "Not as good as the Li-4."

Whatever he planned to do, she knew he wouldn't hesitate to hurt others. The sight of the insane soldiers in the cages was seared into her memory, and she'd barely thought of anything else since. She'd told Tina and Elara about what she'd seen, and they were in agreement. The soldiers had to be saved. Somehow. Seeing as they had yet to think up a plan to save themselves, this wasn't looking great.

The assistant stabbed her in the other trapezius and blood pounded to Romy's temples.

Her mouth twisted as her control on her anger slipped. "It's ironic, don't you think, James? That I was the one who lost my mind, but you're the insane one?"

His head snapped up and he fixed murderous eyes on her.

She grinned. "You don't like being called insane, do you, James? Is it because of your daddy? Little Houston doesn't want to be like his little father?" Romy tested the arm restraints, gaze honing in on the doctor. She smiled.

The assembled doctors stirred uneasily.

"Do you mean to make an army of angry space soldiers, James?" she pressed again. "Is that why you're doing these tests and not focusing on the cure?"

A few of the doctors glanced at Houston uncertainly and this broke him out of his jaw-tight fury.

"There's the Rosemary I haven't seen in a while," he said smoothly. "Observe, everyone, what happens if she is pushed too far. Sawyer, jot this down." He assembled his thoughts, or so it appeared. To her eyes it was a frantic reach for control, and she wanted to see him snap.

Houston dictated. "Subject able to withstand an aggression-inducing spot in isolation, but several of these in a row results in verbal—" His hazel eyes flickered to her straining arms, "and physical displays of aggression."

"Avoidance of any comment that questions his state of mind and absence of ethics." Romy mimicked the doctor's professional voice. "Sawyer, jot this down: It seems to be becoming easier for Houston to justify his depravity over time."

Houston surveyed her. "Clear the room," he said flatly.

The doctors filed out, exchanging wide-eyed looks.

Once they were gone, Houston reached to pick up the blunted needle. Smiling, he rested it in the web area between Romy's thumb and forefinger and dug in down. Hard. She drew in a breath, feeling blood fill her cheeks. But her anger overrode the pain. Romy stared at him, telling him wordlessly that if she were free, he would be dead.

"We had a deal, my dear," he said, twisting the needle. "Elara's safety is guaranteed only by your continued cooperation."

Tina's plans to negotiate a way out for Elara depended on how on easy it was for Houston to keep Romy compliant. "You can't expect a person without an operating lateral septum to control what she says, can you?" she said silkily.

Romy would shove that needle in his jugular if he touched her knotmate.

He withdrew the needle and it was almost more painful without the pressure. The doctor twiddled the needle around in one hand. "Right you are, skyling. That is unreasonable of me."

She couldn't help probing again. "Do you really need an army of soldiers you can control, Houston?"

He paused. "Why yes, I believe I might if all goes well."

Houston strode to the door. "Sawyer," he called into the hall. "Could you fetch me that ball gag from the interrogation room?" He glanced back over his shoulder at her before calling back out, "That's the one."

He ambled back over to Romy. "Problem solved."

She grinned at him until he looked away.

"HE PRETTY MUCH ADMITTED TODAY THAT HE WANTS TO create an ultra-aggressive army of space soldiers," Romy said, lying on the bed, staring at the concrete ceiling.

Tina replied, "I don't know that I trust anything that comes out of his mouth. He continually lies. We know his family history is a definite factor. That reaction was genuine. Everything else . . . I'm not so sure."

Her doubt was understandable. Houston was hard to read, and always had been. "He's testing how to induce anger," Romy said. "It's working on me. I lost control of my temper in there today."

Tina munched on a carrot stick. "Do anything good?"

"Spoke enough crap about Houston to make him gag me for the rest of the day," Romy admitted.

Elara gasped from where she watched the passage for company. "Oh, Ro."

"Worth it," Romy replied. She stretched out an arm, and she and Tina bumped knuckles.

Tina ran her hands through her greasy red hair. "I haven't made any headway with him. He's crazy, but not stupid."

She crouched next to Romy, speaking low. "The only way

I can see us getting out is if all three of us can rush the guards when they open the door."

"Six guards, and we have no weapons," Romy said.

"We'll have the advantage of surprise. If we can take a couple out in the first moments and secure a weapon, the odds will be even."

Romy let out a slow breath. "Risky."

Tina nodded. "Yes, but I can't think of anything else. You're usually strapped down all day. And there's no way I can get back here when I'm out in meetings with Houston to free you guys."

After a careful check down both ends of the hall, Elara came to join them. "We could use the fire alarm, too," she whispered.

Tina and Romy turned to her.

"There's one just down the hall."

Tina and Romy got up and peered out. Sure enough, two metres to the right was a red box fitted between two pipes on the wall.

"If we could get out of the cell, it might create the chaos we need to make it out," Romy said.

"Ideally, we'd sneak out and get a head start with them none the wiser, but it's better than nothing," Tina said, hands clasped behind her back. She paced back and forth for a minute before repeating, "Okay. This is what we'll do."

The three women crouched in the middle of the concrete cell and pressed their heads together.

<small>OVER THE NEXT WEEK, THEY NOTICED THREE THINGS.</small>

One, there was a gap between when Romy or Tina were taken out of the door, and when the door was closed. They were moved out between four of the guards while two locked the barred door again. Romy and Tina couldn't handle six armed guards, but three of them stood a chance against six in a confined space, if they used surprise, and managed to get ahold of a weapon.

Two, Romy couldn't be sure what testing they were doing each day, and whether or not she'd be in a healthy state to escape at the end of the day.

Three, none of them had any idea how to secure a craft to get back to Ireland. If they couldn't find anything to contact the Amach with, the closest allies were in Cuba. They'd have to make it there and hopefully find a settlement to contact Atlas from.

Romy focused on her surroundings—the lab, just for something new.

"Today, you'll be going under for a little procedure," Houston said, nearing her with a mask. It explained why he'd left the ball gag off today.

"What procedure?" she asked. They hadn't put her under yet.

"Just taking a few eggs," he said. "Nothing you'll miss. Fertile as you are."

Her eyes widened and she bucked against the restraints. "No. I don't agree to that."

He shoved the mask over her face and she held her breath, trying to free herself. The pressure in her lungs built, but she refused to take a breath, pushing the last of the air out of her nose.

Black spots appeared before her eyes, but Romy held on to her control. She wouldn't breathe.

Houston lifted the mask in annoyance, and her head lolled against the bed as she took a huge gulp of air.

"Stubborn fool." He turned away. "Inject it into her IV."

Romy screamed at him and the two doctors who appeared at her side.

Her tongue grew heavy, and her words slurred.

Black ebbed over her sight.

"YOU ALL RIGHT, RO?" ELARA ASKED FROM HER BED.

Romy was curled in a ball around her cramping stomach. "Yeah, I'm fine," she lied. She just needed a night to absorb what he'd done to her, and his parting comment in the lab. *"Minus one hymen, Rosemary. My, my, it looks like you and Atlas have been having fun."*

He'd taken some of her eggs, and Romy felt sick, wondering if he meant to build an army out of her children. Or did he plan to use her eggs to find a permanent cure? She had no idea. Romy swallowed down a bout of nausea.

"Are you sure, Ro?"

Romy smiled at her. "I'm sure, just tired." Houston couldn't find out about Elara's pregnancy.

Tina was ushered back into the cell. She'd been behaving for Houston all week, and the guards had stopped pushing her around. Once the soldiers disappeared, she and Elara gathered at Romy's bed.

"Did you ask what they're doing with you tomorrow?" Tina asked.

"They knocked me out today—didn't get a chance."

Tina's brows slammed together. "What'd they do to you?"

Romy hesitated. "I'll tell you when we get out."

"You said you were fine," Elara accused, rolling on her back. The action sent a jolt of pain to Romy's stomach and she winced. Tina and Elara lowered their eyes to her legs, and they glanced back at Romy's pale face.

Elara started breathing fast, her face twisted with anger. "I'm going to kill that fucker," she said.

"Keep your voice down," Tina scolded her.

"He took eggs," Romy admitted. She should have known better than to try to keep something from these two; they were like freakin' bulldogs.

Tina was quick to ask the pertinent question. "Why? Army, or cure?"

Romy shrugged. "No idea."

"Why keep the space soldiers if he means to make his army from you," she mused, then narrowed her gaze. "Hmm, maybe a backup plan."

"You think so?"

Tina sat. "Just thinking aloud. There's no way to know, is there?"

Footsteps sounded down the hall and the women fell quiet. Houston appeared, pacing before the door, in and out of sight. "Evening," he said.

They didn't answer.

"Evening!" he shouted at them.

"Jesus," Tina said. But her instincts clearly told her the same thing as Romy's. *Tread carefully.* "What do you want?"

"Your commander-general is making a few problems for me," he spat. "And the Mandate."

Romy smirked.

"Why doesn't he stay out of it? It's not time yet." Houston muttered to himself wildly. "Gives me no choice." He stopped in front of their door. "Gives me no choice." His eyes landed on Elara. "No choice."

Romy's mouth dried, and she pushed Tina aside to free herself from the blankets. Houston's hand slid to the pocket of his stained lab coat, and he withdrew a gun.

"You." He jerked the gun at Elara. "You're coming with me."

Romy shifted in front of her knotmate. Tina came up next to her. "Why are you taking her?" Romy asked. "This is the first time you've taken Elara out."

Spittle flew from his mouth. "Now!"

"Are you going to shoot us?" Tina asked with a laugh. "Aren't we crucial to your plan?"

He clicked off the safety and pointed it at her head.

Romy's blood ran cold at the look in his eye. Unhinged. He would shoot Tina in this state of mind. She felt it. Just like Feral Romy would've done it without hesitation.

Elara spoke in a firm tone. "I'm coming. Don't shoot her."

"Ellie," she hissed over her shoulder.

Elara spoke. "It will be fine. Won't it, Houston? I'll be fine with you?" She moved forward and gave Romy a pointed look.

Houston didn't answer.

Romy blinked as she deciphered her knotmate's intentions.

Houston was the only person in the hall and he was about to open the door and take Elara out. She sucked in a breath. He had a gun, and he wasn't stupid, but the odds were much better than having six guards to fight.

As Houston trained the weapon on Elara and began to open the door, Romy shot a careful look at Tina, who gave her a barely perceptible nod.

"Commander, sir," a voice panted.

The door froze a quarter of the way open. "What?" Houston snapped.

"Sir, you asked to be updated as soon as possible."

Houston closed the door and spoke without turning to the out-of-breath person.

"We've lost a fifth encampment of Critamal to the bombing tonight, sir. The Mandate's doing."

Five encampments? Her body buzzed with hope. The Amach and Mandate were fighting back. They were attacking Houston's force.

"Five, you say?"

The person gulped audibly. "Yes, sir. We've dispatched our air force to the other main locations. We've also sent out a general warning to ask the Critamal to move underground for now. But . . . you know how they are about being underground, sir. The Mandate is picking them off, targeting the largest encampments."

Houston's fingers tightened around the butt of his gun. "This isn't the work of the Mandate," he said in a voice that made the hair on Romy's arms rise. "It's *Atlas.*" He released the safety and holstered his weapon.

Romy's shoulders relaxed slightly when the doctor moved off down the hall.

"Bring the brown-haired girl to my office," Houston called back to the young man still in the passage.

The young man was more lucid than his leader. He disappeared for five minutes and reappeared with the usual six-strong escort.

All three of them deflated at the sight.

Romy pulled her knotmate close. "Don't let him know."

Elara licked her lips, trembling in her arms. "I won't."

"And don't provoke him," she said quickly.

Elara kissed her cheek and moved to the door.

They went through the same routine, placing her at the front with four guards while two remained to lock the door. Tina approached the bars. "You got this, Spitfire."

In moments, Elara was gone and the passage was silent.

Romy sat on the edge of the bed, clutching the strands of her hair in tight fists.

"Worrying doesn't help her," Tina said, perching beside Romy on the bed.

"Yet, worry I do," Romy answered sarcastically.

"That's your job, mother hen." Tina nudged her. "It's harder to stay behind. Action is easy, but to be parted from someone you love, knowing they're in danger, *that's* far harder. Our girl Ellie has been doing it for nearly two weeks. So, guess what, you don't get to worry about her. You just need to suck it up, be there for her when she returns, and help me get us the fuck out of here tomorrow night."

Romy lifted her head slowly, staring at Tina in the dimness of their cell. "Tomorrow night?" she repeated.

Tina's eyes gleamed. "Houston and the Critamal are distracted. Seems like perfect timing to me."

21

The cell door creaked open and a pale-faced Elara walked through.

Romy waited until the door was closed and the guards were out of sight before running to her and hugging her gently. "Are you okay?"

"Yeah, just tired."

That wasn't surprising; it had to be near morning. "What happened?"

Elara sighed and collapsed on the bed. Tina listened silently from her bed. "He did a big speech on the cameras and made me say a bunch of lies." A ghost of a smile curved her lips. "It didn't go too well, and he ended up holding a gun to my head on live stream."

Tina sat. "You genius."

"Right?"

Romy glanced between them in horror. "You shouldn't have—"

Elara groaned. "Ro, you do it all the time. Don't be a hypocrite."

Her jaw clicked shut.

"All right, Spitfire," Tina called. "Get some sleep. You'll need your strength."

Hazel eyes cracked open. "Yeah?"

The three women shared a determined look. They were going to do their damnedest to get out of this place.

Romy returned to bed, but sleep eluded her. If anything happened to Elara and the baby, she'd never forgive herself. Hopefully, this time tomorrow they'd be out of this place and on their way to Cuba. They would wait until people were winding down and heading to their rooms to sleep. When the halls were emptier. Though it all depended on what happened in Romy's bout of testing today—she might not be in the right shape to run for her life.

. . . If Houston had aimed a gun at Tina's head over the bombings of the Critamal encampments, what would he do if he caught them trying to escape?

She jerked awake as breakfast was shoved under the door.

Romy sat and wobbled toward it.

"Anything good?" Tina asked, awake and alert.

"Cold toast and jam, and lukewarm tea."

Elara was dead to the world.

"Rosemary," a guard said from the door. The usual contingency had arrived.

She shoved a piece of toast into her mouth, and chewed on it as they marched her to the labs.

Doctors milled around the room as she was strapped to the table.

There was no sign of Houston. "Where's the bigwig?" she asked.

They shoved the ball gag in her mouth. Nice to see them following Houston's example. To this day, Charlee was the only doctor she'd ever liked and trusted.

Today they tested combinations on her. Needle jab in her thumb webbing, with a jolt of current. That was the morning. The afternoon was spent on the treadmill, running and being stabbed. They studiously noted the readings from the screens, but she could've told them the jab of a needle while being shocked with electricity made her go from angry to furious in a nanosecond.

Somehow, she managed to refrain from attacking them by focusing on what would be happening that night.

They unstrapped her and removed her gag.

She grabbed a tissue and spat out the gathered saliva into it. She balled it up and threw it in the open bin by the bed. She reached for another one and a radio transmitter caught her eye in the front pocket of a doctor's coat. Sawyer. He was Houston's favourite, likely because he did everything asked of him without question.

Romy wiped her mouth with the fresh tissue. If they had a radio transmitter, they could probably contact the Amach once outside. . . .

Taking Sawyer's was tempting, but the plan was more likely to fail than succeed and if she were searched before going back into the cell, the game would be up. Once they had weapons, it wouldn't be hard to secure one from one of the six guards, if they managed to take them out.

Romy chucked the tissue away and noticed a syringe next to the tissues. The needle was sealed in a packet; it was one that had to be assembled. For the doctors to have left it there was a huge oversight—not that the syringe could be used against them without her opening the packet and assembling it. Romy darted a look around. The guards were at the door and the doctors turned to see who was entering. Romy reached for another tissue and snagged the syringe. She turned so her back was to the raised head of the bed and shoved it down the back of her filthy coveralls, feeling it fall until it reached the elastic waistband.

She held the tissue to her face as Sawyer glanced back at her, and released a shaky breath when he turned away.

The guards marched Romy away from the lab, in the direction of the prison cell. They were more distracted than she'd seen them yet. Hopefully that worked in her favour and allowed her to get the syringe back to the cell.

"More attacks?" she asked them.

A couple of them looked at her and glanced away.

"Does Houston plan to kill the Critamal once the Renegades win?" she tried again.

More than one of the guards threw her a suspicious look.

The head guard answered, "Enough questions."

Romy waited a few minutes. "Whose idea was it to hide under the sand in Cairo and ambush us?"

An uncomfortable ripple moved through the escort. She interpreted that to mean that idea came from the Critamal.

Never once in years of fighting the Critamal had Romy underestimated the aliens' intelligence. In her opinion, it was the scariest thing about them. A poacher's brain was four times the size of a human brain and encased in a skull stronger than steel. Animal species evolved over time to become stronger and take advantage of niches in the environment. They should all be questioning why the skull of a Critamal had evolved to be so strong.

"Enough questions," the head guard snapped. He stopped and rounded on Romy.

Romy smiled at him, and he gave her a look of disgust before turning away.

They neared the cell and Romy tried to keep her cool as she waited for them to open the door. The syringe packet burned against her lower back.

A guard waved her inside.

She entered the cell and walked slowly to the bed, listening as the head guard locked the door and moved away down the passage before relaxing. They hadn't patted her down.

"Nothing bad today," she said to the two others, who watched her.

Tina's deep green eyes narrowed at her odd tone.

Romy plucked the back of her coveralls, shaking her body, and felt the syringe packet slide down her right trouser leg. She drew the packet out, lifting a brow, and shoved it under her pillow.

The other women grinned.

"Is it me, or does Houston usually send for you by now?" Elara asked a few hours later.

"Yes," Tina said, teeth clenched.

She wasn't the only one getting cabin fever. They'd been locked in this room for two weeks now. They'd declared their intention to escape tonight, and it was an itch under Romy's skin. She wanted out of these four walls.

Romy had assembled the syringe and handed it to Tina hours ago. She'd have the hardest job . . . if the guards ever came to collect her.

Footsteps echoed down the passage. Romy lifted her head, then turned to the others. *This was it.*

"You ladies ready?" Tina asked.

"Beyond ready," Elara said.

"Let's do it," Romy whispered.

She shifted so she was at the edge of her bed. Elara sat on the floor by the door, picking at her boots in faux boredom. She'd been sitting there the last few days, so the guards would get used to her position there. The thing about locking Tina in a room and then doing the same thing each day was that she was a natural fighter and a strategist, and also a she-demon. Elara and Romy had been schooled in exactly what to do when all hell broke loose.

Romy tried to keep her shoulders relaxed, staring as a guard called Tina over and put the key in the door.

Tina slipped out and Romy stood, moving to the doors and saying, "I need to talk to Houston."

The guard paused. "Al, you know anything about that?"

The head guard glanced up from where he was ushering Tina to the others.

Tina plunged the syringe into his neck.

Elara was already ripping back the door. Romy closed the gap and thrust the bottom of her palm upwards into the closest guard's nose, leaving him for Elara to finish off. There was a mess of shouts and grunts to her left as Tina erupted in a flurry. Romy ignored it and spun around the howling guard, collecting his handgun and using the butt of it on the next guard's head, and again when that didn't do the trick.

He slumped to the floor.

A speaker crackled. Romy turned and saw the one behind had reached for his walkie. Elara punched him in the face. His head rocketed to the side and she followed him, punching him twice more, until he slid to the concrete ground.

Romy raised the gun, clicked off the safety and pushed it into the base of a guard's neck as he snuck behind Tina, who was engaged with two others in the narrow confines of the passage.

"All right, boys," Romy said between breaths. "In the cell, or this one loses his brains."

The fight in front of them stopped and Tina stepped free of the two men, ducking to collect another handgun from the head guard, who was clutching his bleeding neck and gasping for air.

Elara did the same from the guard at her feet.

"Leave your walkies, guns, and knives behind. Tina, search 'em," Romy said.

The remaining guards shared a look.

Tina laughed. "They don't think you'll do it, Ro. Maybe they didn't see that video of you in Cairo."

"I feel sorry for them if they haven't," Romy said. "Because if so, they might be about to make a big mistake."

"She likes kneecaps," Elara added. "They're her favourite."

"Shooting them is therapeutic," Romy said. "I don't know why."

The guards quickly unclipped their guns and slid them down the hall. They removed their walkies, too, and kicked them toward Elara. Tina patted the men down, removing their other weapons.

"In you go," Romy said cheerfully. "Take your injured friends."

She shoved the guard in front of her, keeping her weapon trained on him as he dragged the unconscious two inside while the others helped the head guard into the cell.

"Yikes," Romy said. "I'd put something on that neck."

Elara went to close the door.

"Oops, hold on." Tina ran in and lifted the top pocket of the head guard's shirt. She pulled out a swipe card. "Thanks."

"You'll never escape," one said as Elara closed the door.

Romy ignored them and leaned down to collect two of their walkies from the passage floor. She clipped one on to Elara, and shoved the other in her pocket. After a hurried deliberation, Romy grabbed the syringe lying on the ground and shoved it down the side of her boot, pressing the sharp end into a roll of her socks.

She caught a rifle from Tina, who then chucked one to Elara and proceeded to store various knives around her body.

"I say we leave the fire alarm for now," Tina said. "There's one on each level. Let's try to get out without detection and use it as backup."

"How long do you think we have before Houston sends someone to check on us when the guards don't return?" Romy puffed.

Tina tossed back, "I'm only counting on twenty minutes."

They wasted no time setting off down the hall, making straight for the elevator. Their prison cell was on the lowest level in the base. They had to get to the highest. Taking the elevator opened up the most options for their escape. After arriving at the top, they could head to the trapdoor through the hangar, or if that was barred, go left or right to the level one emergency exits. If they wasted time running all the way to the emergency stairs at either end of this level, Houston could be on to them because they'd climbed halfway up through the Amach. It was a risk, but a necessary one.

They reached the elevator and Tina swiped the guard's card. The doors slid open. They stood, guns trained on the spot people might appear. The elevator was empty.

Romy pressed number one and the doors closed. The elevator began to rise. They were going straight to the space soldiers. If there was any way to get them out, they would. If not, they'd need to come back for the space soldiers when they had more backup. The exit they planned to use was also on level one.

"Hey," Elara said, peering above. "What does a ring around a number mean?"

"The elevator is going to stop there," Romy said.

Tina lunged for the buttons, pushing number seven. "We'll get off on the level below and wait for them to pass."

The doors opened and they filed off, rifles raised, and moved around a passage corner to wait. Tina craned her head around to check the numbers above the elevator.

Boom!

A huge, echoing blast sounded from the levels above. The walls of their passage shook, some crumbling rock skittering onto the floor.

"What was that?" Elara asked, brown eyes wide.

A high-pitched noise blared overhead and red lights began to flash. The fire alarm was going off, but Romy suspected the current disruption had nothing to do with them, and everything to do with the booming sound they'd just heard.

"Back to the elevator," Tina shouted.

She rammed a fist against the button. The doors opened after what felt like an age. The elevator was empty again, but wouldn't be for long. People poured out of their rooms into the seventh-floor passage. The elevator doors closed on several faces rushing to reach it and ride to the top.

"Was that a bomb?" Elara asked once the elevator was moving, echoing her thoughts.

"Yes. Friends are here," Tina said. She pressed level one several times.

Elara replied, "Houston has the cannons. They can't attack."

"That would've woken people up. Anyone tries to get in the elevator, shoot them," Tina said. "And I don't know what's happening up there, but if Atlas is attacking, he has a plan."

"Is it safe to go to level one when bombs are hitting the top?" Romy asked.

"It will have to be. We need to head the guards off. They'll be rushing down to the cell to get us and we'll be going up. This might be what we need to get the space soldiers out. The hangar will be chaotic. We just need to get up there before we encounter too many guards."

Shoot. The doors slid open on level six, revealing another passage crammed full with panicked people woken by the blasts overhead.

Romy lifted her gun. "Please remain on your level," she called confidently to the Renegades out in the passage who were pushing to get onto the elevator. "The upper levels of the cave system have collapsed. Spread the word, the elevators are not to be used until further notice."

The doors shut on their nodding faces. Only one young woman looked at her oddly.

Romy repeated these instructions on levels five, four and three.

"One more level, ladies. Move with confidence once we're out; use your gun without hesitation. We're going right, directly to the space soldiers. Then continuing to the exit."

"Roger that," Romy said tersely.

The doors opened on level two, and they stared at the empty hallway in amazement. The other levels had been packed.

A canister rolled into the elevator with a soft plink, making a hissing sound. "Gas!" Tina shouted. Elara lunged to kick the canister out.

Her foot connected with it, catapulting it out of the small space, but the momentum of her sprinting kick carried her outside of the elevator. She whirled to jump back inside.

"Freeze!"

The collective click of a group of guns being readied for fire reverberated in Romy's ears. Elara glanced up at Romy, eyes huge, at least twenty red dots trained on her frame.

She raised her hands in the air, holding Romy's eyes.

"No!" Romy lunged for her knotmate. Tina intercepted her, shoving her to the ground.

"Take care of our guys, Ro," Elara whispered.

The doors shut, and Romy shouted, lashing out at Tina. The woman caught Romy's swinging fist in her hand.

"Listen, idiot," Tina shouted. "Do you think you're any use to her if we get caught?" She let her go and stood, lifting her rifle and panting. "You can't do shit if you're caught. Get ahold of yourself."

Romy picked herself off the ground, breathing hard. "I could've pulled her back in."

"Yeah, full of bullet holes."

She glared at the woman, but got to her feet and pointed her rifle at the door.

"New plan," Tina said, palming all the buttons in the elevator as the doors slid open. "Find a hideout point, then save Spitfire."

22

The bombing hadn't abated in the last five minutes.

Tina eyed the ceiling of level one. "Atlas is clearly attacking, but I have no idea what he's trying to do. He can't have been counting on us to get to the cannons from the inside because he'd assume we'd be locked up. What's his angle? The bomb fire seems too spread out. He should be aiming it all at the hangar, but some of it is way off-target."

"Is he distracting Houston from something?" Romy wondered.

The woman shook her head. "No freakin' clue. But I don't want to make a move from the inside in case it screws up his plans."

"Quiet, another group's coming," Romy whispered.

They'd made it out of the elevators and now crouched behind a stack of crates in the first-level passage close to the hangar. In this craziness, they could have easily stolen a craft. But the bombs were still falling far to their left and Romy knew any enemy craft would be gunned down in a second by the Amach and the Mandate. They'd attempted to use the walkie in Romy's pocket, only to find she'd broken it during her tussle with Tina in the elevator. Elara had the other one.

Romy was one shallow breath away from losing her cool. Houston had her knotmate. Her pregnant knotmate.

Marching feet sprinted past them. Another team came from the other direction. "The commander wants three teams sent to escort him to the cannons," a soldier said.

Romy and Tina shared a loaded look.

"We'll head there now. Where are you going?" the leader of the other team asked.

"There's a giant crater over the hangar. Commander Houston said to put the Amach girl in the middle of it."

No. Romy covered her mouth until they were moving away, then gasped, "Elara."

Tina took a breath. "Shit."

"He's going to use the cannons against our side, and Elara to stop them dropping bombs." Romy peeked to where the cannon team was disappearing. They wore gas masks. "We need to risk screwing with Atlas's plans now. We know more than he possibly can. We'll split up. You track the cannons, I'll get Elara."

"Nope, other way around," Tina said.

"I'm going for Elara."

"Whoever goes after her needs to secure a walkie and contact Atlas. Do you know how to use the walkies to do that?"

Romy glared at her.

"Didn't think so. I'll save Spitfire, you go save everyone else." Tina pushed up and poked her head around the crates to check the coast was clear.

Romy latched onto her arm. "Tina, Elara means more to me than my own life. Please tell me you'll do everything you can to save her. Tina, she's. . . ." Romy choked as she reminded the other woman. "She's pregnant."

The red-haired woman hunkered down beside Romy and pulled her into a fierce hug. "We can do this, Ro. You're the best shot I've ever met, and I'm the best at everything else. *We got this.* Yeah?"

She took a deep breath and gave a tight nod.

Tina's emerald eyes shone. "I will do everything possible to keep her safe."

"Thank you," Romy said. She could name the people she'd trust to keep her knotmates safe on two fingers; Tina was one of them.

"I'm out of here," Tina said. On quiet feet, she set off to the left.

Checking her weapons were in place with fleeting touches, Romy poked her head out to check for company, and set off to the right. She ducked into the first-level storage area and went straight to the bottom shelf on the opposite side to pick up one of the few remaining gas masks. The mask would go some way in disguising her, at least.

After a panicked moment at the elevator, wondering which direction the group had gone in, she heard a shout echo from her right and set off in that direction, fitting her gas mask on. The cannons had to be on the top level as well, surely.

She ran, her breath rushing in her ears inside the gas mask, pausing at each corner to check for company. She hid twice to avoid sprinting troops. It seemed they were the only ones up here, and the civilians were being contained on the lower levels.

Romy sprinted to the next corner and peered around.

She wrenched back with a sharp inhale.

Houston was at the end of the next passage—she took another look—with around twenty soldiers. They were outside the doors where the frozen space soldiers were being stored. Her mind flew in circles. Should she just shoot Houston and end this? Romy hesitated, her finger on the trigger. What if someone else knew how to operate the cannons? Until she knew for sure, she couldn't risk shooting him.

"Oi!" someone shouted behind her.

She jumped and spun, spotting a team of soldiers sprinting down the piped passage toward her. With twenty soldiers around the corner, running wasn't an option. Romy waited for the troop of six soldiers to catch up.

"What are you doing here, soldier?" the closest soldiers barked.

"I don't know where I'm supposed to be," she answered, spine straight.

"Who's your captain?"

Ah nuts. She let her rifle hang on its strap, and whipped out both of the handguns, firing rapidly: knee, knee, upper thigh, right shoulder, left shoulder. The last one managed to train his gun on her forehead.

Romy tensed to throw herself to the ground.

"Rosemary," said Houston in surprise.

With a growl, she turned in a lowered crouch and aimed both guns at him.

Two rows of soldiers closed in front of their leader, each training a red dot on Romy.

"Come to kill me?" he asked. "I was most displeased to hear you'd escaped your cell. But I figured, we have your knotmate, where are you going to go? So predictable, space soldiers."

"I came to save Elara," Romy lied. *To kill you.* "Where is she?"

"Not here, I'm afraid. I'm also afraid I don't care. You, however, are coming with me."

"As long as I can keep my guns," she said sarcastically.

The soldiers ripped her weapons from her with rough hands as well as her gas mask, patting her down and shoving her after Houston.

"Nicely, nicely," Houston scolded them. "I have plans for this one."

He led them through the double doors into the lab and Romy looked helplessly at the frozen space soldiers. The empty cultivation tank was still open, and Houston stroked it as he passed. She frowned and looked past him to the glass window and cages beyond.

She stumbled, and looked again.

The cages were empty.

"What have you done with the space soldiers?" she snapped.

Houston called back. "I let them out. Nice little present for the Amach."

The thought of those creatures set loose made her stomach turn, as sorry as she felt for them.

"You know the best thing?" he asked.

"I'm sure you're going to tell me."

"Atlas has brought me back my army of space soldiers."

"You already have three hundred," she said. Though if there was any possible way to change that, Romy would.

"The frozen space soldiers?" he asked. "Oh no, skyling. They are quite dead."

Dead?

He laughed at her horrified face. "I wasn't sure you'd fall for that one. Dr Charlee certainly wouldn't have. Frozen space soldiers still need to be hooked up to medi-tech, dear Rosemary. I killed those soldiers weeks ago. By accident. I really did hope synthesising your blood would work, but alas."

"You killed three hundred of them?" she choked. He shrugged a shoulder, and she forced back her reaction, not wanting to give him anything. He was a monster, and she should have known better than to believe they were simply frozen.

"All for a cause, Rosemary. All for a cause."

"*Your* cause," she said angrily. "All for you! To cure your insanity. To keep your power."

His eyes slid to the empty tank and then back at her.

Her lips parted as she replayed her words, looking at the cultivation tank. They'd been blind. Houston always acted for himself. She'd thought the cultivation tank was for her, but. . . . "You're going to cultivate yourself," she guessed.

His eyes sharpened and she knew she'd hit home.

"You're going to reset yourself somehow," she whispered quickly. "The cure isn't holding and you're running out of time. You know you're losing your mind."

Houston's smile dropped and he made toward her.

"But you'll be vulnerable for a long time in the tank. It takes a full year for space soldiers to reset. You can't be sure you'll be protected. Is that what your new army will be for, Houston? To protect you?" she demanded. "Or is that for when you wake up?"

He slapped Romy, and her face rocketed to the side.

"Your time is running out," Romy panted, straightening to look at him with a grin. "You're getting desperate. The noose is tightening. Soon, you'll be like your father."

His eyes widened and he whipped out a hand to grip her throat. "You know *nothing* of my father."

"I know you're mad, just like him," she wheezed.

He laughed. "You don't know anything about madness," he answered. "Madness is when you run away from your wife and child and then return months later as if you never left. Madness is forgetting to dress yourself and becoming the laughing stock of the base. *Madness* is taking a scalpel to your son's body because you forgot he wasn't a cadaver, and that you weren't in the lab any longer." Houston let go of her throat and drew up his T-shirt.

Romy's chest heaved as she took in great gulps of air. She stared at the thin scars all over Houston's torso.

"That is madness," Houston said, dropping his shirt.

"You're hurting people, Houston," she said softly. "If you don't want to become your father, then stop what you're doing and let us help you. This doesn't have to be hard."

The doctor leaned in close, and she smelled his rancid breath. "You were right before, skyling. Time is running out. The noose *is* tightening, but I still have enough time to make sure those who oppose me die. I didn't want this, you know. If Atlas had stayed out of my way, I would have welcomed the Amach with open arms after winning the war." He looked into her eyes. "But I can't stop now. Not when I can end it all —the suffering, the inequality, the insanity."

"People won't remember the things you did after winning," she replied. "They'll remember how you won the war in the first place: how you welcomed alien invaders in, tested on innocent space soldiers, killed any in your path. How you turned on your friends."

Houston turned away. "So be it. The people of Earth don't have to agree now. They'll see my point of view in time, and they'll thank me." He nodded at the guards. "Take her."

The guards grabbed Romy and pushed her through the rows of dead, frozen soldiers to the back of the long room. Houston swung a door open ahead of them to reveal ex-Amach techie, Tyson, furiously typing on a keyboard.

"The coordinates are locked in," the techie said. "Just awaiting your thumbprint and the satellites will shift into place."

She'd been right not to shoot Houston in the passage. Tyson was ex-Amach. He'd been the one to rewire the cannons from the Mandate and give Houston control. He had to be contained as well. Tyson noticed Romy and she smiled at him, forming her hands into a gun and shooting him. He paled and turned back to the screen.

"Ingenious, isn't it?" Houston said to her. "Locating the Mandate's cannons when we seized control of them was simple. They'd been bluffing, did you know?" Houston said. "They could only reach a small fraction of the world from Everest. When we seized control of them, I thought, why limit myself like that? Space was empty, meaning the technology couldn't be stolen. Why not put them there?" He flashed a grin at her. "Brilliant, wasn't it?"

She would have never guessed their location. "Very clever, James," she said sweetly. Houston was setting up the scene for his show. He had the cannons, and he had Elara out there. He had his audience.

Romy's mouth dried as she finally understood what Atlas planned to do.

One of the soldiers stepped forward. "Sir, the Amach air force have pulled back, as you expected."

Houston didn't miss Romy's jerk. "Oh, so you do know I had Elara tied right above the hangar area they've been bombing for the last hour? It is the weakest part of an Amach's structure. Something Atlas is well aware of, but my sacrificial lamb, Elara, appears to have done the trick."

Without ceremony, he turned back to Tyson and swiped his thumb over a small scanner. The screen blinked green.

"Twenty-four minutes until the cannons are within range, sir. The optimum window is open for five minutes; after that, accuracy will be affected," Tyson said.

The doctor tapped his mouth. "I'm thinking a few people are going to turn up to save Elara, am I right?"

Romy kept her face smooth. Atlas had been right about him, about his need to display his genius. If Romy was correct, Atlas was banking on one tiny thing to win.

"Where is Tina, Rosemary?" he asked her. A boyish grin split his face. "No, don't tell me. It's more fun if you don't. But I'm *hoping* Atlas turns up. I'd like to keep Tina. It would be nice to have Deimos in the mix, too, and Gwenyth. But I won't get my hopes up."

"It won't work," Romy answered vaguely. She wanted to suggest that the final show wouldn't be quite right *unless* everyone was in the right place, but she didn't dare raise his suspicions.

Houston's face clouded. "No?" he asked. "I hope you're wrong. However, just in case, I've set a cannon on the Irish Amach, and on the area around this base, where, if you wanted to know, a large force is creeping up on us. All of your little space buddies, as I said before. They're coming up the southern end. But there are ten thousand of the Amach and Mandate forces around us, at least."

Atlas was giving Houston everything he wanted, forcing the doctor to bring all of his pieces into action on the Amach's terms. Because Atlas knew one thing about the person who was once his best friend.

He knew Houston would want front-row seats to the anarchy his cannons and traps caused.

Atlas was luring him into the open.

Romy struggled to remain impassive to Houston's gloating. Tyson passed a remote to him and her eyes tracked it.

"You recognise this?" Houston held up the black remote. Two months ago, she'd shot off Mandate Tony's finger to stop him from pushing it. He came closer. "Do you recognise it?"

Romy looked into his wide eyes. "I recognise the look of madness. I've seen it in the mirror enough times to never mistake it. You are mad, James, but you still do the right thing. Tell the Amach what you plan, and they'll leave peacefully. Negotiate a truce. You need time to go into the cultivation tanks. If you have me as a hostage, you can demand that from Atlas. You know you can. I will willingly stay if you let Elara go."

His eyes sharpened. "I don't have a permanent cure yet."

"You'll have years on the other side to figure it out. And if not, you'll just keep going back into the cultivation tanks. This is your chance to take care of yourself and do the right thing."

His eyes lost focus. "No," Houston said, backing away. "No, no, no! That's not how today is happening. It's all set out."

He pushed in close, his breath hitting her cheeks. "I told you I have a plan. I have time to get in the tank. Be as I was. I won't be like him. Soon the others will be gone. I'll be able to work." He whirled, hand over his mouth. "My mind, it wants to always be formulating, planning, researching, discovering. But I did it for the people. Because they needed someone who could see what had to be done. I did it, but once I take everyone else out, it will just be me again, my mind, my research."

She let out a slow breath. "James," Romy said very softly. "You'll never be you again. Not the person who had friends and people who loved him. That person is long gone. That's what you're feeling. Using the cannons won't fix that. Atlas was your friend once. Doesn't that mean anything to you?"

Houston rushed her, backhanding Romy across the face. "They are here on my doorstep with their armies. I'm not the one at fault!"

Blood pounded to her face, and Romy laughed. "You

know how I know you spend your time in a lab, James? You hit like a bitch."

She was still laughing when he grabbed a handgun off the soldier next to her and brought the butt of the weapon down against her temple.

23

She groaned, shifting onto her back.

"Sir, she's awake."

"Gotta love those nanos." Houston cackled.

Romy was dragged upright with a suddenness that nearly made her vomit.

Taking several deep breaths, she cracked her eyes open.

They stood on top of a small hill; around twenty soldiers, Houston, and Tyson. Romy peered down to the ground and her heart stopped. One hundred metres out from their position and down the bottom of the hill, Elara lay tied in the middle of a gigantic crater in the ground. She was struggling to get free.

They were finally out in the open, which meant Atlas would have eyes on them, but how could he move when Elara was trussed up below, and Romy was right next to the man he wanted to gun down?

"There are eight cannons," Houston said to her. "They have a fifty-metre radius and will incinerate anything in that distance. I have one on Elara, two trained on Ireland, and five on the bush surrounding this base, where they are creeping up on me. Not on the area with my space soldiers, of course. How many of my enemy do you think I can kill at once?"

"Three minutes until the first cannon comes into view. The first press will target the girl," Tyson said.

Elara was going to die. She had to get more than fifty metres away. Tina had to be there, somewhere in the treeline, waiting for the Amach to reach her and help.

"Two minutes," Tyson called.

"There doesn't look to be much of a turnout," she observed. The comment was a risk.

Houston laughed. "Oh, don't you worry, skyling. They're there. Hiding in the trees. Not for much longer."

Her knotmate was about to die. Panic worked its way up her throat.

Romy wasn't restrained. They thought there were enough of them to keep her docile. That was their mistake.

She rushed the nearest soldier and punched him in the liver. Seizing his gun, she shot him in the head, hearing Houston scream in fury behind her. She reached for the guard's walkie and hoped harder than she'd hoped in her life. "They have the cannons set on Ellie and the surrounding trees. Get fifty metres away. One minute—"

She cried out at a savage kick in her lower back.

Coming to her feet, she trained her gun on Houston. "Drop the remote," she said.

"No, I don't think so, Rosemary."

A searing bolt of electricity hit her in the back and her body shook against her will as the current burned through her. She fell to the ground, immobile, and felt someone kick the gun away.

She could see down the hill. Could see Tina sprinting into the middle of the crater. A tear fell from the corner of her eye. Tina got the message.

"Oh, look. It's Tina," said Houston as though from a great distance. "Do you think she'll make it in time?"

Romy's body shuddered with aftershocks, and she blinked slowly.

Tina dropped by Elara's side and swept a knife through her restraints. She jerked her up, her shouts a wordless mess from up here.

"Twenty seconds," Tyson said in a voice tight with excitement. "Sir, victory is nearly yours."

"And you will be my right-hand man, Tyson," Houston replied.

Tyson's eyes gleamed.

Tina was shoving Elara, all but dragging her from the centre of the crater. Romy's toes and fingers twitched, but she couldn't move her eyes from what was happening below.

They were going to make it. They were halfway.

But something was wrong with Elara; she wasn't running straight. She was injured.

Elara tripped and Romy screamed wordlessly down to her knotmate, tears leaking from her eyes as she lay immobile.

Tina doubled back and picked up Elara. The woman thrust her away with all her strength.

"Boom," Houston said.

Romy jerked as a huge column of blue hit Earth with a sound so overwhelming, Romy rolled on the ground in agony.

The effect of the Taser began to wear off as she lay panting in the wake of the cannon blast. Her legs unlocked and, shaking, she got to her knees.

Romy glanced down the hill, and the air whooshed out of her chest. She couldn't see a thing through the smoking mess down below! Where was her knotmate? Romy screamed.

Where were they? Where was Elara? Where was Tina?

Someone dug sharp fingers into her upper traps and she lost it. She spun, kicking out a leg in a circle and the soldier lost their grip, falling with a thump onto the patchy grass. Romy scanned the area. The cannon blast had forced most of the other soldiers to the ground.

Beyond them was the most amazing sight she'd ever seen.

Amach soldiers running up the hill.

Those enemy soldiers still standing charged at the Amach lines, shooting. Soon, the Renegades who'd fallen over were rising to their feet and joining them.

Romy had to do something.

Colt.

She dove for the gun. A groan sounded directly behind her and Romy whirled in time to see a Renegade dropping to the ground, clutching his stomach. She looked back and almost burst into tears at the sight of Atlas fifty metres away, gun still pointing at the fallen man who'd snuck up on her.

He started toward her, but dove to the ground when the enemy soldiers before her opened fire at the line of Amach soldiers, a desperate attempt to hold them back. Already, Romy knew the enemy soldiers would lose, and she couldn't be in their midst when that happened. They'd threaten her to control Atlas.

She quickly glanced around in a crouch.

There was a roar of shouts and screams from down the other side of the hill where Elara and Tina had been, but she couldn't think about that now.

Romy kept low, firing on a soldier who ran toward her. That was when she noticed Houston was missing. She turned in a full circle, spotting people pouring out of the trees below.

Where are you, you bastard?

There! Running down the other side of the hill. She glanced back at Atlas and saw the Amach were advancing, steadily pushing forward against the Renegades. But by the time they got here, Houston would be gone.

Tilting her head to the right, Romy shot a soldier in the face and took off after Houston and Tyson, running faster than she ever had. Her lungs burned, her calf muscles ached, but steadily, she gained on the small group ahead through the trees.

Three soldiers accompanied them. Romy waited until the branches cleared and shot once, twice, three times.

Houston dove behind a thick tree trunk. Tyson wasn't smart enough. He screamed, grabbing his side as her bullet caught him.

Sprinting, she reached the tree where Houston hid. Rounded it.

And fired.

He blinked in shock, and she did too . . . as the chamber clicked empty.

He grinned and pushed the remote button again. She jerked, eyes going to the sky as it filled with blue. Mass screams echoed to her from afar.

The air whooshed out of Romy's lungs as Houston tackled her to the ground. The remote skittered away behind a tree. She gasped to breathe, raising her arms to protect her face as Houston knelt on top of her chest. One of his fists got through her guard and pain exploded in her jaw.

His body weight was gone in the next instant, and she rolled, head spinning. Houston was on his feet, staring to where one of the dead soldiers lay close by, a gun resting by their side.

A sharp pain dug into the side of Romy's calf, clearing her head and spurring her into action. She got to her knees, black edging her vision from his blow. Houston ran for the gun and she dove, just catching his feet.

Grunting with the effort, ignoring her blurred vision,

Romy slowly climbed up over his body. Houston was reaching for the gun, his finger scraping the edges of the weapon.

Romy focused on him. She felt inside her boot, the source of the sharp pain, and drew out the syringe.

His eyes caught on the shining point and he renewed his struggles, screaming.

She dragged in an inhale, and pinned him with her knees over his shoulders. Romy lifted her hands, drawing back on the syringe handle to fill the large canister with air. She watched Houston's eyes widen on the glinting needle.

He bucked. "This isn't how it ends. You'll see."

She blinked back the white spots filling her vision. Smiling unsteadily, Romy held his hazel eyes and jabbed the syringe into the throbbing pulse in his throat.

"It's over, James."

She pushed down on the end, slowly emptying air into a leaping artery.

The effect was almost immediate.

His eyes rolled back and his grip loosened, his hands sliding off of her arms as he lost the strength to fight back. His head lolled to the side. Romy didn't move, watching his feathering pulse, the screaming and shots around her blurring into an indiscriminate wall of sound.

The pulse in his neck grew weaker, and Romy, swaying on top of him, grew stronger.

Crawling, she retrieved the gun Houston had failed to reach in time, and dragged herself back to him. She fumbled for his pulse and could only feel a faint stirring as the embolism blocked the blood flow to his brain.

It was how his father had died.

Her vision filled with white and Romy wasn't as successful in blinking it back this time.

She stared with unfocused eyes at the man who had caused so much needless pain.

You can never be too sure.

Clicking off the safety on the gun she'd picked up, Romy pressed the butt against Houston's chest and fired a bullet into his heart.

"There's your cure," she slurred.

The white seeped across her vision and her body filled with a buzzing sensation as she fell forward across him.

24

"Rosemary!"

Someone was shouting and Romy felt a wrinkle appear between her brows, but she couldn't move.

"Oh, god," the man sobbed.

She was rolled onto her back, and did her best to open her eyes, but her body didn't seem to belong to her for now.

"Atlas, let me see her."

"She's got blood all over her," the first man said, breath catching. "Where is it coming from?"

"I can look, but you need to let her go."

He didn't, not completely. But Romy felt new hands on her. They ripped open her clothing and checked. "There's no blood underneath. That's not her blood," the woman said curtly. "Move now; let me check the rest of her."

The man's hold tightened, before he resumed breathing. "She's alive?"

"Yes!" the woman snapped. "Now move yer sorry arse."

Romy turned her head to where the male had been, vaguely registering the movement of hands over her body.

Someone whistled. "Houston's dead. She did that to him?"

There was the click of a gun and then six shots were fired a few metres to her left.

"He was already dead," someone said.

The man replied, "And now he's deader. Charlee?" His voice was strained.

"Her body has taken a toll. Some of it seems older, and some recent. But she's not bleeding from anywhere, Atlas. I need to get her to medi-tech and run a complete scan."

The man fell to his knees.

"She's going to be all right," the woman said softly.

Romy twitched her fingers, a tear rolling from her eye at the man's distress. The man was Atlas. Her Atlas. He was here. And he was hurting so bad because he thought she was injured.

Gathering her strength, Romy pushed at the fuzziness filling her from head to toe. Then, with colossal effort, she moved her lips. Atlas. *Dammit.* She swallowed and tensed her throat. "Atlas," she sighed.

"She spoke," he said, bending over her. A wave of eucalyptus hit her senses. "Rosemary, darling. Can you hear me? Open your eyes. Open them for me."

For him, she'd do anything. Romy cracked open her eyes. They closed almost immediately, but she did it. Enough to catch a glimpse of shining grey eyes and dusty tear-stained cheeks.

Enough to know she'd somehow made it.

He kissed her gently on the lips before pressing his forehead to hers and shaking uncontrollably. She would be, too, if lethargy didn't infuse her so strongly.

"Atlas," Charlee interjected. "She needs attention."

He nodded and placed an arm under Romy's head and at the crook of her knees, lifting her into his arms.

"Behind tree," Romy croaked, eyes closed.

"Behind the tree? What do you mean?" Atlas urged her.

"Remote," she breathed, cracking her eyes open.

Atlas's face hovered between caring and not caring. He finally said, "Where?"

She directed him to it.

"Dr Charlee?" he called.

The doctor joined them behind the tree.

"Kindly pick up that remote there and keep it out of sight? Oh, and I wouldn't recommend pushing the large black button."

Charlee gasped. "This isn't what I think it is."

Atlas's face smoothed. "Probably not."

Their voices faded as she closed her eyes again.

Romy woke as Atlas placed her in a bed.

"Send word to her knot," he was saying over his shoulder.

"Yes, sir." Footsteps receded.

Charlee began hooking her up to medi-tech, eyes riveted on a number of monitors.

"Stable," she announced, with a curt nod.

Atlas's shoulders sagged. When he saw Romy's eyes were opened, he kissed her again. "You're okay. You're safe now."

He was here; of course she was.

Charlee whirled away from the bed and wrenched open cupboards, selected the supplies she needed, and moved back and forth to deposit them on the table next to Romy's head.

The doctor pulled open a fridge, taking out several bags of blood, but she paused her frantic movements, staring at something inside. Charlee reached into the fridge. There was a long hiss and a small white fog swirled out around her.

Atlas tensed. "What is it? We have enough blood, don't we?"

"Yes," Charlee said, staring at something they couldn't see.

"There's something in this freezer." She flicked Romy a glance and strode to a drawer where she selected a long, thin instrument. Returning to the white cloud emanating from the freezer, she dug around for a few seconds and then drew out a small cylinder.

"What is it?" Romy croaked.

The doctor stiffened. "Romy, did Houston take anything from you?" She shut the freezer and the fridge it was stored within, and crossed to the bed.

Romy could barely remember the last five seconds. "I don't know."

Charlee sat on the bed. "Romy, did Houston take eggs from you?"

As she heard the words, Romy wasn't worried in the slightest about the eggs. Her eyes were drawn to Atlas, who had stiffened, his gaze hard and frozen on the small cylinder Charlee held.

Crap. Romy tore her eyes from Atlas, saying, "Yes, he did. Are those them?"

Charlee swallowed hard, whispering, "Yes. That's what the label says. What would you like me to do with them?"

Houston's plans had died with him, but Romy didn't doubt for a moment that he'd had some sort of plan for her eggs. "I don't trust that Houston didn't do something to them. Please . . . please destroy them."

She ignored the sharp inhale from Atlas's direction, fixing the doctor with a firm look.

Charlee tilted her chin, which only wobbled slightly. "Consider it done." She replaced the eggs in the fridge and began working on Romy's immediate problems once again.

"I wish he was still alive. I'd kill him all over again," Atlas whispered, gripping her hand.

He and Romy stared at each other for a long time, unspeaking.

Eventually, she nodded. "I know you would." Then Romy asked the question she'd been too scared to ask.

"Atlas," she said. "Elara? Did she—?"

She couldn't watch three of her knotmates walk through the door and wonder if Elara was just at the back and yet to come through. She had to know before they arrived. The cannon fire had been huge. Romy had been one hundred metres away and the sound of the blast had thrown those around her to the ground.

He looked into her eyes. "She made it," he said. "They all did."

He hesitated.

There was a commotion at the door and three men raced through, one of them pushing a woman in a wheelchair.

"Romy!" Deimos said, reaching her side first and taking her hand.

Atlas snapped, "Careful."

"Where did you find her?" Thrym asked, blue eyes on her.

Atlas quickly relayed what had happened.

Phobos kissed her on the cheek, concern filling his green eyes. He glanced over at Atlas. "Houston's dead?"

"Yes," Atlas said, peering at her. "Romy killed him. With a syringe, by the looks of it."

"What about Tyson?" Romy asked, the blur of events coming back to her. "I only shot him in the arm."

Atlas's brows rose. "We found Tyson trying to sneak away from the base through the forest."

He'd snuck away, probably thinking she was dead. Or maybe too scared to actually pull a trigger himself.

"We brought him back, so we can use him to rewire the cannons over to us."

Romy shifted on the bed. "That's why I only shot him in the arm."

Her eyes landed on Elara.

They burst into tears. Elara got out of her chair and stood next to the bed. "Ro," she choked.

"Tina got to you in time," Romy said, shaking like a leaf as they hugged. "They'd just tased me and I couldn't move. I was so far away, and all I could think of was that Tina might've gotten to a walkie, and might hear me."

A terrible silence filled the room.

"Ro," Elara sobbed. "Tina didn't make it."

"What?" Romy said, a deafening murmur filling her ears. *No.*

Tina wasn't gone.

"Tina can't be gone," she said adamantly.

Tears poured down Elara's cheeks. "They'd drugged me, and I couldn't see straight. I tripped. And she, she picked me up and *threw* me out of the way."

Romy's eyes widened in an attempt to keep the tears from tipping over. She'd seen Tina do it. "The cannon caught her?"

"There were only three metres between us. I thought I'd died when the cannon struck. But I rolled over when I came to my senses, and she wasn't there anymore. She was g-gone, Ro. Just gone."

"I made her promise me she'd do everything she could to save you," Romy said quietly, wiping her eyes with a trembling hand. "I didn't mean that."

"I tripped." Elara's head hung low.

Atlas reached across the bed and lifted Elara's chin. "You were drugged, soldier. That's not on you. Tina was a grown woman, she knew the risks, and she decided to save you and your child. Don't belittle her sacrifice by blaming yourself."

Fresh tears squeezed from her hazel eyes, but she gave him a small nod. Phobos gave him a grateful look over Elara's head.

"Tina's gone," Romy said in a stupor.

Half of the people in this room wouldn't be alive if not for the red-haired commander.

. . . Tina was gone.

NONE OF THEM SHIFTED FOR THE NEXT TWO HOURS. EXCEPT for Charlee, who spun around the various screens hooked into Romy's body. She told Romy, unnecessarily, that her main problems were exhaustion and what looked like regular physical abuse on top of the night's events.

Though her body began to feel better, Romy's mind wouldn't rest.

"Houston planned to reset himself and then use a permanent insanity cure so his madness didn't come back," she said into the quiet. Romy stared at the white blanket over her legs, feeling the eyes of Atlas and her knot on her. "But he backed himself into a corner when he formed the Renegades. He didn't have time to enter the cultivation tank. He knew he needed to step away, but he couldn't."

"If he'd truly inherited his father's psychosis, the constant pressure of that situation probably made his mental illness accelerate," Charlee said, pausing to listen.

Romy sighed. "Do you know he truly believed that what he was doing was the right thing?"

Atlas's fist curled, and she reached out to hold his hand.

"If he'd told me what was happening before he betrayed the Amach and hurt you, I would've done everything I could to help him," Atlas said, staring at the far wall.

"He probably didn't see how bad he was until later," Deimos said. "He got bad fast after we left."

Elara shivered. "I'm just relieved whatever terrible plans he had never happened."

Romy shivered, too, thinking of the testing he'd done on

her recently. "We need to make sure the Mandate can't just take his place," she said, throwing off her blankets. "We have things to do."

"You're not leaving yet," Atlas and Charlee said at the same time.

Romy glanced around the lab. "No offence to what you do, Charlee. But if I ever enter another lab, it will be too soon. I'm leaving." Atlas wouldn't go to work until she was okay, and they couldn't afford to delay. "We need to secure the cannons before the Mandate attack. If we don't do it now, we'll regret it, and I am not fighting any more damn wars."

Ten minutes later, they rolled into the large room with the frozen space soldiers. Earlier, Romy had told Atlas the three hundred soldiers were dead, but now she recalled the five caged soldiers. "Atlas, did anyone come across five space soldiers outside? They would've been extremely violent," she added.

He tore his eyes from one of the upright cases. "I haven't received any reports of the like. Why?"

She looked toward the glass window. "Houston let out five insane soldiers. . . . You had this place surrounded?"

"We did." He put a walkie to his mouth. "Commander Cronus. There's a possibility we have five violent space soldiers lurking around. Please set two teams to do a thorough search of this base, and make our people outside aware they need to be on their guard."

Cronus's crackled *'roger that'* came through a few seconds later.

Atlas pushed the button again. "Krystal, please have Tyson escorted to the control room."

'Yes, sir,' came an answer.

They made for the small room at the back, where Tyson had set the cannons from earlier. Romy was on Elara's lap in the wheelchair, Phobos pushing them along. Atlas led the way, with Thrym behind him, and Deimos and Charlee bringing up the rear.

They reached the room and Atlas withdrew the black remote from his pocket. He set it out of sight behind a computer.

Tyson was forced into a seat not long after, arm in a sling. His eyes landed on Romy. "You were dead."

"I have super powers," she replied.

He opened his mouth to speak, and Atlas cut him off. "Tyson, I'm about to make you a one-time offer to save your life. Do you accept?"

Tyson's mouth bobbed open and closed. "Y-yes," he said.

Spinning the chair to face the computer, Atlas said, "How many cannons are there?"

"Eight," Romy said. "Fifty-metre diameter. They're in orbit."

The people in the room blinked at her.

"I want one pointed to Cairo, one to Dublin, another on Sydney, Rome, Moscow, Japan, Beijing, and Toronto. Get that?"

Tyson began typing with his right hand.

Atlas picked up a walkie and turned the top dial to a different radio frequency. "This is your commander-general. I will be making a public announcement in the next ten minutes. Could the tech team please bring the necessary equipment to the control room on level one."

They waited in tense silence.

Three techies arrived a few minutes later, and busied themselves setting up the camera equipment. No one asked Atlas what was happening—it was clear from his eyes.

He was about to end this.

"Live in three, two. . . ."

"Good morning, people of Earth," Atlas announced,

standing dusty and bloodied in his black T-shirt and cargo pants. "I bring good tidings for you today, and some change. At 0400 hours, the Renegades were defeated, thanks to the combined effort of the Mandate and the Amach. The leader of this movement is now dead. His work destroyed, and his depravity at an end. Those who followed him have been gathered, and are being removed to a secure location as we speak. We offer amnesty to any of them who are willing to dedicate their lives to a peaceful future, proving this to us by helping to clear North America of any Critamal. The cannons, for so long in the Renegades' control, are now in the control of the Amach. Soon these cannons will start systematically attacking the Critamal encampments before our new ground force moves in. I hope we can make this area of New America safe once more."

He paused. "Currently, however, these cannons are pointed on eight different cities. The vast majority of humankind came together in recent weeks to take down a larger foe. We got a chance to see we aren't really that different from each other. For more than one hundred years, the Amach has worked to take down the tyranny of the Mandate. And this has not changed." He looked directly into the camera. "I ask the civilians within the cities not to be alarmed. The Amach has always strived for the most peaceful solution, and this has not changed, either. We wish to bring equality to Earth, an equality it hasn't had since global warming tore through our world and split us apart. I now speak to the Mandate's armies. I speak to those with families, with a child, and finally, to those who have lost someone to the Mandate's cruelty. Bring me the Mandate members within twelve hours and I will turn my attention to eradicating the Critamal from this world. If they are not delivered to the Mandate's island prison in Madagascar in twelve hours, please note that you have a further twelve hours from that point to make sure all of your cities are evacuated. I will be destroying them one by one, if the six people who have lied and manipulated you all are not in my possession. Twelve hours. You will not get another chance."

His grey eyes softened. "Good change is coming," Atlas said, emotion filling his words. "Great change is coming."

25

"Guys," a hushed voice said. "Wake up."

Elara kicked out viciously and settled back into sleep.

"Does she always do that?" someone asked.

"Yeah, you've got to keep your distance when you wake her. I have a stick in our room that I use," another answered.

Romy cracked an eye open at the gathered group: her knot, Nancy, and her small gang. "Whadisit?"

"What language is that?" Nancy asked.

Romy shut her eye again.

Phobos shook her shoulder. "We're going to see something you won't want to miss. You've been asleep for seven hours."

"The army are handing the Mandate over," Thrym said.

Romy sat up and set to getting on her boots. There was no way she wasn't watching that.

After twenty-five minutes spent trying to wake Elara, Knot 27 boarded a craft with Atlas, Charlee, Nancy, and her crew to travel to Madagascar.

"The army just handed them over?" she asked. "Even Mandate Tony?"

Thrym replied, "Six people or one billion? It's an easy choice, and it's not like we're executing them. It wouldn't do us any favours, seeing as they helped us beat Houston."

"Why didn't the Mandate storm the Florida base last night?" Elara asked.

"Because Atlas leaked intel that the cannons were held at a 'secret location' in Canada," Phobos replied. "The Mandate offered to handle the Critamal encampments because they thought it put them in an advantageous position to take the cannons once Houston was beaten."

"Outmanoeuvred," Romy said, fiercely proud of Atlas.

"We should be executing the Mandate members," Deimos said. "While they're in the prison, their friends can conspire to free them."

Phobos shook his head. "A martyr is a much greater force. Killing them won't achieve anything. Let them rot in jail; execution is too quick."

Their green eyes met and Deimos smiled slowly. "I do like the sound of that."

Romy said, "We'll be able to focus on getting that cure for the space soldiers."

"Already done," Deimos quipped.

Romy demanded, "How do you know that?"

"I'm sleeping with the head of research," he replied, adding, "regularly. You've been away for more than two weeks, remember?"

Romy screwed up her nose. "So?" she asked impatiently.

"So, Char found your genetic mutation and mimicked it. She said the results are showing completely different. She's going to wait a few months, but she's quietly confident it will provide a permanent fix."

"Ha!" Phobos snorted. "She gave you the dumbed-down version."

A frown creased Deimos's brow. "She did, too." He grinned to himself.

Romy stood and moved to sit beside Atlas. He gave her a tired smile and wrapped an arm around her shoulders. "Have you slept?" she asked.

"No, I hoped to catch some sleep on the way there."

She bunched up her jacket and placed it on her shoulder. "Well, sleep then."

He was too exhausted to put up a fight. But he managed to say loudly, "I'm worried about enemy craft fire when we land."

Deimos and Phobos glanced over, and Deimos answered, "Should we get the bazookas out?"

Atlas pursed his lips and then nodded, his eyes closed. He was fading fast. Romy smiled at her knotmates, saying, "Could you get them out? I don't think Atlas will be conscious much longer."

The twins made their way to the trapdoor in the cargo area, which was located before the cockpit. The trapdoor led to the belly of the craft, where the heavier equipment was stored.

Phobos pulled on the lever.

"Don't worry, it's not real," Atlas whispered.

What?

A Critamal exploded from the floor, launching at Phobos, and collecting Deimos on the way. A terrified scream lodged from Romy's throat, but Atlas clamped down on her lap as the entire crowd in the craft launched to their feet, guns raised and shouting. The twins swung their arms frantically, yelling at each other as they both tried to fight off. . . .

. . . The dead Critamal.

"It's not alive," Deimos said after that fact became clear. He grabbed his chest. "*It's not alive.*"

A deep laugh rumbled in Atlas's stomach and worked up through his throat, bursting out of his mouth. Romy looked down to see he was staring at the twins, head still resting on her shoulder.

Phobos unwound his arms from where he'd been gripping around his twin's waist to throw him out of danger. Deimos let the water canister he held drop to the floor.

Then both of them turned to stare at Atlas, who now had tears streaming down his cheeks. Romy was unsuccessful at biting back the grin spreading across her face. She'd never seen Atlas laugh so hard.

"He just . . . *got us*," Deimos said.

Phobos blinked. "Really good." He shifted to look through the trapdoor. "Spring system. Ingenious."

Atlas's chuckling began to trail off.

The other occupants of the craft weren't as forgiving. Elara was clutching her chest. "I almost had my freakin' baby!"

Deimos's chest puffed out as he inspected the spring contraption beside his twin. "Taught him everything we know, don't you think, Pho?"

"We sure did. You picked a good one, Ro." Phobos glanced back at her with a grave nod.

They sat down, and Romy shared a long, confused look with Elara and Thrym, feeling as though some rite of passage had occurred, but she wasn't entirely sure what it had meant, or why it had happened. Flinging a Critamal at the twins seemed to have earned Atlas their acceptance.

Atlas wiped his eyes, and readjusted on her shoulder. "Sleep now."

"Okay," Romy drew out. She sent weak smiles to the disgruntled members of the craft, hissing at Atlas, "You set me up."

There was no reply.

Thrym began talking excitedly with Nancy. "They're absorbing the Mandate's army into our own, pardoning them because they moved to bring the Mandate in. Cronus is in charge; he knows pretty much all of the officers. The Amach bases will be emptied and the cities expanded to accommodate the civilians from the settlements and the Amach."

Nancy sighed. "It's a good thing; who knows how long it will take to hunt the Critamal down. The cities are easier to protect."

"Work details will go out from the cities," Atlas mumbled.

Romy looked at his closed eyes and grinned.

"Is he sleep talking?" Nancy asked her.

She bit her lip. "Apparently. Making sleep plans."

Atlas sighed and shifted. "Equal resources and opportunity. Three-month ground plan to eradicate Critamal. Destroy cannons for good."

The others sniggered and Romy tried to still her shaking shoulders so she didn't wake him. With a weary sigh, she glanced around the light faces, some still streaked with dirt and blood. Many of them appeared slightly bewildered, like they weren't sure what they'd been through, and didn't believe it was over.

Over five hundred lives had been lost last night, most of them with the second cannon blast Houston managed before Romy killed him. It would be a few days before they knew what the total toll had been . . . but thousands could have died yesterday.

Each of the deceased Amach fighters deserved to be here now, looking light and bewildered like the rest of them.

One person in particular.

Romy clamped down on her grief, knowing Tina would punch her in the gut for crying. There would be a time to remember her friend soon, but they had to consolidate their position first.

There, Tina, you happy?

"Hey," Romy said to Phobos as the craft landed a couple of hours later. "Can you check if the Mandate is here yet? I don't want to wake Atlas until I need to."

"I'll come and get you when they're close." He winked and helped Elara down the ramp.

Charlee had done a full body check. The baby was fine. None of the books said that going through a war was healthy for a baby, but Romy was inclined to think nothing the books said about pregnancy was true, except for the hole the baby came out of.

She sat in the empty craft with Atlas snoring gently on her shoulder for another hour before Phobos reappeared.

"They're due in ten," he said.

"Thank you," she mouthed.

He blew her a kiss.

"Atlas," Romy said gently. She reached around and stroked his cheek. "Time to wake up." His mouth tugged up in a smile and then relaxed again. After another few minutes of coaxing, his eyes were opening.

He sat, rubbing his eyes. "Where's everyone?"

"I wanted to let you sleep until the Mandate were in sight. They're five minutes off," she continued, sensing his next question. His eyes were blinking, still half closed. His jet-black hair in an adorable mess.

She unhooked her harness and went to him, straightening him up. Grabbing a canteen, she led him off the craft and waited while he splashed his face, drying it on the bottom of his black T-shirt and revealing a lot of bruised torso.

"It's over now," Romy blurted suddenly.

He replaced the cap on the canteen, echoing her. "It's over now."

They stared at each other, eyes full of everything they felt but were unable to voice.

She leaned in to kiss him. "Come on, they'll be here in a couple of minutes."

The small crowd parted to let them through. The invitation had been opened to all of the Amach leaders. They hadn't wanted to make a fanfare, but wanted a display of power. Atlas looked marginally more awake now. He weaved his way through the crowd, holding fast to Romy's hand as he nodded and briefly clasped a shoulder here and there.

"Mother," he said, walking over to Gwenyth.

The always-put-together woman burst into tears at the sight of her son. "You're safe," she said. "It's finally done."

He pulled her into his arms, and said, "We did it, Mum."

"You did it," she said, holding a hand up to his cheek.

He shook his head, saying in a vehement tone, "No, *we* did it. You, me, and Dad."

"He'd be so proud of you," she whispered, hands shaking. "*So proud.*"

"You have no idea what it means to hear you say that," he said. "I love you."

"I love you, too, my boy."

Atlas drew Romy forward, still holding her hand and with no sign of letting go anytime soon.

"Romy," Gwenyth said uncertainly. "I'm so glad you're safe."

That sounded entirely sincere. A few seconds went by as Romy absorbed that startling fact. "I am, and I'm happy to see you well, Gwenyth."

"Please," she replied. "Call me Gwen."

Romy smiled. "I'll do that. Would you like to come to the front and watch with us?"

The older woman dabbed underneath her eyes. "Of

course. I don't want to miss a single second of seeing those fuckers locked away."

Atlas lifted a brow, glancing back.

"What?" Gwen said defensively. "They are."

He pursed his lips and she did the same.

They arrived at the front of the procession, nearest to the prison entrance. When Romy had imagined Madagascar, she'd thought it would be small, but the island was massive and the building on it was huge as well. "Didn't Houston empty this place?" she asked.

"And now we've filled it up again," Cronus said cheerfully, coming up on Gwenyth's other side and taking her hand.

Atlas inhaled and cut a look at Romy, who nearly burst out laughing at his horror.

"Here they are," Cronus said, jerking his head.

A large craft was coming in to land.

The crowd roared, stamping and hugging one another. Romy felt her knot come up behind her, and relaxed inside at their silent and strong presence.

How had Knot 27 made it through this war intact? She shivered at just how easily this all could've been different. One push of a button a second earlier; a single stray bullet. She could've lost her mind. Deimos could've stayed with Houston. Elara could've fallen inside the fifty-metre radius of the cannon.

But somehow, they were still here.

The craft came to a halt in front of Atlas, and the cargo door lowered. The crowd surged forward, trying to look inside. The cameras were at work, one tracking the Mandate, one on Atlas and her, and the others on the crowd.

The Mandate shuffled out in a row, their hands and feet chained.

They weren't dressed in white anymore, or rather, their clothes had been white once, but were now covered in dirt and grease. A loud booing broke out from the Amach. Romy glanced at Atlas, but he didn't seem bothered by it. These people had waited generations for this moment. Booing was tame, in comparison to what many of them wanted to do.

The guards stopped the six dishevelled Mandate members in front of their group.

Mandate Tony's eyes swept across them and landed on Romy.

She tilted her head to the side, feeling blood rushing to her head. She wanted to end this man's life. Romy wanted to exact revenge on this man for everything he'd done to humanity, to her knot, and to her personally. She wanted to take her gun and hold it right to his forehead as she shot.

"Looks like you won," Tony said.

If there was anything she'd learned since her time on Earth, it was that there were more important things than revenge. As much as she wanted to put a bullet in every person who had done her harm, war didn't work like that. The end of a war wasn't neat; its threads weren't trim and tidy. Romy could waste her energy being angry that this man wasn't dead at her feet, or she could accept that he would never see the light of day again. She held his brown gaze. There was so much she could say to him. He'd torn her life apart. She might not have existed but for a bit of luck. If she'd fallen into the Mandate's hands she would've been tested on and tortured for the rest of her days. Her knot would be dead. She would be Feral Romy.

But she wasn't. She'd beaten all of that. She'd beaten them, and she hadn't *become* them to do so. Her family was safe. The world would be safe, too. This man no longer had any power.

If she'd met him in battle, if *he'd* been the one holding the remote, things would be different. But it had been Houston, not Mandate Tony.

"Looks like I did," she replied mildly.

"Look at you." He eyed her hair in disdain and, no doubt, took in the array of scratches and bruises covering her.

Romy tilted her chin. "That's the point, Tony. I *can* look at myself."

Something flickered deep in his hard eyes, and Romy let her lips curve, holding his gaze until he dropped his.

Atlas addressed the six fallen Mandate members. "At a critical time in our history, you chose to betray Earth's people. Thousands were killed on your orders. On behalf of the Amach, I hereby sentence you to prison for life."

"How many have you killed, Commander Atlas?" Mandate Tony spat. The red dot on the camera blinked and Romy's stomach churned with fury at the question.

Someone shifted behind her and Romy turned to look back at Deimos. His eyes were fixed on the Mandate. Her gaze dropped to the grip he had on his holstered gun, and she tensed.

Deimos stared at the Mandate, jaw clenched, unbreathing.

He blinked after a few seconds and released his grip on the gun, shoulders relaxing. He caught Romy watching. She reached back and squeezed his hand, and he gave her a sad smile in return.

"Too many," Atlas said in a straightforward voice that didn't fully cover the rawness underneath. "I remember each and every one of them, every person who has died so that the world may finally have the peace it deserves. Do you remember the people you've killed, Tony?"

His brows raised in faint astonishment. "Of course not."

Atlas smiled without humour. "That is the difference between you and I." He gave the guards a nod and the Mandate were escorted away.

The crowd continued to cheer as the Mandate were led into the single-level concrete prison.

They cheered for a long time after.

"Romy." Gwenyth had moved to stand beside her. "My son deserves a break now."

"Gwen," she replied, "I couldn't agree more."

EPILOGUE

One year later. . .

"Wait for me," Atlas called.

Romy ran ahead of him up the narrow and steep path. "Not my fault you're slow. You've gotten slack."

'Slack' wasn't a word anyone would apply to Atlas. She turned and spotted him coming around the next corner in a white T-shirt and black sport shorts and sneakers. As broad-shouldered and toned as ever. He had sunglasses on and a backpack slung over one bronzed and muscled arm.

"What is this place again?" he asked.

"Machu Picchu. A fifteenth-century citadel."

He reached her and she started off again.

He called after her, "Why is it on a hill? The other places weren't on a hill; Niagara Falls, the Taj Mahal, the Colosseum, and the Great Wall were all flat."

"The Great Wall wasn't flat."

"Flat*er*," he muttered.

They reached the top and stood overlooking the ancient remains of the citadel.

Atlas whistled, eyes wide. "That's some view."

"Yes," Romy started, throwing her long braid back. Her platinum hair reached to the bottom of her shoulder blades now. "Northwest of here we have New Cusco, the Urubamba rivers border us on three sides, and the mountain at our backs is almost impassable. It's interesting to note that while. . . ." She trailed off, catching Atlas pursing his lips.

He coughed. "Never mind."

"I'm *informative*," she said with a hand on her hip.

He laughed and closed in on her, pressing a kiss to her lips. "It's damn cute is what it is," he disagreed.

"Informative," she repeated.

"Whatever you say, darling."

Three months after removing the Renegades and the Mandate from power, Atlas had decided to take an indefinite break from his work, and he and Romy had disappeared the next day. They took a craft—with permission, though Atlas had fooled her into believing it was stolen for a full week—and set off. Romy guesstimated they could have her list completed in another three years if they kept up this pace, though she kept adding more destinations with each stop.

By the time they reached their craft again, the sun was low in the sky.

Atlas threw himself down on the mattress set up in the back. Inside, it looked nothing like it had a year ago. Their wardrobe was on one side of the cargo area, and a kitchenette was set up on the other side with various pots, pans, torches, cards, matches, and camping equipment shoved into every available space. They'd converted the craft into a mobile home.

Romy jumped on top of him and he caught her, pulling

her in close. His stubble scratched at her cheek and she giggled.

"Want to watch *Bridget Jones's Diary?*"

He grimaced. "You know I hate rom-coms. What about *Remember the Titans.*"

"How many times have you watched that now?"

"I like it. You should make those cucumber avocado snacks."

Atlas had taken it as a personal challenge to get to know himself, now that he had the time. He had a very decisive list of what he did and did not like: he did like sport movies, he didn't like hills, he did like orange chocolate, he didn't like curly pasta. He hadn't made peace with his past entirely, but he was working on it.

"We could play strip poker again," Romy said, rolling to the side and propping up on an elbow.

He snorted. "You want to play that every night."

"Don't you?"

"Do I want to be tortured for hours before I get all your clothes off?"

Her mouth dropped. "You don't always win." She felt her temper begin to rise.

He lay flat, staring at the craft's ceiling. "Depends how you look at it," he said with a small grin. "As long as we end up in bed, that's a win."

Her irritation disappeared and she grinned back.

"But," he said, "I would think you'd be wanting to start back to Jimboomba tonight."

She stilled. "We aren't leaving until tomorrow morning."

"You don't want to see your knot a day earlier? Silly me." He clambered to his feet. "I'll get the cards."

See her knot? A month had passed since their last get-together.

Romy scrambled to her knees. "No, I do want to see them a day early," she said. "Unless you really want to play cards?"

Atlas threw the cards away and picked her up, wrapping her legs around his hips. "Leave in an hour?"

"Always negotiating," She pressed her lips to his, sighing as he held her tight and kissed her right back.

Just like the first time, just like every time. His arms and his lips were her favourite place in the world, and none of these places they'd gone to would have been anything without him there.

"Ro!"

Romy heard Elara's scream all the way across the packed Jimboomba settlement. They'd landed in Australia last night, but Atlas said she shouldn't wake everyone at three in the morning.

"Ellie!" Romy squeezed through the crowd, dragging Atlas behind her and ignoring the disgruntled looks.

There was a huge turnout for the occasion.

Elara hit her running and took them both to the ground, despite Atlas's efforts to save her. Romy's knotmate peppered kisses all over her face. "I've missed you so much."

The worst part of travelling was being without her knot. She cried each time she saw them, and every time they left.

"You, too." Romy assessed their position and decided the timing was perfect. She licked Elara's eye.

She screamed. "That's sick!"

"Yeah, well, that's what it feels like when you do it to me," she shot back. Romy's revenge was slightly ruined by the happy tears she was shedding.

Strong arms picked her up from behind. "You made it!"

"I wouldn't miss it for the world," Romy said, turning to give Phobos a hug. "Where is she?"

His green eyes danced. "Aren't you just happy to see me?"

"Where is my niece?" Romy gave him a flat look.

He reached down to where a crawling golden-haired child was clinging to his legs. "Jane, your Aunty Romy is here to see you."

Romy sobbed like crazy, holding her arms out. "H-hey, Janey."

"You gotta stop crying when you see her, honey," Deimos said, slipping behind them. Romy turned and gave him a kiss on the cheek, which he returned.

"I can't help it," Romy sniffed. "She's just so adorable. She's our Knot 27 baby." With golden ringlets, Elara's pixie features, and Phobos's green eyes. This child would get whatever she wanted, *when* she wanted with that combination. And her name, nothing like their mythological names. Jane. Such a unique name.

"Babies," Elara corrected.

Deimos glared at her. "Ellie."

Elara gasped. "Sorry, I forgot."

He disappeared briefly and reappeared with Charlee. "We have some good news, Ro. Char and I are having a baby."

Romy calmly gave Jane to Atlas, who began tossing her in the air. She then screamed as loudly as she was capable of.

She threw herself at the couple. "How far along are you? Are you feeling okay?"

Charlee placed a hand over Romy's mouth. "I'm a doctor."

Relief coursed through her. "Oh yeah."

The doctor snorted and added, "I'm six weeks along."

Romy groaned. "I hate waiting for babies to come. It's the worst." She glanced at Atlas holding Jane upside-down. Jane was howling with laughter.

He glanced up and waggled his dark eyebrows at her.

"Uh-oh, that's a 'reproduce with me' look if I ever saw one," Charlee whispered.

Romy laughed, her cheeks warming. "Yeah, he wants kids. I told him he can wait until we travel the world."

"Good on you." Charlee pulled her in for a hug. "And hello, how are you? You were at Machu Picchu, yes?"

Romy launched into a recount of the last month, one eye scanning for their last knot member. Someone tapped her on the shoulder.

"Thrym!" she shouted, turning.

He covered his nearest ear and hugged her tight. "It's so good to see you, Ro. What do we need to do to convince you to stay here?"

"You're one to talk. I hear you and Nancy will be in Sydney for the next six months running a space soldier integration course."

"Sydney is a lot closer than. . . . Where are you off to next?"

"Antarctica."

His sky-blue eyes danced. "I can't believe you're actually travelling Earth. It's what you always wanted."

She nudged him with her shoulder. "Never thought we'd get here, huh?"

"Honestly?" he asked. "At one point, I wasn't sure if any of us would make it. You were bonkers, Deimos was a dick, Phobos was being tormented by the others, Elara wouldn't get off her ass as usual, and I couldn't see straight."

"Is that what you call it?" she teased.

He made a face. "Don't be gross. You're my sister."

They grinned at each other.

Atlas passed a wriggling Jane back to Romy. "I've got to go up now."

He still spoke at gatherings such as these when asked. Romy suspected Atlas could only last so long on his 'indefinite break' before he was lured back into some kind of lesser commanding role. Whether from the meticulous grooming he'd gone through or because of who his parents had been, the drive to lead was in his blood, and Romy truly didn't think he would be satisfied in any other job.

"Ba ba ba," Jane said, reaching after Atlas.

"Why doesn't she ever do that to me?" Romy asked Phobos.

He raised both brows. "Because you cry every time you hold her."

Romy sniffed, wiping her eyes with one arm. "She's just so cute."

Phobos rubbed Romy's back as she played with her niece.

The crowd quieted and faced the front as a microphone was tapped.

"Welcome," Atlas's voice rang out, "to the first Peace Memorial Day. I am honoured to join you all here in Jimboomba to remember our fallen, and remember what they fought for." Cameras zoomed around his face and the crowd. Romy spotted one camera trained on their knot. Knot 27 usually made an appearance at events.

Jane spewed down Romy's front.

Phobos laughed. "Hilarious. I hope the cameras got that."

"Can you get her a towel instead of just standing there?" Elara snapped, rifling through a nappy bag.

Romy smiled at Jane. "I don't mind. She can spew on me."

Deimos and Thrym shared a disgusted look.

Elara patted down Romy's white blouse and took Jane to clean her.

"For the last nine months, our new computer system, the Tina 2000, has been running smoothly, distributing resources around the world—"

"That name gets me every time," Deimos wheezed.

"She'd hate it." Romy grinned.

"That's why it's so amazing," Charlee said.

"—A poacher has not been sighted in several months," Atlas said. "This means we are resettling in North America, and our armies have largely been disbanded."

A cheer went up.

"Do you remember wondering what Earth would be like if we ever got here?" Romy asked her knot.

"No one did that but you," Thrym reminded her.

Romy sighed happily, glancing over her family. "I thought it would be like this."

Smiling, Deimos wrapped an arm around her. "We got there in the end, honey." He squeezed her to his side.

"This brings me to mention one person in particular who is not with us today," Atlas said, dropping his voice. "There is no one on Earth that doesn't know her name. The person I speak of was once the commander of this very settlement. She would have been a Mandate member one day, if she hadn't possessed an inherent self-need to do what she believed to be right. This saw her enter the ranks of the Amach after suffering greatly at the hands of the Mandate. Many of you respected her, or at least respected what she'd do to you if you didn't respect her."

The crowd laughed quietly.

He peered down at the podium for a long beat. "In Tina Lyons' last days, she did more to consolidate peace than any person on Earth. The groundwork she put in back then formed the foundations of our future. She carved the beginnings of a path that allowed the peoples of Earth to begin to understand each other. One year ago, we won a war. One year ago, Tina Lyons put plans in motion that would win us what we really wanted: happiness. I once said to Tina that there was no one I trusted to get a task done more than myself, but that wasn't true. If a job was humanly possible, Tina Lyons would get it done. Today, as we have five minutes of silence for our lost loved ones, I want you to spare a moment to remember a woman who possessed a heart as large as any I have ever seen."

Romy closed her eyes and thought about Tina. About all the good times.

. . . And that time Tina told her she was useless at everything she did. Romy frowned. Or that time she punched her in the throat for not paying attention. Or that time she'd said men only liked her because she was genetically enhanced.

Romy snorted through her fresh tracks of tears, drawing a scandalised look from those around her.

"Sorry," she wheezed at them, going bright red in a bid to contain her laughter.

Thrym cracked an eye open. "You okay?"

A hysterical giggle escaped, and Romy said with as much serenity as she could, "I just remembered what a bitch Tina was."

He barked a laugh and hastily covered it as a few people hushed him. "She was the meanest damn person I ever met."

The five minutes finished and Romy let her laughter out, finally.

Recovering a minute later, she nodded to herself. *Tina, you were the meanest, but you were also one of the best. I'm honoured to have known you.*

All of her favourite people were right here. Thrym, who had finally loosened up and had someone he loved more than duty—Nancy would keep him honest. Phobos, who had returned to his plants with glee, and Elara, who was the settlement mechanic and driver when she wasn't chasing Jane. And Deimos, the founder of Co-exist, a massive organisation which worked alongside Thrym and Nancy to ensure prosperous peace for all.

She looked across the crowd at Atlas, who was watching

her, grey eyes very rarely like hard stone these days and more like the soft rainclouds she loved. The right side of his mouth tugged up into a half smile, and he held her gaze as he leaned back to the mic and said, "Now, let's party."

The crowd erupted and Knot 27 shifted back as tables were brought out and piled with food and drink.

"Hi, Commander Cronus." Elara greeted him as he came to get some food. "How are you?"

Cronus looked up with surprise. "Eh? Oh, it's just Bill now, soldier." He paused. "Knot 27, isn't it? You were always one of my favourites."

Something came back to Romy, and she found herself asking. "Comm— uh, Bill? When you first came to the Amach, you mentioned something about our knot. . . ."

"Yes, you went from one of our top teams to the worst," he said sadly.

Deimos and Phobos shared an evil look.

"Do you know why it happened, uh, Bill? There's no doubting our knot is different from others. Dr Charlee said it might be a naturally occurring mutation?"

Cronus barked. "Science! They always have the most complicated answers. I'm always telling people, why look for a zebra when you should be looking for a horse."

Knot 27 stared at him.

"No, soldier. I don't believe in mutations, science, and whatnot. I remember it well because I'd been waiting for your team to be harvested so I could put you to use again."

Romy wasn't the only one who leaned forward to hear him.

"There was an incident with your tanks in the early days," he said. "The trolley carrying you overturned."

Thrym's jaw fell open.

"What are you saying?" Elara demanded, switching Jane to her other hip.

"He's saying we're different because we had the space soldier equivalent of being dropped on our heads," Deimos said drily.

Cronus shrugged. "Yes, soldier. I am. Exactly that."

They watched him saunter over to Atlas's mother, now his wife, with varying levels of horror and disbelief.

Knot 27 turned to each other.

"That can't be why we're different," Romy said.

Phobos snickered. "Hey, Ro. You don't have a super brain —you just got dropped on it."

"Those in favour of forgetting we ever heard that and going with Charlee's mutation theory, say 'aye'," Deimos called.

As one, the five members of Knot 27 chorused, "Aye."

I hope you enjoyed Romy's story. She has a special place in my heart! Read on to check out my other series.

**Your honest feedback helps other readers to decide whether or not to take on Romy, Knot 27, and Atlas.
Please take a moment to leave a review.**

ACKNOWLEDGMENTS

Romy, Atlas, and the rest of Knot 27 came to me on a bus trip from Derry to Dublin in late 2014. These characters waited two years (Romy, Atlas, and Thrym patiently, and Elara, Phobos, and Deimos not so much) to get their turn on the page. By the time I got around to penning *Earth's Warrior*, I was desperate to start *Last Battle for Earth* and sank into the tale with relish. The research involved in portraying their story was particularly enjoyable (such a nerd), and the antics of Knot 27 have never ceased to bring a smile to my face during the last two years.

I would like to thank Deimos for not breaking my heart entirely, Romy for being the nicest crazy person with a residual temper ever, and Atlas for being . . . cargos, eucalyptus, grey eyes, can't form coherent sentences . . . *Atlas*.

Thank you to:

My advanced reader team and my book barracks. You guys are way too much fun!

My beta team: Michelle, Kayla, and Hayley.

My manuscript team: Melissa Scott (editor), Robin Schroffel (copy editor), and Patti Geesey (proofreader).

To my friends and family, thank you yet again for being so very supportive of what I do. If I liked talking about feelings, I would tell you all how much I appreciate your encouragement to your faces, but as it turns out, you just get to read about it with every release.

Many thanks and hugs to Jo. You know who you are.

To my readers, who allow my stories to fill their imaginations for hours on end. What an honour to write books for you all.

To Scott, my husband. Thank you for doing the things you do. Thank you for being the person you are.

Happy reading!

Kelly St. Clare
Escape into Fantasy

BOOKS BY KELLY ST. CLARE

Supernatural Battle

Vampire Towers (Paranormal urban romance)

Blood Trial

Vampire Debt

Death Game

The Darkest Drae (Dragon shifter romance)

with Raye Wagner

Blood Oath

Shadow Wings

Black Crown

The Tainted Accords (Royal fantasy romance):

Fantasy of Frost

Fantasy of Flight

Fantasy of Fire

Fantasy of Freedom

Novellas:

Sin

Olandon

Rhone

Shard

Pirates of Felicity (Pirate fantasy romance):

Immortal Plunder

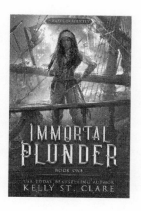

When I'm caught eavesdropping on the pirates of *Malice*, they retaliate with violence, and my fathers become set on revenge.

But simple payback cascades into magical misfortune.

An intense russet-haired landlubber seeks to help me. A savvy silver-eyed Malice pirate strives to hinder me. But the further I drift, the more I wonder—am I helping or hindering myself?

Complete Series Available Now

Made in the USA
Coppell, TX
12 August 2020